"This was a good read, and I love the author's style, which was warm and friendly . . . I can't wait to read the next book in this wonderfully appealing series."
—**_Dru's Book Musings_**

"I am happy to admit that some of my expectations were met while other aspects of the story exceeded my own imagination . . . This mystery novel was light, fun, and kept me thoroughly engaged. I only wish it was longer."
—**The Young Folks**

"_If the Shoe Kills_ is entertaining, and I would be happy to visit Jill and the residents of South Cove again."
—**_MysteryPlease.com_**

"In _If the Shoe Kills,_ author Lynn Cahoon gave me exactly what I wanted. She crafted a well-told small-town murder that kept me guessing who the murderer was until the end. I will definitely have to take a trip back to South Cove and maybe even visit tales of Jill Gardner's past in the previous two TOURIST TRAP mystery books. I do love a holiday mystery! And with this book, so will you."
—**_ArtBooksCoffee.com_**

"I would recommend _If the Shoe Kills_ if you are looking for a well-written cozy mystery."
—**_Mysteries, Etc._**

"This novella is short and easily read in an hour or two with interesting angst and dynamics between mothers and daughters and mothers and sons . . . I enjoyed the first-person narrative."
—**_Kings River Life_** magazine on _Mother's Day Mayhem_

Books by Lynn Cahoon

The Tourist Trap Mystery Series

Guidebook to Murder * Mission to Murder * If the Shoe Kills * Dressed to Kill * Killer Run * Murder on Wheels * Tea Cups and Carnage * Hospitality and Homicide * Killer Party * Memories and Murder * Murder in Waiting * Picture Perfect Frame * Wedding Bell Blues * A Vacation to Die For * Songs of Wine and Murder * Olive You to Death * Vows of Murder

Novellas

Rockets' Dead Glare * A Deadly Brew * Santa Puppy * Corned Beef and Casualties *Mother's Day Mayhem * A Very Mummy Holiday * Murder in a Tourist Town

The Kitchen Witch Mystery Series

One Poison Pie * Two Wicked Desserts * Three Tainted Teas * Four Charming Spells * Five Furry Familiars * Six Stunning Sirens

Novellas

Chili Cauldron Curse * Murder 101 * Have a Holly, Haunted Holiday * Two Christmas Mittens

The Cat Latimer Mystery Series

A Story to Kill * Fatality by Firelight * Of Murder and Men * Slay in Character *Sconed to Death * A Field Guide to Homicide

The Farm-to-Fork Mystery Series

Who Moved My Goat Cheese? * Killer Green Tomatoes * One Potato, Two Potato, Dead *Deep Fried Revenge * Killer Comfort Food * A Fatal Family Feast

Novellas

Have a Deadly New Year * Penned In * A Pumpkin Spice Killing * A Basketful of Murder

The Survivors' Book Club Mystery Series

Tuesday Night Survivors' Club * Secrets in the Stacks * Death in the Romance Aisle * Reading Between the Lies

LYNN CAHOON
Six Stunning Sirens

Kensington Publishing Corp.
www.kensingtonbooks.com

To my sister, Reana Gardner. Thanks for being there, even in the beginning.

CHAPTER 1

Fall was imminent. The season always arrived too fast in the mountains of Magic Springs, Idaho. At least for Mia Malone's wishes. The bright sun that warmed Mia as she sat outside her constantly remodeled schoolhouse would soon just be a memory until next May or maybe as late as July. But she wasn't worried about fall's colder temperatures just because she was holding on to summer.

Today, she was drawing out plans for hosting the Miss Magic Springs Harvest Pageant here at the school, outside, at the end of the month. The backyard was still beautiful with a row of mums in alternating colors circling the area. Her herb garden was still a vibrant green. Pumpkins, cabbages, and gourd plants had replaced the summer's bounty in her main garden.

All she had to worry about was a sudden freeze, or worse, an early snowfall. She stared at the craggy mountains that bordered the town and wondered if there was a spell she could do or ask Grans to cast to keep the cold weather away until the festival was over.

Who knew, maybe the local coven, the Magic Springs Society for Magical Realism, already had the weather spelling covered. They had been the ones to set the date and to choose Mia's schoolhouse for the pageant and the opening reception. She could be worrying over nothing.

She quickly drew out a staging plan for the part of the three-day event hosted by Mia's Morsels. On the weekly planning call that morning, her boss at the Lodge, Frank Hines, had been snippy about Mia's Morsels getting the Harvest Queen contest contract. Mia worked hard to present the Lodge's proposal, but the coven had gone with Mia's Morsels proposal that Abigail Majors had submitted instead. And they'd rented the school for the event.

James Holder, the Lodge's head chef, had come to her defense on the call, saying Mia's Lodge proposal had been solid, even better than the one they'd submitted last year. Abigail Majors, the current manager of Mia's Morsels, just knew the right people.

In a small town like Magic Springs, it was all about networking. Abigail had connections in the town and the coven. And after living here for more than a couple of years, Mia was still a newcomer.

Mia had the feeling that she couldn't serve two masters much longer. She'd taken the job as the Lodge's catering director because Frank had banned any outside caterer from using the Lodge's facilities. Which had cut Mia's annual catering by more than fifty percent. Until the company could stand on its own, she needed the income from the Lodge job to keep the mortgage paid on the old school, as well as buy food and pay the utilities.

Christina Adams brought out three plates with what looked like a ham and turkey sandwich, potato salad, and a dill pickle and set them on the table next to Mia. The only other employee of Mia's Morsels, Abigail Majors, followed Christina out of the kitchen with a tray holding glasses of ice and a pitcher of iced tea.

"You need to eat something," Christina said as she sat next to Mia. Christina was her best friend and now was also a full-time employee for Mia's Morsels. Once, she had almost been Mia's sister-in-law, but their friendship had lasted longer than Mia's engagement to Isaac. Mia knew that Christina had gotten several higher-paying job offers when she'd graduated in June that she'd turned down. Christina was dating Levi Majors, Abigail's youngest son, and the couple had decided to wait at least a year before moving out of state.

Christina brought her back to reality as she poured the iced tea. "You've been stewing on that setup since your catering department leadership meeting ended at nine. Frank must have been his usual charming self."

"He basically called me a liar when I said I didn't give Abigail our contract estimate. He thinks we underbid the Lodge." Mia closed her notebook and put it on the ground under her chair.

"Our bid was higher than any other bid, according to the coven. We just had a few boutique offerings that no mortal company could offer. Like a room for spell detection during the competition. Last year, the coven had to park an RV in the Lodge's parking lot, and still, there was an incident with a judge and a contestant's mother." Abigail poured the tea, sitting down at the table afterward. "Don't feel bad about losing the contract. They came to me because we understand the problems having an active coven in town has on a beauty competition."

"All great information, but nothing I can tell Frank to ease his mind about my loyalty." Mia sent a blessing to the Goddess for the food she'd been provided, then opened her eyes to see Abigail and Christina watching her. "I'm fine. I just don't think I'll be able to keep the Lodge job much longer after Mia's Morsels becomes solvent. I understand why it could be seen as a conflict of interest."

"Which is why I'm doing the management for the company. Don't worry about Frank. He isn't going to fire you because he knows what an asset you are to the Lodge." Abigail had run Majors Groceries for years with her husband before officially retiring. When Mia offered her a cake decorating job, she'd jumped at the chance to get out of the house again. Then that job had turned into managing Mia's Morsels a few months ago. Oh, and she was Trent Majors mom as well. Mia and Trent had been dating for the last few years. Magic Springs was a typical small town. Everyone knew everyone.

Mia met Christina's gaze. They both knew that sometimes Abigail was a little bit of a Pollyanna. Especially for a witch. But they loved her anyway.

"So, I think we'd be fine having the reception and the competition out here. Especially since we ran lights around the yard. We'll have to have a dais built over in that corner. But if it's too cold or rains . . ." Mia paused, glancing at the large mountain peak behind the yard again. She shook her head. Focusing on the negative was a great way for that unwanted outcome to come to pass. "We can move to the gym if there's a weather issue. I wish we'd painted it this summer."

"We replaced the van with that money," Abigail reminded her. "Anyway, eat. I don't want to talk about problems while we eat lunch. It upsets the digestion process."

Mia knew Abigail was right. Good or bad, the school was going to host the competition this year. And if they didn't totally blow it, Mia's Morsels could probably count on the annual contract. Small towns didn't like a lot of change.

"Where's Trent taking you for dinner tonight?" Christina asked, trying to change the subject.

"The new restaurant in Twin. We'll probably be late getting back." Mia took a bite of her sandwich. Christina still lived with her and would probably be there until she and Levi moved in together. Or got married. Christina's parents weren't pushing for the wedding vows because Mother Adams was still hoping that her only daughter would see the errors in her dating choices and find someone more suitable with a few seven-figure bank accounts. "Can you babysit Cerby? The last time Trent left him alone, he manifested a goblin to play with."

"Hellhounds can be a problem to raise. Especially if you're not with them all the time." Abigail sipped her tea. "If I wasn't working full-time now, I would have insisted that Trent let me raise Cerby. I bought him the *How to Train Your Hellhound Puppy* book last week."

"Where did you even find a book like that?" Mia set down her sandwich.

Abigail shrugged. "Off the internet, of course. They have everything. Of course, most mortals think it's a joke book, but it's by the most respected hellhound trainer in the world. Well, the only one who's actually still alive, that is. There was a guy in France who had more experience, but well, he's no longer with us."

"Old age?" Christina asked.

Abigail glanced up, nervously. "No, a training accident with a new student. The host animal was a Bengal tiger. Cats don't seem to assimilate hellhound spirits quite as well as canines."

"And with that, I'm texting Levi to come over tonight and help babysit. I love Cerby, but I'm not equipped with all the extra magic stuff if something goes haywire in his head." Christina picked up her phone.

"He's a six-month-old Maltese," Mia reminded her.

"Small dogs can be vicious. Think of Mr. Darcy's safety." Christina grinned and held up her phone. "Besides, it's already done. Levi says he'll be glad to be my knight in shining armor. Especially if I cook him dinner."

"And there's my youngest son, always looking for his next meal." Abigail turned toward Mia. "So what else is going on with you guys? We don't get a lot of time to chat now that the Lodge has you busy."

The three women talked about their days. They'd

just finished eating when several cars pulled into the parking lot. "Is it a food sell day?"

Abigail shook her head. "No, those are the parents and contestants for the contest. The contest coordinator called me last week and asked if they could come to walk through the school today. I'd totally forgotten about them stopping by."

"I'll clean this up, you guys go play hostess." Christina took the trays and quickly cleared the table.

Abigail went to greet the organizer, and then the group moved toward Mia and into the backyard. Mia could hear the parents talking as they walked in her direction.

"We'll need to build pathways, so the girls' heels don't get stuck in the grass if the competition is held outside," a tall woman in a blue suit said into her phone. Mia assumed she was taking notes.

The woman next to her said, "The grass will ruin the evening gown competition. You know how thick the dew gets this time of year. Maybe we should focus on the gym, or better yet, go back to the Lodge. At least there they aren't trying to hold the event outside."

"You just want the Lodge because some of your family works there. You think you'll be able to glamour your girl to the winner's circle," another woman, dressed in a pink dress and standing on the other side of the Blue Suit woman, chimed in.

"That's not why." The other woman, who she now saw was dressed in upscale jeans and a cropped sweater to show off her toned stomach, stopped and reached for Pink Dress woman. There was going to be a fight.

"Stop it. We're the adults here," Blue Suit said, marching the group forward. And then they were in front of Mia.

Abigail took Mia's arm. Mia could tell she was ignoring the conversation between the women. "Ladies, Mia's the creator and owner of Mia's Morsels. She owns this entire property and has done amazing things restoring the outside, including planting an herb garden."

"Miss Malone. Thank you so much for meeting with us. I know you have a busy schedule." Bambi Parry, the event coordinator, smiled. "I'd like to introduce a few of this year's contestants for the Magic Springs Harvest Queen contest and their mothers. Crissy and Tatiana Evans, Rachel and Marnie Carter, and finally, Kristin and Carla Manson. Oh, and Melody Sellers. Melody's mother was an MSHQ back in the day."

"An MSHQ?" Mia was confused by the acronym.

"Sorry, we shortened the title years ago. Who wants to say Magic Springs Harvest Queen a hundred times a day?" Bambi shrugged. "Besides, it doesn't fit on the sashes."

Mia welcomed the group to the school. The woman in the blue suit was Tatiana Evans. The one in the jeans was Marnie Carter, and Carla Manson was in the pink dress. She knew she'd remember the moniker she'd given them long after she'd forgotten their names. But Mia needed to try. Abigail played these social graces games well. Maybe Mia should keep her on as an assistant when she came back. Maybe the head of marketing or some cool title like that.

Mia kept her gaze unfocused, hoping she wouldn't show that she'd heard their earlier argument. "I bought the Academy a few years ago so it wouldn't be torn down and turned into a strip mall. I'm still renovating the building and lands, but I hope to have it totally remodeled sometime next year."

"A strip mall would have brought in a nail salon and probably a Starbucks." A blond teenager in the back glanced around the backyard.

"Crissy," Tatiana chided her rude daughter. "Please let Miss Malone talk."

Mia shrugged. "It's okay. I get it. Sometimes it's easier to just wipe away the past and create something new. But when you remodel old buildings rather than destroy them, you don't lose the spark that the building held. You keep the shared history and the town's story. When you tear down the past, you forget the lessons that our ancestors have already paid for, sometimes in blood."

Crissy stared at Mia like she had three heads. Then her phone beeped with a text, and she dropped her gaze.

"Well, wasn't that an amazing social history lesson of why historic buildings should be preserved? Thank you, Miss Malone. Tell us, what were you thinking about for the setup?" Bambi asked, moving the conversation back to the contest. Bambi had a large name tag pinned onto her off-white vintage Chanel suit.

Mia walked them through the setup ideas she'd created for the outside, using her sketchbook as a guide. Now she was glad she'd taken the time to outline the event that morning. The indoor setup was more traditional, although the moms were right about the high heels and the grass. She needed to set up a walking path around the yard as well as crisscrossing the area. But that wouldn't get done before the contest happened. Maybe she could ask Trent to figure out a temporary fix.

Abigail stood by the doors to the gym as the group finished looking around the backyard. Mia pointed the group toward the open doors, then trailed behind them, her sketchbook tucked under her arm. Christina had come back out and met her at the door. To Mia's delight, Abigail had taken over the tour.

Christina rolled her eyes when one of the moms asked about lighting for the pageant. "I used to be that kid following her mother around. I would be so embarrassed when she'd say things like that."

"Mother Adams put you in pageants? What was your talent? Cooking?" Mia teased as Abigail took them out to the lobby area, where they would hold the Monday introduction reception. Mia closed the doors to the gym and walked toward the other set of doors.

"Actually, I sing." Christina blushed at the memory. "Mom wanted me to play the piano, but even my teacher told her I'd never be good enough to make it in that world. And don't get me started on ballet. I wanted to learn to ride horses, but Mom told me I was never going to be a Rodeo Queen unless she was dead and buried. Honestly, I don't think she would have let me even after her death. Vengeful spirits would rise and all that."

Mia wondered what it would have been like to have a mom who'd pushed her to do things. Mia liked reading and cooking, and when she was in high school, she had participated in track. She enjoyed being outside and alone with her thoughts as she ran. Her mom would drive her to any extracurricular club or activity she wanted to join, but she didn't push one thing over another.

And when Mia said she didn't want to do something anymore, like when she quit Girl Scouts, they'd talk about it, but mostly, her mom had agreed with her decision. Not like these moms who seemed more committed to the contest than their daughters, who were on their phones checking social media.

Only one girl stood alone and took in all the views as well as the bones of the old school. She walked over to Mia, who was standing by the fireplace. "Do you know if this works?"

"It's original to the school, and yes, it works, but we don't usually have fires downstairs. Maybe I will this winter if we host a smaller event." Mia watched as the girl took in the elaborately carved woodworking around the room. "Do you like old houses?"

"I adore them. I live with my grandmother in an old Victorian on Main Street. It's been here since Magic Springs was a gold rush town." She smiled at Mia and held out her hand. "I'm Melody. I think they ran out of senior girls who could fit into the dresses when they chose me to participate."

"I'm sure that's not true. Is your grandmother here?" Mia swallowed the laugh and looked at the crowd of mothers around Abigail and Bambi. She assumed Melody had been included since her mom had won the competition. What did they call those kids, legacies?

The group was fawning over the staircases and how lovely it would be to use them in the contest. Maybe for the evening gown competition.

"No, my grandmother isn't well. And well, my mom isn't around." Melody looked over at the group, and a touch of sadness showed on her face. "Besides, Crissy is going to win. She's the queen bee at the high school. Head cheerleader, president of the student body, etc."

"You never know," Mia said as they watched the group.

Bambi seemed to collect herself and appeared to be looking for a way out of the conversations. "Okay, ladies, I told Mrs. Majors that we wouldn't take up much of her time and we've been here five minutes past the time I'd promised we'd be out of her hair. Say goodbye and thank you for letting us tour the area. I'm sure it was very helpful to both the moms and their lovely daughters."

"I'm being called back into the cow herd." Melody touched the carved monk and his large belly that sat on the fireplace. "See you at the contest."

"I'll be here. Good luck." Mia watched her walk away, toward the girls. No one greeted her or even acknowledged her existence as she rejoined the group. Mia wondered what had happened to Melody's mom. Melody didn't seem happy to be part of this group.

No one knew what went through the mind of another person. Especially the underdeveloped mind of a teenager. Wild and varied couldn't begin to describe their emotions or thoughts.

Mia hoped this event was going to be worth the trouble she could already see coming.

CHAPTER 2

The lighting in the restaurant was muted, making the candle in the iron moose holder on the table sparkle even more. Mia loved eating at new places and trying to figure out what the owner was thinking when they made décor decisions. Working in the catering department rather than running a full-menu restaurant day in and day out was more her style. By focusing on catering, she could change the menu she offered to fit a client's needs or her whims. But sometimes, she wondered what it would be like to know exactly what she was going to be cooking each day.

"I'd offer you a penny for your thoughts, but from the look on your face, it would probably be much more expensive. What's got you dreaming again?" Trent sipped the wine they'd ordered that had been produced at a new vineyard just down the road. "A bad day with Frank?"

"Are there any good days with Frank?" Mia picked

up her glass and took a sip of the rosé. The sweetness was surprising, especially considering the hot desert climate where the grapes grew. "That's tasty."

Trent nodded his agreement but didn't speak. He knew that sometimes she just needed a little more time to format her thoughts.

She looked up at him, wanting him to say something. Anything. If she said it twice in one day, the chance she'd quit sooner than she'd planned would be more likely to occur. She knew herself. Finally, she gave in. "I don't think it's fair to Frank for me to be at the Lodge, knowing I've got one foot out the door already."

"Frank gets what he paid for. You're the best catering director in Southern Idaho. Probably in all of Idaho, if not the Pacific Northwest. He's getting your expertise for a steal. Don't let his negativity drive you out of a job you need to support your business. You have things under control. Mom's getting a kick out of working again, and she loves planning parties." He smiled at their waitress as she dropped off their dinners. "You do what *you* need to do. Stop worrying about other people."

She cut into the steak and checked its doneness before taking a bite. She rarely ate beef, but this was a special occasion. It was their dating first anniversary. "Easier said than done, I'm afraid. There's a reason our clan is called 'kitchen witches.' Historically, we're all about peace and harmony."

"You need to take better care of yourself rather than focusing on the needs of others. That's all I'm saying."

He bit into his steak. "This place is wicked good. I'm glad we could get reservations."

"Thank you for dinner. I appreciate you making time for us. I know you're busy with the store." Majors had been undergoing a major remodel for the last few months with most of the work being done at night when the store was closed. Trent's father, Thomas Majors, was working with the architect company that had designed the changes. Trent was all excited about the new services they were going to be able to provide. Trent's dad, not so much.

Change for change's sake didn't quite fit Thomas's personal motto. He was more of a traditionalist with the "if it's not broke, don't fix it" axiom. It didn't matter; Thomas wasn't making the final decisions. Trent was in charge.

Trent chuckled as he wiped his mouth with his napkin. "Dad's all upset about the deli case. He doesn't think anyone would even want to purchase sandwiches or frozen dinners without being part of your delivery system."

"As long as they have money to buy the food, I don't care if they want to meet me in person before they buy. I'm glad you're going to have a spot for my products. A sale is a sale." Mia played with her lobster mac and cheese, using her fork to move the pieces around her plate. "I haven't tried to make this for delivery yet. I'm tempted, but I worried about how the lobster will freeze."

"That's the problem with fresh ingredients. It's an 'it's not you, it's me' situation. Sometimes serving things made to order is the right recipe." Trent reached over and scooped up a bite with his fork. "This is excellent."

Mia took a bite, then another before Trent's fork could return. She didn't mind sharing, but this was awesome. "Did your mother tell you she landed the coven's queen contest account? That's going to fill the business' coffers for quite a few months. And if the delivery business stays busy, I might not need to work at the Lodge for much longer."

"Then Mom will have to go back down to cake decorator. Dad will be happy." Trent shook his head. "I don't know about their relationship. It feels like one person has to lose for the other to win."

"I hope we're not that way." Mia thought about what she'd said. She hadn't thought about what it took for a couple to work for a long time. With Isaac, he had to be first and the one in charge. He had to be the power side of the equation. He would have hated watching Mia grow her business. He'd discouraged her from starting a catering company for the entire time they'd been together. He liked being her boss. And now that the company was semi-successful, he would have been talking about the best way for her to sell out and exit the business. Something she didn't have to or even want to do. She wanted to keep growing her business. And remodel the entire Academy building. And so much more. Mia knew she'd probably never want to close the business, but she could slow it down if she needed to limit her hours for maybe a baby or two. She hadn't really thought about couple dynamics since she'd started dating Trent. That had to be a good sign.

"We're definitely not that way. I don't know if Mom

mentioned it or not, but they almost divorced when I was in middle school. Mom was working at Majors, and Dad was hunting a lot. She reeled him in, and they set some rules as a couple. They have never taken each other for granted since."

A woman paused at the table. Mia looked up into Tatiana Evans's smiling face. "Oh, my, isn't this a coincidence."

"Hi, Mrs. Evans. Nice to see you again." Mia wiped her mouth with her napkin.

"We came down from the mountain for dinner. You can only eat at the Lodge so many times, right?" Tatiana smiled and held her hand out to Trent. "Please call me Tatiana. Mrs. Evans makes me sound like my mother-in-law. And this is Jack. I know who this handsome guy is, Trent Majors. I just saw your mother, but how's that handsome father of yours, Thomas?"

"He's fine. Nice to see you again, Tatiana. Jack." Trent stood and shook the man's hand.

Jack still hadn't said one word, nodding at Trent instead.

"I was so happy to hear that Thomas had agreed to judge the queen contest this year. With Majors as a sponsor, we desperately needed someone from the family, although I'm sure the girls were hoping for you or Levi. Someone closer to their age." Tatiana smiled like a satisfied cheetah who'd just bagged her prey.

"Your dad's judging the queen contest?" Mia sat back in her chair. She didn't know why the news had taken her by surprise, but it had.

Trent met her gaze. "This is news to me too."

Tatiana giggled and covered her mouth. "Oops. I

hope I didn't spill the beans. I'm sure I'll see you both soon. This harvest festival is the crown jewel of Magic Spring's fall season. I just hope that Crissy does well in the contest. I've been waiting for my chance to be on the council for years."

The couple walked away, and Mia tried to process the information.

"Mia, I really didn't know that Dad had told them yes. Both Levi and I told the coven representative that we were too busy, but I guess Dad said yes. Is it a problem?"

Mia pursed her lips together. "Frank's going to think your dad being a judge is why Mia's Morsels was chosen. That we had an in when the contract was awarded."

"You did have an in, but that was Mom and the fact that she knows so many people on the board. Not Dad being a judge." Trent sipped his wine. "I hate it when a perfectly good date night turns into a business discussion."

Mia reached for his hand. "Don't think that way. We can deal with this when we get back into Magic Springs. Right now, it's just you and me at this table. And we're having a great dinner."

A few minutes later, a different man approached the table. He was dressed in chef whites. "How was your meal?"

"Perfect," Trent said while Mia looked up at the chef.

She gasped, then stood and hugged the man. "Brad? Is that you?"

"Well, I hope so, but maybe you just give hugs to all the chefs who feed you well. However, the lobster mac and cheese is hug-worthy." The chef, now known as

Brad, squeezed her back, then let go. He reached over and shook Trent's hand. "Before you decide to hit me, let me introduce myself. Brad Heinrich. I knew Mia in Boise. We had both taken the same cooking class. No one expected me to do anything with the information, but Mia, she was voted most likely to succeed that year."

Mia sat back down. "Now, Brad's being modest. He got a scholarship for the Boise State culinary arts degree. The full ride. The award worked out well for him."

A crash sounded from the kitchen. "I better go. They work better with me in the kitchen leading the troops. I play the best music. Thanks for coming tonight. I'll make my way up to Magic Springs tomorrow, and we can catch up. I'm off on Wednesdays."

Another crash made him hurry away. Mia watched as he disappeared back into the kitchen.

Trent cut another bite off his steak. "So, Brad, huh."

"Don't even start. He was just a friend. Well, we went out to pizza one night without the group, but there was never anything romantic between us. He was a total food geek, which is what we had in common in the first place. Getting both of us in the same room is horrible. We can name all the ingredients in a soup by taste." Mia grinned at the memory.

"Sounds like a fun time." He grinned as Mia threw a napkin at him. "No worries. You do you, boo. I'm just glad I'm at the table. And that we're not talking about my dad anymore."

As they drove back to Magic Springs, Trent turned on the music, and Mia found herself lost in memories of high school. Before she knew she would have to take on the family mantle of a kitchen witch. She'd known her mom wasn't keen on her learning the craft, but she'd thought maybe she'd change her mind. Her grandmother had known it would be Mia for years, though. That's why she'd started training Mia when she came for summer breaks. Her grimoire had grown each summer as she learned potions and spells.

As a side benefit, Grans let her cook and experiment. She made her own recipe book that first summer, starting with cookies and then expanding into savory dishes. If she wasn't under Grans's tutelage for witchcraft, she would be in the kitchen, cooking or baking something. Gran's herb garden was planted right next to the house, and as the plants grew, Mia learned more about ways to store the bounty for the winter. She must have read every cookbook in the library over those summers.

She felt the truck stop and looked up from her day-dreaming. They were back at the old school.

Trent looked over at her. "You've been quiet. Everything okay, or am I about to be dumped for Chef Brad?"

She laughed and slid out of the truck cab. "You can't get rid of me that easily. I was thinking about high school, and then that rabbit trail led to the summers I spent here in Magic Springs with Grans. I need to find my old recipe book and see what I was making back then."

"That's why you and I mesh so well. I bring the food; you make it delicious." He walked her to the front door. "I need to go up and collect Cerby."

"Levi's up there with Christina. They made baby-sitting a date night." Mia unlocked the door to the old school and stepped into the foyer, turning on the downstairs light. A figure stood near the fireplace. Mia froze in place. "Who's there?"

But instead of answering, the figure just disappeared.

Trent stood next to her. "That's a new ghost, isn't it?"

Mia nodded. Either the wards the coven had placed on the old school were slipping, or this ghost had just taken a while to show up. Some of the library ghosts had hung around, even after they'd been shown the way out of this plane. "I think so. It looked like a woman. She reminded me of someone, but I can't place it."

"I can't say I knew her. But most of the ghosts here are from years ago, when the school was running, right?" He checked the door lock. "Do you want me to ask Mom what she knows?"

"That's okay." Mia headed upstairs. She didn't want to overreact to seeing a ghost. Especially since she already knew the school was haunted. She'd be freaking out all the time. "I don't go to work until noon tomorrow, so I'll see your mom before they start the delivery process."

He put his arm around her, and they walked up the three flights to her top-floor apartment. She went to open the door, but he stilled her hand from turning the key and turned her toward him. "Do you want me to stay for a while?"

She reached up and touched his face. She could see the weariness on him and knew his morning would start early tomorrow when the delivery trucks arrived. Running a small business was a lot of work. "I'd love for you to stay, but I think you need to go home and get some sleep. Isn't Cerby sleeping through the night, yet?"

Trent groaned and rubbed a hand through his short hair. His go-to move when he was frustrated. "No. And I've tried everything. I've even threatened to send him home with my mom after work. He went outside by himself when I finally fell asleep last night. And when I woke up, he was playing with a pile of newspapers he'd gathered from the subdivision. He's a pain."

"He opened your front door?" Mia tried to keep the grin off her face.

Trent pushed her hair off her shoulders. "I wish. He actually made a portal. I watched him as he did his trick in front of me. One of these days, he's going to make a portal to somewhere he can't get back from. Like Antarctica."

Mia reached up and gave Trent a kiss. "Maybe we should talk about moving in together sooner than next spring."

"We agreed we'd wait for Christina to move out with my brother. I know you don't want to hurry her leaving along. You're already doing the mother hen dance when her baby chicken is leaving the nest." He leaned on the doorway. He was beat.

"I know, but that conversation happened before Cerby arrived into our lives. Maybe having one more pair of hands to shoulder the weight might help." She rubbed his chest. "Besides, Christina's a big girl. Having you sleeping in my room isn't going to send her to a therapist."

He leaned in and kissed her. "You're assuming I'll

move in here. I have a huge house out by the river. Anyway, we'll talk about this later. Are we still on for dinner on Friday?"

"As long as I don't get a surprise catering gig at the Lodge, of course." Mia reached back down and turned the key. "Next weekend is out of the question. I think we'll have people here with the contest for a full week, if not longer. Oh, and I need to talk to you about a temporary walkway out in the backyard for the competition. I don't want to spend a lot since we'll be tearing it down later."

"A runway? You want me to build a runway?" He laughed as he followed her into the living room. He nodded to the occupants. "Hey, Levi, Christina."

Cerby barked and jumped off the couch. He ran to Trent, then levitated into his arms, reaching up to lick his face as Trent pulled him close.

"I can't take you anywhere without you using your magic. We've talked about this. No magic in front of mortals." Trent pointed a finger at the little Maltese.

"Wow, that's hurtful. Cerby loves his aunty Christina." Christina got up and rubbed Cerby's head as she walked into the kitchen. "There's leftover barbecue if you're hungry."

"We ate in Twin." Mia followed her into the kitchen. "How was the pup?"

"Cerby was great. That levitation act was the first batch of magic we'd seen all night. I was really worried about taking him outside, but he just played in the yard, did his business, and then came back in. I think he knows I'm human so he gives me a break." Christina grabbed something off the shelf near the television.

"And he found this. I'm assuming it's one of your grandmother's?"

Mia took the small potion pouch from Christina. It felt different. Not like anything Grans would make. It felt like a glamour spell. One a witch would add to her makeup routine. Maybe it had fallen out of one of the mothers' pockets from the queen contest. "I'll ask, but I don't think so."

"Well, I didn't think he should be eating it." Christina rubbed Cerby's head. "He could choke on something like that."

"You're a good babysitter. And of course, he knows you're mortal. He's a hellhound. He can smell magic miles away," Trent said as he and Levi followed them into the kitchen. "If I'm going to play carpenter for you, I guess we need to get a schedule set up. Levi, I could use your help as well. What are you planning for the next few days?"

Mia pulled out her planner. "Anyone need a piece of paper or a pen?"

The other three held up their phones.

Trent grinned. "We live in the digital age. It's all in one place."

"Until you lose your phone. Then you'd be wishing you had a planner." Mia pointed to the calendar on the wall where she and Christina meal-planned around all their activities. "And a calendar. And a computer calendar."

"You double-booked yourself twice last week alone," Christina pointed out.

Mia shook her head. "That was because Frank added

something to my work calendar without asking me first. It wasn't a problem with my system except for the fact that I allow him to make changes."

"Face it, Christina. Mia's old-school when it comes to planning. I bet she doesn't know what she's doing the day after Christmas this year." Levi opened the app on his phone. "I know I'm going to Hawaii."

Christina punched him. "You are not."

He held out the phone. "Seriously, I am. See. Seven days in a swim-up suite on the main island."

"Thanks for inviting me, you jerk." Christina made a face at him, then turned back to Mia. "So the competition is two weeks from Friday night, but they need time to practice on the 'runway,' as Trent calls it. Which means, you need to start next week."

"Yeah, I see that." Trent was making notes on his phone as quickly as Mia was writing them down on her planner. "Make sure you send this schedule to Mom too. She likes to be included since she's technically the one in charge of this event."

Mia looked up from her notebook. "I'm overstepping, aren't I?"

Trent shook his head. "It's your business. And you're the one who has to eat the costs of the dais and runway. Just keep Mom in the loop so I don't get comments from her."

"I'll send her an email as soon as we finish our planning session." Mia made a note on a Post-it. "Okay, what nights will you be here? I want to try to be here to watch Cerby and make you dinner."

"There's more than just you, Mia." Levi put an arm

around Christina. "We'll be here for you. Of course, I'll be Mr. Slavedriver's assistant, so Christina is going to have to pull the dog-sitting or dinner cards."

"Well, since I'll be here and not on some tropical vacation, I can do that." Christina looked at the kitchen calendar. "All my stuff for the next two weeks is up on that calendar. Just tell me if you need me for something. I've got a headache, and I'm heading to bed."

Mia watched as Christina departed the room. It wasn't quite stomping out, but it was close. She shook her head at Levi. "Leave her be. She'll be more rational tomorrow."

Levi grinned. "I'm not sure. I think she's going to be even madder when she finds out she's coming to Hawaii with me and I didn't ask her first. I've already made the reservations."

CHAPTER 3

Abigail was on her cell phone as she walked into the apartment the next morning. She rolled her eyes at Mia as she handed her a cup of coffee. "Of course, you can come by again and look at the backyard. I'm sure our solution for the walkway will be perfect for the girls. And we have a way for the audience to be able to see everyone clearly as they do their evening gown walk."

Mia opened her planner and held up a pen.

Abigail sat at the table, listening to the other side of the call. "Eleven o'clock today would be perfect."

Mia wrote down the time and pushed a fresh cinnamon roll toward Abigail as she hung up the phone. Lucky for her, Mia had to go into work this morning.

"Thanks, I need this. I'm sorry I got Mia's Morsels involved in this event. You wouldn't think that a beauty contest would be so high maintenance. Bambi is bringing the moms back over, this time without the daughters. They have other obligations, like school." Abigail sipped her water. "I'm so glad I didn't have daughters who had to go through this rite of passage."

"Is participating in the pageant required of coven girls?" Mia hadn't realized it wasn't voluntary.

Abigail shrugged. "Yes and no. Of course, a girl can bow out, but all the families know the winner gets a seat for a family member on the council for a year. And that's good money. It can change someone's life."

"Which is why Melody Sellers is participating. Okay, now that makes more sense. She didn't seem like the pageant type." Mia took a fork and pulled off part of a cinnamon roll still in the pan. She didn't want a full roll. She'd already had one for breakfast. She just wanted another taste.

"Melody might not be, but her mother was. Sherry was raised to win the competition. After she died, Melody's grandmother kind of lost it. She's on our delivery route. I don't think Mrs. Sellers has left the house in years." Abigail opened her paper planner. This one had a flowered cover, but at least it was paper. Not like the people last night, who'd made fun of Mia's system. One of the reasons that Abigail and Mia were friends. "Thanks for updating me last night. My job is easier when we communicate."

"I just hope I didn't overstep by hiring Trent." Mia pulled out the plan they'd sketched out last night and showed Abigail the flow with the dais and the walkways. "This way, they can use the entire yard as their runway."

"It's perfect." She held up the sheet of paper. "Can I

make a copy of this for the tour today? I think seeing this might calm down the pageant moms."

"Just put the original back in this folder. I'll keep a folder up here so if I make any changes or have suggestions, I'll have them here."

A noise came from the hallway, and Christina came into the room. Her eyes were red. Whatever Levi's game was, Mia hoped he'd tell her the truth before Mia spilled the beans. She didn't like seeing Christina this upset. Even if the trip was supposed to be a surprise. "Good morning," Mia said.

Christina didn't answer, just poured her coffee.

"Oh, my. What has my son done now?" Abigail leaned forward and tucked a strand of hair behind Christina's ear.

"Nothing. I'm fine." She stood and picked up her coffee cup. "I'm heading downstairs. That van isn't going to pack itself."

Abigail and Mia watched as Christina stormed out of the apartment. "Whatever he's done, he has to fix it. Now. I have to work with her," Abigail said.

"He's your son, you might want to talk to him." Mia left the discussion at that. She wasn't responsible for reporting back what Levi and Trent did to their mother. Especially since Abigail was also part of her business. There needed to be some boundaries. "Anyway, I need to get ready to go to the Lodge. We're having a lunch meeting to talk about this quarter's earnings as well as next quarter's events. I'm sure Frank's going to have some not-so-subtle comments about Mia's Morsels and their winning the bid for the queen contest."

"Just tell him what I said. That we were told we had the highest cost proposal. I don't think he wants you to fight with unsustainable budget projections. The point of his business model is to make money. I just want you to have a sustainable block of business so you can come back to just doing your passion." Abigail stood and put her now-empty plate into the sink. She refilled her coffee cup and paused. "Don't worry so much. Everything is going to turn out."

Mia cleaned up the dining area and then put the rest of the rolls away. She spied the potion bag on the counter. She'd forgotten to ask Abigail about it. Mia was almost certain Abigail didn't use glamour spells in her everyday life, but she could be wrong. She set the bag in the middle of the table so she'd remember to ask her tomorrow or the next time Mia saw her.

Then she went to her room to get ready for work.

Two hours later, the meeting was finally over. James, the kitchen manager, pulled Mia toward his office. "Let's grab something to eat. I'm trying out a new recipe for Cobb salad, and I need a taste tester."

"How many versions of Cobb salad can you make?" Mia asked. She didn't keep the grumpy out of her voice. Frank had been in rare form. Every time she'd opened her mouth, he'd made a face or called her out on something simple, or worse, just ignored what she'd said. "He's a five-year-old, throwing a tantrum. I'm sure he tried to get the corporate guys to let him fire me, but I've been too good at my job. And I've made him look good."

"Yes, you're right, and you don't have to have any salad. I just need you to eat something and calm down before you throw your resignation in Frank's face. I don't know if I could do this job without my partner in crime around." James gently pushed her into his office and then stood at the door blocking the exit. "So, what do you want?"

"I want to wring his neck." Immediately, Mia saw the distressed look on James's face and felt bad. Maybe Trent was right. She did try to please everyone else. "Fine, get me a French dip and lots of fries. With fry sauce."

"Ooh, a French dip sounds amazing. I might order one as well." James started to leave to put the order in the kitchen. Then he popped his head back in the office. "You're staying put, right?"

Mia gave him a pained smile. "I'll be right here when you get back. I have a mortgage payment to make."

"Perfect. About you staying, not the mortgage." James disappeared, and Mia opened her laptop to check her emails. All the other department heads had sent her emails railing about how Frank had treated her. The housekeeping manager—who had been there longer than anyone—even said she was reaching out to corporate to report his bad behavior. Mia scanned the other emails that had come in when she was in the meeting and answered several quick questions about possible bookings. Frank was a jerk, but he'd get over this. She just needed to ride the storm out. Besides, if she loved this job, maybe she'd never leave and take back over the reins at Mia's Morsels. And that would be a shame.

Day jobs paid the bills. Passion projects took a while to be successful.

Especially in small towns like Magic Springs.

James came back with a tray with what looked like a pitcher of mimosas and one of iced tea. And four glasses. "Our food will be ready soon, but I thought we deserved a pick-me-up. Then we'll drink iced tea during our meal. You're working here this afternoon, right?"

"I am. So, give me a mimosa, and we can toast to what a jerk Frank is and how we survived another meeting." Mia closed her laptop. "I got emails from everyone in that room today about how inappropriate he was. I'm saving them in my 'Frank' file. If I go down, he's going to go down first."

"See, that's my girl. You have a plan." James poured the mimosas and handed her one. "I have to say, I'm glad you're hosting the queen contest over at the school. We have the out-of-towners coming into the hotel for the festival, so we're going to be busy enough in two weeks. Frank never sees the good in not getting a catering event."

"The mothers came over again today to check out the venue. The school isn't that big. And they were just there yesterday," Mia complained as she sipped her drink. "I'm just glad Abigail is dealing with them. I had my fill yesterday when they came to see the setup."

"The event coordinator, Bambi, she's a sweetheart. She tries to rein in the mothers from hell, but sometimes even she can't control them. This contest is a big deal in Magic Springs. I didn't even think anyone still did beauty pageants." James refilled his glass and Mia's, draining the small pitcher completely.

James was mortal, so he didn't know about the coven connection. Mia wasn't going to be the one to out the coven's traditions. "I guess being a small town is why they still do the pageant."

"I get tradition. I just don't get why the moms are so brutal during this process. I really hope they don't treat people like this all the time." James drained his mimosa, then turned to the tea. "But they've been this way since I moved here to take over the kitchen. I'm surprised you didn't get involved last year."

"I remember going to the festival the Saturday after the competition and watching the parade, but no, queen contests aren't my cup of tea." She set the half-empty mimosa on the tray and poured herself a glass of tea. "The corn dogs at the festival were amazing."

"My friend Tanner owns that food truck. He's always trying to perfect the lowly corn dog." James continued talking about the festival and the brief history he had around the event. Mia needed to chat with her grandmother tonight. One, to see if she'd left that potion bag. And two, Mia wanted to know what they were getting into with this catering gig. Maybe they could be prepared for any bad actors causing problems.

After lunch, Mia headed home and wasn't surprised to see Grans's old car in the school's parking lot. Her grandmother seemed to know when Mia needed to talk. As she parked her car, a truck with the logo of the Magic Springs Police Department pulled in after her. She got out of the car and smiled at Mark Baldwin, the local police chief. "Hey, Mark, did you come for a frozen dinner or two? I've got a stuffed meat loaf in there that will knock your socks off. And how's the little angel?"

Mark closed the door and held out his hand. "Give me some room, Mia. Abigail called in a suspicious death. I need to check this out."

"Wait? Who's dead?" Mia stayed near her car, not wanting to be locked out of her own home.

"Abigail didn't say. Just stay here, and I'll clear you as soon as I find out if this is an active shooter situation." Mark wasn't focused on Mia anymore. He had drawn his gun, and he and another officer were moving toward the old schoolhouse door.

Mia said a quick prayer for everyone's safety as she watched her house become a crime scene. Again.

CHAPTER 4

After what seemed like hours to Mia, the other officer returned to the doorway and waved her inside. She hurried to his side. "So, what happened? False alarm?"

The officer shook his head. His name tag said *Officer Forester*. "Sorry, ma'am. There has been a death. Chief Baldwin wants to talk to you about the deceased. Please come with me."

"It's not Christina, is it?" Fear made Mia's heart race. "Pretty blonde, early to mid-twenties."

"I know Christina Adams, and no, it's not her. Or Abigail Majors, before you go there. This woman attended my church. It's Carla Manson. Her daughter is going to be heartbroken." Officer Forester turned back into the school and headed for the stairs. "Chief Baldwin is up here."

Mia followed him into the school, closing the door behind her. Then she followed him to the second floor.

"The moms were here this morning, checking out the school. Carla must have really wanted to use the stairs for the evening gown competition."

The officer didn't say anything else, just led her to an empty schoolroom near the top of the stairs. Baldwin stood over a body on the floor. Or a body-shaped blanket. Maybe Mia had had too many mimosas at work. Maybe she was asleep at her desk, and this was just a dream. She pinched her forearm, and pain flowed up to her brain. "I guess I'm awake."

Baldwin looked at her strangely. "You thought you were dreaming?"

"There's a dead woman in my school. I can't think of any other alternative." Mia glanced around the room, trying to figure out what had happened. "It doesn't look like there was a struggle."

"We don't know what happened. There are no stab wounds or any other marks on her body. It could have been a heart attack. Abigail Majors said the woman was very upset during the tour that Bambi Perry set up earlier today. Maybe she just got too excited."

Mia blinked, once, twice, then three times. "You think she got hysterical and just died? Didn't that diagnosis go out for women in the Roaring Twenties?"

"Mia, I'm not a doctor. I can't even deal with giving Sarah a shot. Or watching the baby get her immunizations. I'll send the body to the county morgue. Then we'll have a cause of death. But you're right, usually, people just don't fall over dead." Baldwin took off his cap. "We'll be out of here in a few hours. Your grandmother and the rest of your posse are up in the apartment."

"Thanks, Mark." Mia turned to leave and almost didn't see the small white bag in the corner of the doorway. She checked to make sure that neither man was watching her, then picked it up. Another potion bag.

What was going on? Did Carla's death have anything to do with the potion bags she'd been finding around the school? Or was that just another coincidence?

She went up the final flight and found the apartment door opening. No one was nearby until she looked down and saw Mr. Darcy with Cerby in tow. She shooed them back into the apartment. "No going outside until the police are gone. Sorry, guys."

Trent came into the room and scooped Cerby into his arms. "I told you to stay inside when I got here a few minutes ago. Sorry, Mia. I've already said my piece, but he doesn't seem to be listening."

"I think he and Mr. Darcy are up to something." Mia picked her cat up. "Just give us a few minutes until the mortal people leave, and then you two can go on your mission."

Mr. Darcy blinked at Mia, then jumped out of her arms.

She called after the cat as he disappeared down the hall, probably heading toward her bedroom, "I'm taking that as a yes."

One loud *meow* was all she got. Mia went to the kitchen and grabbed the other potion bag. Then she set both of them in front of Grans on the coffee table. "What are these?"

Grans looked up from the book she was reading. She dropped her glasses farther down her nose as she studied them. "Potion bags. Not mine, if that's what you're thinking."

Mia nodded. "It was. So, can you tell who they belong to? Or better, what they are meant to do? I've found two of them now on the school property. I don't think that is a coincidence, and I think one of the queen contestant moms must have brought them."

"I'll look into them. Why on earth was Carla Manson in a second-floor classroom?" Grans set her book aside. "Abigail said their group left at noon. That was hours ago."

All gazes went to Abigail. "Don't ask me. She left with the group. I saw them all get into Bambi's van. Then I went to the kitchen and worked with Christina, cleaning up after today's deliveries. We have a class tomorrow night on fall casseroles. I wanted to make a shopping list so I could give it to Trent."

"It's just weird that she would come back, just to wind up dead. Did Baldwin have a cause of death?" Grans turned to Mia, who shook her head.

"Not yet. He says there are no visible wounds." Mia leaned back in her chair. "At least the cleaning of the room will be easier that way. Wait, that sounded bad. I must be tired. Are we still sure we want this catering client?"

"You want to give it back to Frank, even after all the trouble he's caused you?" Christina asked. "You've always been able to turn the other cheek, but this feels excessive."

"No, you're right. I'm not going to turn down the gig. It was just a long day at the Lodge." Mia looked at

Abigail. "Did you know that Thomas is serving as a judge for the queen contest?"

Abigail jerked up her head, and Mia could have sworn fire burned in her eyes. "No, but I'll have a chat with him as soon as I get home."

"Uh-oh. Dad's in trouble." Trent grinned as he held Cerby.

His mother's attention diverted to him. "What are you doing here and why aren't you at the store?"

"Measuring for wooden runways for a bunch of spoiled high school seniors." He pulled his measuring tape from his pocket. "I need to make sure that Twin Falls Lumber is going to have the materials."

"Sounds like a good excuse," Levi said as he walked into the apartment. "Hey, everyone. Christina, I think we need to talk."

Mia noticed the same look she'd just seen on Abigail cover Christina's face. She stood and walked back into her room through the main hallway.

Levi looked at the people left in the living room. "Wish me luck."

Abigail sighed. "I'd hoped that my heart-to-heart this morning had some effect on him."

"Mom, what you call a heart-to-heart, we refer to as the 'beatdown'. I'm sure he'll do the right thing and stop playing with Christina. He adores her." Trent stood and checked the outside monitors. "I hope the police release the crime scene soon. I need to get out in the yard before it gets too dark to see."

"I probably should make some dinner since every-one is here." Mia thought about standing, but before

she could, Abigail popped up and waved her back
down.

"I'll make dinner. I've just texted Thomas and told
him he was on sandwiches tonight." She winked at
Mia. "I need some time to cool off before I talk to him
about this judge thing. He knew we were doing the
catering. I figured that, along with the generous spon-
sorship from Majors Grocery, would be our family
contribution. He doesn't need to be in the mix if magic
starts getting thrown around like it has in the past."

"Okay, now you have to tell me what happened."
Mia pushed herself off the chair. "I'll help with dinner.
What are you thinking about making?"

"Comfort food. Either some kind of soup or my tuna
casserole. I was going to check your fridge to see what
you had available." Abigail glanced back at Grans, who
was using a pen to poke at the potion bags. "Are you
coming?"

"I'll be there in a few. I want to check these out.
They feel new. Like someone just made them. Maybe
the contest group was trying to spell the school in
someone's favor." Grans looked up at Abigail. "Like
they did for the old Mill restaurant in 1998."

"Didn't that place burn down?" Mia asked, watching the conversation between the two women.

"Yes, it did. Right after the competition, where a
long shot took the crown." Abigail's lips pressed together in a line. "If someone is trying to sway the results, we might have a problem. And that might be why
Carla's dead."

Mia looked at her grandmother and then back at

Abigail. "Seriously? People would kill over this beauty pageant?"

"I told you, for the coven members, it's a lot more than just a beauty pageant." Abigail shook her head. "I'm afraid I didn't pad the proposal enough to save us from having to put on the competition."

"You tried to sabotage the bid?" Now Mia didn't know what to think. Frank hated her for Abigail winning the bid. But now she knew that Abigail hadn't wanted it in the first place. She couldn't win for losing.

Abigail nodded. "But it's too late to cry over spilled milk. We have the contract. Let's just try to keep anyone else from dying over this stupid contest."

"Or the school from burning down," Grans said under her breath as she studied the mixture in the potion bags.

"Great, now I feel worse about getting the contract than I already did." Mia followed Abigail into the kitchen. Gloria, the kitchen witch doll who was also a familiar and a connection with the Goddess, giggled as they came in. Mia gave her a look. "I don't need any comments from you, missy."

Abigail frowned, then saw Mia looking at the doll. "I didn't realize she was your connection. I guess I should have."

"Grans gave me Gloria when I was ten, with my grimoire. I suppose my connection with her was supposed to break when I got Mr. Darcy, but it stayed just as strong. They have conversations about me when I'm not around. I walk in on them sometimes." Mia stroked Gloria's straw hair and adjusted her plaid dress. "I know it sounds weird, but they have always been there for me. Even during my time with Isaac."

"There's nothing wrong with being attached to your familiars. It's the way we keep in contact with the Goddess." Abigail opened the fridge and started pulling out vegetables. "Do you have plans to use these?"

Mia shook her head. "I went overboard at the farmers market last weekend. Everything looked so good. I made a huge salad on Sunday, but then we went out last night. Now the rest of the veggies need to be used or frozen before they go bad. What are you thinking about?"

"An old recipe I got from Girl Scouts back in the day. They called it hobo soup, but that's probably a little too politically incorrect these days. Anyway, everyone just brought a can of something. We got a slip the week before listing out our contribution." Abigail opened the freezer and found a package of hamburgers. "Perfect, now I'll just start chopping."

Mia reopened the fridge and grabbed two quarts of the homemade beef broth she'd made. "Is this enough?"

Abigail smiled as she took the quart containers. "It's perfect."

Soon the two of them were chopping and mixing and stirring. That was the good thing about cooking; it took your mind off everything. Even having a dead woman one floor below them.

They'd just finished putting the stew on to simmer when Trent walked in the door. "Everyone's gone but Baldwin. He wants to talk to you. Levi and I are heading outside to get the measurements for the walkways and the dais. Do you have that drawing you made?"

Mia handed him the folder she'd kept in the kitchen. "Everything is in there. Make sure you have the lumber-yard charge my account and not Majors."

"Yes, ma'am." He kissed her before heading out of the apartment. "Oh, I'm taking Cerby outside with me. And apparently Mr. Darcy too. I'll watch and see what those two are up to."

"Sounds good." Mia looked up when Christina came into the kitchen. Her hair was pulled back into a pony-tail, and she could tell she'd been crying. "Everything okay?"

"Kind of. Levi said he was trying to keep the Hawaii trip a surprise. He was being funny when he pretended to be going without me. I didn't think it was humorous at all." Christina poured a glass of water out of the fridge's filtered tap and sat down at the table. "Am I overreacting?"

"From someone who has a history with your par-ents, you probably are dealing with some of the stuff your mom and dad pulled on you. Remember when they told you they'd take you out to the hot springs on Saturday if you cleaned your room?" Mia poured hot water over her loose tea holder and sat at the table with her.

"Yeah. Then on Saturday, Mom went shopping with her best friend and left me at home while I was getting my swimsuit on. I loved that pool." Christina sighed. "So, why are you bringing up old memories?"

"I think that is what happened between you and Levi. You expect people to tell you the truth. Some-times they don't. For a lot of reasons. But not all of them are bad." Mia smiled. "Besides, if he doesn't take you to Hawaii now, we'll go on a girls' trip."

"You and Isaac took me swimming at the hot springs the next day. Mom was furious because she had reservations for all of us for brunch at that fancy hotel." Christina squeezed Mia's hand. "You've always been there for me. I'm so lucky to have you in my life. Even if we aren't sisters."

Mia frowned. "What are you talking about? Of course, we're sisters."

"Stop fighting, you two. I swear I'll turn the car around." Abigail gave Christina a hug. "Family is what you build after you find out what's missing in the one you were born into. I think that's why we go out and develop our own lives as adults. To build better families."

Christina hugged Abigail back. Then she shot a look at Mia. "She started it."

They all started laughing.

"Let's make some biscuits to go with that soup." Abigail smiled at the two at the table. "It's good to have daughters in my life. No matter what happens between you two and my sons, you're still the daughters of my heart. Remember that."

When Grans came into the kitchen, she looked around the room. "This room reeks of female bonding. I'd tell you to knock it off, but I think we're going to need all the good vibes we can get in the school this next week while we host the contest. Those potion bags were set to mess with the intended victim's self-confidence. If a contestant had brushed up against one, they would have freaked out trying to present themselves during the event."

"Oh, no. We'd talked about having that room on the second floor as the room where the girls got ready for the evening gown competition. We were going to film them coming down the stairs, then the spotlight would take them from the house out to the dais." Abigail looked at Mia and shrugged. "It was a compromise from having the audience tucked into the lobby. And Tatiana said she would hire the cameraman."

"So, that's why Carla came back. To sabotage the dressing room." Mia sighed as she got the flour out of the cupboard. "Since she's gone, maybe this contest will go off as planned."

"You think Carla Manson was killed while she was setting up potions to scare the competition away so her daughter, Kristin, could win the queen contest? Are you all crazy?" Mark Baldwin stood in the doorway to the kitchen. "Sorry, the door was open, and no one answered my knock. That soup smells amazing."

Abigail glanced around the table. "The soup will be ready in about an hour, and we're making biscuits to go with it. Do you want to stay for dinner?"

Mark shook his head. "Sarah and Elisa Marie have dinner waiting for me. Or Sarah does, I'm sure she has Elisa Marie in bed by now. Having a family to go home to makes my days feel normal. Even though I've found out recently that both my family and Magic Springs are far from normal."

"Mark, it's not that bad. It's just when the coven gets involved in things that it gets messy." Mia tried to soothe

the police chief, who had recently found out that witches existed and that his wife, well, she had powers that she'd given up to be with him. Except, as Mia was finding out with Trent, sometimes power didn't leave just because you wanted it to. "Besides, this is a great town to raise a child." Especially one as special as his daughter. But Mia didn't add that part. Mark was dealing with enough now. He didn't need to worry about the future.

"Anyway, we don't know that Carla Manson was murdered or if she just died. As soon as the autopsy comes back, I'll let you know. Then you can do your 'society' investigation if it was a murder." He rubbed the top of his head. "And I sound like an idiot. I wouldn't believe any of this if Sarah hadn't been the one to expose your group."

"The coven is not my group," Mia tried to explain. But she guessed it didn't matter. To Mark, there were now three types of people: good, bad, and witches. And she was a witch.

CHAPTER 5

Work went better on Wednesday, mostly because that was Frank's day off. Mia sat in her car for a few minutes girding herself against his torment until she realized Frank was heading to Bozeman for the corporate retreat that weekend. The last hotel manager had taken all the department heads to this retreat, but no, not Frank. He wanted all the praise for their increased sold nights and catering jobs to go to him. They were supposed to funnel down to the actual departments, but Frank didn't like to share.

Mia grinned as she got out of the car and headed to the front door. She waved at the valets, calling out personal greetings as she went. Then she did the same to the front desk. As she made her way through the huge lobby, she was next to the floor-to-ceiling fireplace when she heard her name being called.

By Frank.

She turned around, the smile dropping from her lips

as she saw him powering down on her. "Frank, I thought you were on your way to Montana?"

"My plane leaves this afternoon. I got a call from the Davis family last night. They have a daughter-in-law who is expecting, and they want to throw a surprise baby shower for her this weekend. That won't be a problem, right? You can pull something of that scale off in less than three days, correct?"

Mia must have nodded because he grinned. "Perfect. I told Mrs. Davis you'd be here at nine. She's waiting in your office. Bad day to be four minutes late."

Mia spun around and hurried to her office. If she knew Frank, he'd had this party confirmation in his pocket for days now. Maybe weeks. But he'd held it back to make it difficult for Mia to give the Davis family the event they wanted. He wasn't just messing with her. He was messing with their customers. If there was a way to prove it, she'd send the information up the line and see if good ol' Frank didn't get his butt fired. She tried to slow her breathing down as she opened the door to her office. Not only was Mrs. Davis there, but four other women crowded the room. Mia had hit one of them with the door when she'd opened it.

"Oh, my, this won't do at all. Please come with me, and we'll set up in the conference room. That way you can get a feel for the room we'll be using for your party." Mia held open the door and shooed them all to the closest conference room. She and James had set it up yesterday as they were planning on getting the new servers together later that day for a training session.

She opened the door and then used the intercom phone on the wall to call James while the family came into the larger room. They looked like they could breathe again. Her office could get stuffy with just herself inside. Mia didn't want to think about how hot it had been with all four women. "James, would you be a dear and bring a tray of treats along with some coffee, iced tea, and a large pitcher of mimosas?" Mia saw the older Mrs. Davis smile at the mention of drinks. "We're in the conference room. You may want to bring a notebook and chat about your thoughts on what to serve at a baby shower too."

She closed the door and sat down at the table. She pulled her planner and a notebook out of her tote, which she hadn't left in her office. Digging for a pen, she asked, "So, tell me what your vision for the party will be? I'd like to give you exactly what you want."

Mrs. Davis nodded and opened her own planner.

A girl after my own heart. But she didn't say anything. She wanted Mrs. Davis to make the first move.

"We'd like to have the event on Friday. My son and his new wife are flying in on that day and I'm sure that no one in our family will be able to keep this a secret, so it's time to get this party going." Mrs. Davis put her hand on the table. "Your boss didn't want to schedule this meeting even though we've been talking for a couple of weeks. He said you worked better under pressure. I hope that's true."

Mia wanted to say so many things. She rubbed at her forehead, hoping she wasn't frowning. "That's water under the bridge now. Let's just focus on what you want for the party so I can go browbeat my suppliers to get the materials and ingredients here by Friday."

"I thought he was messing with us. From now on,

when we have an event, I'm going directly through you. Or maybe your new catering business. Have you remodeled the old school yet? I used to love going there. Everyone knew everything. And the library, well, it was divine."

Mia stuttered, "I didn't say . . ."

"Don't worry about it. I have friends in the corporation that owns this hotel. One of the reasons I agreed to have the party here and not at my house. Well, that and the cleanup afterward. I really don't like a lot of people in my house." Mrs. Davis shrugged. "What can I say? I'm picky."

James came in with the trays, and everyone grabbed a drink and a sweet treat. Mia asked James to sit after she introduced them and then focused on Mrs. Davis. "Tell us what you need to make this shower special. Do you know the gender of the child yet?"

Mia listened as Mrs. Davis described the party she envisioned. "We'll just be family, but that's enough. There are thirty-four of us now. When the new baby comes, we'll be thirty-five. My parents and my husband's parents are still alive and will be attending, so the smaller ballroom will work perfectly. They need something close to the bathrooms and near the elevator to their rooms. You can expect family to start checking in later today."

"That's wonderful," Mia tapped her pad. "How many rooms do you think you'll be using? If it's more than ten, we can give you a reduced rate on the ballroom rental."

"Lucky thirteen, from my count. Several of us live in the area. We may need more depending on my daughter-in-law's family." Mrs. Davis glanced over to a young woman who appeared to be her daughter.

"We haven't received any RSVPs from them." The other woman shrugged.

"Well, I'll alert the front desk to keep a running tally." Mia glanced at James. "So, what do you want for food?"

The meeting lasted over an hour, and by the time the Davises had left, Mia had a basic outline of what she needed to get done on what days. James walked with her to escort the family out and then waited while Mia talked to the front desk, alerting them to the upcoming guests. She met him, and they started to walk back to her office.

He didn't look at her when he asked, "Frank?"

"Frank. Mrs. Davis even knew she was being delayed just to mess with my schedule. He makes it impossible for me to like him. At all." Mia wanted to scream, but she held it in.

James laughed, and a housekeeper walking by jerked her cart away from him.

"It's not funny. Anyway, I bet he didn't know the Davises knew people on the board of the corporation. I bet they're going to get a call about his customer service. And if we do a great job, praises about ours." Mia paused at her office door. "Karma gets everyone in the end."

"Yeah, but sometimes you get to watch it do the smackdown." James held up his notebook. "I'll have a menu and a budget for you this afternoon with some alternatives, both up and down in price."

"Perfect. I'll get the rest of the proposal done, and

we can send it to Mrs. Davis before I leave for the day. I'd like her to have an idea of what this is going to cost sooner than the day before the event."

James smiled. "I'm not sure it matters. And it's only one additional day. I bet Frank told them some crazy high number, anyway. So we should be able to look like stars when we give them the final accounting."

"Maybe. Or he might have lowballed us so we would look bad when we gave her the actual cost. You never know with our devoted leader." Mia stepped into her office. "I've got to work."

Mia texted Trent to let him know that she was working on Friday night and asked if they could change their date night to Saturday. By six, she had a plan and a contract sent to Mrs. Davis. Somehow she and James had pulled it off. At least the planning of the event. Tomorrow she'd make sure that she had enough staff for the event scheduled, and James could deal with the food. The baby shower would be a hit, and Frank would have another satisfied customer to report to his boss.

Even though he'd almost blown the entire thing by not telling Mia about the event until the last minute. Sometimes life wasn't fair.

As she got in her car, she heard Gloria's giggle from the apartment. "Not funny, missy."

But as usual, Gloria's interventions lightened the mood around her. Mia found herself smiling and singing along with the radio as she drove home. Tomorrow she'd have Mrs. Davis's signed contract in her email, and she'd deliver an upscale event.

Trent called just as she was getting out of the car at the school. "Hey there, did you see my text?"

"Yeah, that's why I'm calling. Sorry, I'm not going to be able to get away Saturday during the day at the store, so Levi and I are working on the runway Saturday night. I'll be around the house if you want to order something. Maybe we can sneak away to the library or somewhere and eat for an hour or so."

Mia tried not to sigh. "That's fine. I know the runway has to be done."

He chuckled. "Mom about had a hissy fit when I asked if I could postpone the work. I think she and Dad are fighting about this judge thing. I wasn't going to tell her. I'm not sure you should have either."

"If it affects my business, of course I'm going to tell her." Mia unlocked the door and paused, seeing Abigail's SUV pulling into the driveway. "Hey, your mom's here. She must have forgotten something. I thought the class was this afternoon."

"That's not good," Trent said as Mia watched Abigail park her car and then open the back hatch door. She pulled out a suitcase.

"No, it's not good at all. Trent, I think she's moving in," Mia whispered into the phone as Abigail stormed toward her. "I'll call you later."

"Mia, I need a favor. Can I use your spare room for a few nights?" Abigail looked like she'd been crying as her makeup was smudged, but her face was stone if you ignored the raccoon eyes.

Mia held the door open. "Of course. Is something wrong?"

Abigail shook her head. "No, I just need some space. I'll put these in my room, then I'll make us some dinner. Do you have anything set out?"

Mia laughed. "I just got here. Frank blindsided me with a baby shower on Friday. I don't even know if Christina is here."

"She said she was staying in tonight when we talked after the class." Abigail nodded to the elevator. "I'll meet you upstairs. I don't know if I can carry this monster up three flights of stairs today. I'm beat."

Mia locked the door and then headed up the stairs. The next few weeks were going to be crazy. Especially if Abigail and Thomas were fighting. Christina was still mad at Levi's little prank. Thank the Goddess that she and Trent were solid. At least one couple in the family wasn't arguing.

A knock sounded at the door. Abigail was still waiting on the elevator. "If that's Thomas, I'm not here."

"Okay, I'll see who it is." Mia walked back to the door. She didn't want to lie to Trent's dad, but on the other hand, Abigail was her friend and ran her business for her. Maybe she could just say that she didn't want to see him. He could tell she was there since her car was in the driveway. Mia swung open the door. "Oh, it's you."

Brad Heinrichs stood there with a bouquet of flowers. He handed them to Mia. "That's a warm-ish welcome. It is I, Brad, your friend from high school who followed you and Laurie around like a puppy dog while we avoided the mean kids."

Mia leaned into the flowers, enjoying their scent. "Everyone liked you, Brad. It was me that they were on the hunt for. Laurie was amazing at shooing them away. Are these for me?"

"Yes, if your boyfriend isn't going to hit me for

bringing them. If so, you just found them on the doorstep." He glanced around the outside of the building. "It's Wednesday. I did mention that I was coming by, right?"

"Yes, you did." She took the flowers and opened the door wider. "Sorry, work was crazy."

"Well, let me take you to the Lodge for dinner. We can catch up, and you don't have to do anything but tell me what you're doing with this amazing building. I can't believe you own this."

Mia hesitated, then nodded. It would be nice to catch up. "Let me run upstairs and put these in water. I've got some company that I need to let know where I'm going, then I'll be down."

"Okay if I wait down here and check my email? Work has been blowing me up today due to shipment problems. I think I'm going to need to change tomorrow's specials on the fly." He held up his phone and grinned.

"I got a new event for Friday night this morning, so I feel your pain." Mia hurried up the stairs, not looking at the second-floor landing. If Carla's spirit was hanging around her death site, she'd just have to wait. Mia needed to chat with Abigail and try to explain why she was going out to dinner with a guy who wasn't her son. Even though it was just dinner, Abigail might see it differently.

Mia didn't have to explain anything. Abigail was still in her room. Christina sat in the living room, reading. "Hey, I'm going out tonight."

She looked up from her book. "Oh? Abigail was going to make us finger steaks."

"Sounds great, but a guy I went to high school with just stopped by, and he's taking me to the Lodge." Mia went to the kitchen and put the flowers in a vase. Christina followed her.

"Nice flowers."

Mia smiled at the unasked question. "It was a nice gesture. Anyway, I should be home no later than nine, and apparently, we have a new roommate for a bit."

"My dream has always been to live in an apartment with both my bosses." Christina glanced up at the security monitor. "Do I need to write down the plate for that BMW before you leave?"

"I don't think a Twin Falls chef is going to kidnap me. Unless he's working for Frank. And if he wants my job at the Lodge that bad, I'll give it to him." Mia glanced at her suit and took off the blazer. "I'm grabbing a sweater, then I'll be leaving."

Christina followed her into her bedroom. "Wear the blue one. It's warm enough, but it's dressy too. Was Frank horrible today?"

"I'll tell you about it later, but yes." Mia exchanged the blazer for a sweater. "He's trying to force me to quit."

"Probably. Look, I don't have to take a salary if that would help." Christina put a set of silver chains around Mia's neck. "That looks better."

"It's not a date. And no, you're not going without a paycheck. How will you pay the rent I charge you for this mansion?" Mia squeezed Christina's arm. "It will all work out."

"I got some money for graduation presents. I put it away for a house fund once we decide where we're

moving. Although Levi's not being serious about helping me to pick a place." Christina leaned on the doorway. "You and Trent okay?"

"We're fine. It's just dinner with an old friend." Mia
glanced at the guest bedroom. "I'm heading out. Let
Abigail know not to make me dinner, okay?"

"You could knock on her door and tell her yourself."
Christina followed Mia out to the apartment's front
door.

"I could, but I'm not going to." Mia waved her fingers. "Bye."

When she got back downstairs, Brad was wandering
through the lobby area, looking at different pictures on
the wall. "Did you get everything settled for your
menu?"

He grinned and shrugged. "Kind of. I turned my
phone off. I'll deal with whatever they bring me tomorrow. My sous chef just gets all worked up if things
aren't exactly as we planned. I like having a bit of a
curveball to up the creativity at times. You look amazing. Let's go."

Mia opened the front door and set the lock behind
her. Tonight she wasn't going to think about the death
or the queen contest or her job or Abigail's relationship. Tonight was just about remembering old times
and more than likely, talking food.

It was one of her favorite subjects.

CHAPTER 6

James greeted us as we entered the lobby. He pulled Brad into a bro hug. "Dude, I can't believe you're living here. I didn't think you'd ever leave Tucson."

"I decided I wanted more than hot and hotter for seasons." Brad slapped him on the back. "Oh, do you know Mia Malone?"

"Oh, Brad, you are so out of touch. Mia's our catering director. I'm the one who begged her to take the job last year." James grinned at Mia. "What are you doing back here, slumming?"

"Brad offered to feed me," Mia teased. "Actually, Brad and I knew each other when I was going to high school. He was one of the few people in the group I hung with who I could talk to about a future in food. Everyone else just wanted to get out of Boise and live the magic big city life."

"A life that's not as wonderful as it's made out to

be." James glanced at his watch. "I'd stay and chat, but I've got a date tonight."

"I'll be expecting a report tomorrow." Mia was happy for James. Sometimes she didn't know if he fit in with the more conservative human population in Idaho. And since he wasn't magical, his choices were limited.

"Hey, what happened to that girl you were dating? Did she stay in Tucson?" James paused before leaving the group. "I should have asked earlier. I'm a horrible friend."

"You're an amazing friend." Brad shook his head. "I haven't heard from her in years. Sometimes even soul-mates break up."

"Now, that's the saddest thing I've ever heard you say." James put his hand over his heart. "I'm less optimistic about my date now."

"Go, have fun. Don't worry about tomorrow." Mia made shooing movements with her hands. "You can never win the lottery if you don't buy a ticket."

"Now, that's why I love you, girl. You're always positive." He grinned at Brad. "Tell Carol to put your dinners on my account. And I'll come to your restaurant sometime next week. I've got some free time now that Mia's business stole our client for the week."

"That's a low blow." Mia laughed, knowing that James was kidding. "So, Frank has wooed you over to the dark side."

"It's funny what a raise in pay will do for your interpretation of events." James hugged her. "And now you know I'm kidding. Frank would never raise my pay. There's my ride. See you tomorrow."

They watched as James almost ran out of the lobby and got into a red Corvette. Mia couldn't see the driver, but she sent a prayer up to the Goddess to keep James safe. She turned back and pointed to the right. "The dining room is over there. Shall we get seated?"

After the waiter had taken their orders and brought them a glass of wine, she considered the man in front of her. "So, you know James. That's a coincidence I didn't see coming."

"My wife was from this area. My ex-wife, although we haven't finalized any legal paperwork. She's been gone for years. At this point, I'd probably have to declare her dead to get the divorce." He sipped his wine. "Brit was amazing, but after she had the third miscarriage, she changed. Maybe it was depression. Maybe something else, but one day, she just disappeared."

"So, do you have other children?" Mia's heart almost broke, hearing the story.

He barked out a laugh. "No. Well, I gave up a daughter for adoption, but that was years ago. I've been too busy building a career—I haven't had time for a family."

Mia leaned back as they brought their dinners. After the waiter had left, she met Brad's gaze. "Is that why you're back here in Idaho? To try to start building a family?"

He stared at her, then nodded. "You don't beat around the bush at all. Do you, Mia?"

She took a bite of her dish. Maple-covered salmon with a wild rice base. So good. James knew how to cook fish. And he'd taught his staff the same process. "If I see something like a giant pothole, I don't let my friends fall into it without at least a warning."

They spent the rest of the evening talking about the past. A past that was easier for Brad to talk about since Mia had never known his life before. Brad had rebuilt his life, just like she had, and now he was happy. Or at least on the path to happy.

When Mia got back to the apartment, Christina was the only one in the living room. Mr. Darcy ran over to jump on Mia's lap as soon as she sat down. "Hey, big guy. Did you miss me?"

Christina set down her book. "He wasn't the only one. Trent came by to visit."

"Let me guess, he wasn't happy to hear I was out with Brad." Mia leaned her head back on the couch. It wasn't like she hadn't been planning on telling Trent about her dinner. Now it looked like she was hiding something.

"Actually, he just kind of brushed it off. Mia, he knows you. He's not concerned about any other guy." Christina picked up her book again after looking over Mia's shoulder at the hallway to the bedrooms. "Levi's the same way. He trusts me. I think they learned from their parents how destructive jealousy can be."

"Did Thomas show up?"

Christina shook her head. "Abigail was cool about it. She made dinner, insisted that Trent stay, and we had a nice time talking about everything but you or Thomas."

"I hope they're going to be able to fix this." Mia stroked Mr. Darcy's gray fur. At times, he looked like he had stripes, but at night, he looked almost black in color. "Speaking of fixing things, have you heard from Grans? I thought she was days away from the potion that would release Dorian from Mr. Darcy's body?"

"She didn't come by or call me." Christina was now focused on the book. "Of course, she wouldn't. You might ask Abigail. She might still be awake."

"I'll call her in the morning." Mia rubbed between Mr. Darcy's ears. "It's about time that he goes back to being just a cat and a familiar. Last week I caught him using magic to write a note for more cat food and what kind they would prefer."

"I already know that. They like anything with seafood." Christina picked up her ringing phone, then rejected the call. She stood, tucking the book under her arm. "I'm heading to bed."

"Everything okay?" Mia had seen the name on the caller ID. Christina was avoiding Levi. That couldn't be good.

"Fine. I'm just thinking out some things. Hey, Mom needs me tomorrow, so since we aren't starting the contest until Sunday, I'm staying in Boise for a couple of nights." Christina rubbed Mr. Darcy's ears as she walked by. "I've already cleared it with Abigail. I just didn't want you to worry."

"Is your mom okay?" Mia didn't know anything but hospitalization or the plague that would get Christina to stay with her mom for more than a few hours.

"She's fine. Isaac's getting married on Saturday. I'm supposed to watch him and make sure he doesn't make a break for it." Christina paused. "He gave me an invitation for you. Against Mom's wishes. I think she believes you'll stand up in the church and whisk him away."

"Not on your life. Jessica is welcome to your brother. And your mother. And that life, in general." Mia squeezed Christina's arm. "But if you need someone to talk to, just call. Is Levi going with you?"

Fire flashed in Christina's eyes, and too late, Mia realized what the fight was about. But to her credit, Christina held it together as she answered. "Levi's not good at those types of things, so he's declined to attend the wedding."

"Oh." Mia wasn't sure what to say. Levi's presence would have been a safe haven for Christina among her family, who were less than nice to her. The fact that he'd turned down her invite wasn't okay. "Do you want me to talk to Trent?"

Christina pressed her lips together and shook her head. "He pulled me aside tonight when he came over. He offered to talk to Levi, but I told him no. If Levi can't figure out why this is important to me, that's on him."

Mia watched as Christina strolled to her room. Mr. Darcy jumped off Mia's lap and followed her, just making it before she closed the door. With the prank Levi had played a few days ago about the Hawaii trip and now this, he was batting zero for two. Mia hoped he'd figure out what he needed to do before the third strike would make Christina think her mom had been right. That Levi wasn't the one.

For Mother Adams, Christina's mom, it was about

the money Levi didn't make as a part-time ski instructor and full-time EMT. Levi valued his time off to ski more than money. Christina had thought he valued *her* more than anything, but this wasn't a good sign.

"Not your problem, Mia," she said to herself as she walked through the apartment, turning off lights and checking the security system one last time. Mark Baldwin had warned her that she might have more issues at the school before the queen contest was over. The trouble was, she'd thought the problems would come from the outside, not from the friends inside her sacred circle. She'd get over it if Christina and Levi broke up. She just didn't know if Abigail would. She already treated Mia and Christina like they were daughters-in-law rather than just women dating her sons.

She checked the lock on the front door of the apartment and went into her bedroom. She'd draw a hot bath and read until she fell asleep. As she started filling the tub, she saw she had two missed messages. The first was from Brad, thanking her again for a lovely night. The second was from Trent. He asked if she'd had a nice dinner and said he'd call in the morning. She took a chance that he was still up and called him back.

"Hey, I was just thinking about you." Barking came from his side of the connection. "Hold on, I'm letting Cerby out the back. I need to grab the flashlight and make sure he doesn't run into something bigger than he is."

"In that form, everything is bigger than he is." Mia smiled as she sat on the bed. "I hear you came by tonight. How's your mom?"

"You didn't talk to her?"

Mia looked toward the guest room even though she couldn't see through the walls. "She'd already turned in when I came home. I wasn't even that late. Nine at the latest."

"She says that until Dad tells them that he can't do this contest judge thing, she's not going to talk to him." Trent called out to his dog, "Cerby, come back into the light."

Mia smiled. Trent was such a dog parent. He loved that little guy, even as he complained about him. "Well, it looks like I've got company this weekend since Christina is staying in Boise."

"I just hope she comes back," Trent muttered. "I've got to go track down that dog. He loves going back by the woods. I think he put a hole in the fence so he can escape when he wants to go exploring."

"Raising a hellhound is tricky." Mia went to check on her water. The tub was almost filled, but the water needed cooling down a bit. She turned off the hot and let the cold run. "Have a good night. And if you need help . . ."

"I'll track him down. But I'll see you tomorrow morning for breakfast. Mom has already invited me and Levi. She wants to thank us for putting in the walkways." Trent paused. "I'll be at the school all day tomorrow. Will that be a problem?"

"Not for me. I'll be at work. I got a new event for Friday night. I'm going to kill Frank. Just so you know. Please don't rat me out to Baldwin."

Trent laughed. "You won't be the first one on the long list of suspects Baldwin will have if Frank's body shows up in the river."

"I was thinking something a little more cathartic. Like a million paper cuts with one of those stupid reports I have to produce every week." Mia kicked off her shoes. "I'll see you tomorrow, then."

"It's a date." He paused. "I love you, Mia."

"I love you too." Mia let the silence build between them. Finally, she broke it. "I've got a bath calling my name, and you need to find your dog."

"Already in my pocket. I'll see you in the morning. Sleep well." This time Trent hung up, and Mia plugged her phone into the charger on her nightstand. Her phone was also her alarm clock, so she didn't want it to die and give Frank another reason to yell at her for being late.

She slipped into the water and tried to think of anything but her job and the upcoming events. Both the one at the Lodge and the one here at the school. Just because she wasn't in control of Mia's Morsels right now didn't mean she wouldn't be working the event on her time off.

The smell of cinnamon woke Mia out of a crazy dream. She was the one marrying Isaac, and Trent was his best man. Christina was at her side as maid of honor, and she kept saying, "I told you that you were my sister."

She pushed the dream away and got ready for the day. First up, an uncomfortable breakfast with the Majors and Christina. Or most of the Majors. Trent had an older brother who lived out of state. And of course, Thomas was at home being stubborn. Mia wondered what caused people to dig their heels in the sand over an issue. She didn't know who was right and who was wrong, but she had to be Team Abigail mostly because she was her friend. And she ran Mia's business.

"I told you we were going to be sisters." Christina's words from Mia's dream came back to her.

Mia wasn't marrying Isaac in any version of this world. But Christina could become a sister-in-law if the girls both married into the Majors family. Of course, that version of the future was becoming less and less a possibility the longer Christina and Levi kept fighting.

Her phone buzzed with a text. It was from Baldwin. "What did your contact at the coven say about Carla?"

Mia pulled on her sweatshirt, then typed an answer. She didn't tell him she'd forgotten her promise, just that she hadn't heard back and would reach out today. She didn't say "again" since that would be a lie.

She quickly found one of the board member's contact information in her phone. Sabrina was responsible for membership, but she could find out what the coven knew about Carla's death. She asked Sabrina to meet her at the Lodge for lunch today.

Surprisingly, the answer came back quickly. *How's one?*

Perfect, Mia typed. *See you then*.

Mia looked at her image in the mirror and brushed her hair back into a clip. Sabrina would think the meeting was about joining the coven. That wasn't Mia's fault. She'd never said that.

But her stomach still hurt a bit at the omission.

Abigail and Trent were already in the kitchen drinking coffee and talking. Trent motioned her into a chair, then filled her cup. "Good morning. Why do you look like you just stole your best friend's last dollar?"

"That obvious?" Mia took the cup. "I'm meeting Sabrina today, and she's going to think I want to join the coven."

"So, why are you meeting her?" Abigail put a cinnamon roll in front of Mia with a fork.

Mia took a bite of the roll before answering. "Baldwin asked me to find out if the coven was involved in Carla's death."

"And you think, even if they were, Sabrina would tell you?" Abigail laughed and took a bite of her roll. "Sabrina's been around the block. Make her buy lunch. It will look good on her expense account this month."

"Even if I don't join?" Mia didn't understand the coven politics. And the more Abigail explained, the less she understood.

"Especially if you don't join." Trent gave Cerby a piece of sausage from his plate. "They love a hard sell."

"Have either of you heard anything about Carla's death?" Mia asked as she devoured her roll.

Trent shrugged. "The talk around town is that Carla would do anything to see Kristin win the competition. No one's surprised that she got caught in one of her own traps."

"You think she was setting up death traps with the potion bags?" Mia's eyes widened as she reached for the phone. "Oh, no. Is that why I haven't heard from Grans?"

Abigail gently took the phone from her. "No, she's okay. I talked to her yesterday. But this time, the rumor mill is right. The potion bags did have a curse on them. But it would only be activated by someone who was in or had someone competing in the pageant. This is why I don't want Thomas anywhere near this event. As a judge, he'll be targeted. Just because Carla's gone doesn't mean someone else isn't doing the same things."

"Mom, Dad knows what he's getting into." Trent reached over and squeezed her shoulder. "He says if you have to be at the queen's contest, so does he."

"That's just stupid. He's going to get killed." Abigail shrugged Trent's hand off. "If I have to petition the coven to get him off the judging panel, I will. These women aren't playing around. Carla's death should have proven that."

"Wait, so you're saying Carla died from her own spell?" Mia groaned. How was she going to explain that to Baldwin? Murder by suicide? No, suicide by murder? That was it. But he'd never believe her.

"You all are up and chatty this morning." Christina came in with Mr. Darcy in her arms. He jumped down, and after hissing at Cerby, went to the front door and opened it with Dorian's magic. Christina turned back to the group. "Is there coffee?"

CHAPTER 7

At the Lodge, Mia was just glad she wasn't still at the academy. The tension between Christina and Levi was crazy-high. Abigail was focused on her husband's mistakes, and Trent was caught in the middle. About ten that morning, she got a text from him. *Save me. Do you have lunch plans?*

She giggled as she texted back, reminding him she was meeting Sabrina.

Her phone rang almost immediately. It was Trent. "I don't think bringing the coven into our lives by joining right now is a great idea."

"I agree with you, which is why I'm not joining the coven." Mia put Trent on speaker as she reviewed Friday's budget for the baby shower. Mrs. Davis had signed the contract and dropped off a sizeable deposit that morning. "We talked about this over breakfast."

"Then why are you"—Trent paused—"oh, you're checking into Carla's death. Mom's got me all messed up. She keeps asking me to call Dad and tell him it's a bad idea to judge the contest."

"Yes, I'm checking into Carla. And no, I don't think it's a good idea for you to call your dad. I'm sorry I mentioned it to Abigail in the first place. Maybe she wouldn't have found out until the night of the contest, and we could have been saved from all of this angst." She closed the folder and put it all in a scan basket. Someone would come by and grab the folders she'd worked on at the end of the day and scan them all into the computer. Having them accessible digitally gave everyone the information they needed. One of the truly helpful changes that Frank had implemented since his arrival. Maybe the only one. "Just calm down the house. Christina is leaving tonight to go stay with her mom for a few days. When she comes back, by then this will have blown totally over."

"Geez, I hope so." Trent hated all kinds of conflict. He'd rather be poked with a hot fire stick. "But if Mom had found out we knew and didn't tell her, that would have been worse."

"Just keep your focus on those walkways. I don't want anyone tripping in sky-high stilettos during the contest." A knock came at the door, and Mia waved James inside. "Look, I've got to run. Oh, would you tell Christina that there's a wedding present for Isaac on the downstairs table?"

"What did you get the happy couple? Knives?"

Mia giggled. "If I didn't know that Isaac only used a high-end expensive knife, that would have been an excellent gift. As it was, I spent way too much on an ex-fiancé and his new bride."

"You're not going to tell me, are you?" Trent asked.

Mia watched as James refilled her coffee mug from the carafe he'd brought with him. It was going to be a long meeting. "Not right now. I'll see you tonight. Tell your mom to pull out something from the freezer if she doesn't feel like cooking. Or if she's going home?"

"Oh, I don't see that happening. Dad showed up this morning, and they got into it again. I think she's planning on making a roast. She's been talking about the side dishes to go with it since he left." He lowered his voice. "And she's heading this way. I need to look busy."

Mia set the phone down on her desk after saying goodbye. James leaned back into his chair. "Things going well with the contest? The hotel has a food truck at the festival grounds next Saturday and Sunday. Frank told me not to bother you with the details."

"He's a butt." She pulled out her planner. "Do you need help planning the staffing?"

"Does a butterfly come from a caterpillar? Of course I need help. The restaurant is going to be crazy that week since all the families are staying in the hotel. Or at least the out-of-towners are. This is the biggest weekend of the year for Magic Springs, and Frank thinks it's just business as usual." He opened his notebook. "Now, who on your staff can I call in for the food truck? I need ideas on cooks, as well, since most of my staff will be working overtime at the hotel."

As they made plans for the next week's events, Mia wondered how they could beat Frank at this information-limiting game he was playing. She knew he was doing it to make her fail. Then he could fire her for cause.

Working under these types of conditions wasn't helping her stress levels, but she couldn't keep the school if she didn't have the second income. She'd run the numbers last night before she went to bed. Even if she downsized to just her costs and no payroll, she needed the Lodge job to eat. It wasn't fair that Frank had the power to ruin her life. Of course, life wasn't fair.

"Are you okay?" James's question poked through the pity party she'd been having in her head. "You know, as long as we keep talking, Frank can't get away with these things."

"I know. It's just hard when you don't know when the next shoe is going to drop." She heard a text come over her phone. She checked, and it was Baldwin, wondering if she'd heard anything. She'd answer him after lunch. Maybe at least she'd be able to help him close this case, since from what Abigail was saying, Carla was just unlucky in her sabotage.

After they finished the food truck planning, Mia went over her schedule with James to make sure she wasn't missing any other events that would need her expertise for this month and the next three.

James stood as he checked his messages. "We need a standing planning meeting for just the two of us on our calendars every two weeks. And if I hear of any events, I'll mention them in the department heads meeting. Oh, and I'll go check with lodging and see if they have any big groups coming in. You know they usually book the events then too."

"Good idea. You're good at finding out information." Mia wished she could ask him about Carla's death and see what he'd heard, but that was Baldwin's side of the investigation. Talking to humans. Her phone buzzed again. "Good timing. My lunch appointment is here."

"Have fun. I'm going to go chat with the front desk staff before I go talk to any of the other department heads. I want to make sure they are all on our side with Frank. He can be a little sneaky with gathering followers to the cause." James paused at the doorway. "I feel like I'm a double agent."

"Well, we're kind of spying for our careers." Mia wondered what game Frank was playing with the hotel. Had he done this at other places he'd worked? Maybe she could call in some favors with people at his old hotel. "Know your enemy" was one of Grans's favorite sayings. Before she stood from her desk, she wrote a note. *Call Grans*.

Then she followed James out of her office and to the lobby area to find Sabrina Clay. She wasn't hard to spot. Sabrina loved the glamour of being a witch, and she used her spell craft wisely. Men and women found her hard to ignore with her long, straight, raven-black hair. Her body had just the right ratio of curves and lean for her six-foot frame. And she knew how to dress to accentuate her curves and her narrow waist.

Sabrina smiled and stood to hug Mia as she came out to the lobby. "I'm so glad you called for lunch. The Lodge has so many great memories for me. I got married the first time here in this lobby."

"I didn't know that." Mia wondered when that had been since the Lodge had always limited the lobby to receptions since they had a lot of walk-in traffic. At least that had been the policy for years. Mia had dreamed about getting married next to that fireplace, but Isaac had nixed the idea, wanting to use a popular church in North Boise instead.

Isaac, weddings. It all was getting in her head. She really needed a spirit cleansing soon. Her grandmother did a cleansing once a month, but Mia had always felt that was indulgent. Now she wished she'd accepted her grandmother's invitation last week. She might be more clear-headed now.

Luckily, Sabrina hadn't noticed Mia's lack of attention and was talking about her first husband and his unlucky death at his coven job. He'd been looking for signs of the Northern Idaho werewolf colony encroaching on Magic Springs's circle of protection. The power barrier went ten miles out from the town limits to keep other covens or tribes from getting too close for comfort. No melting pot for this group of townspeople. She didn't know why they were so stuck in their old ways, but that was one of the reasons Mia had been hesitant to join. Because they were wrong in some of their tightly held beliefs. Like how power only transferred to one sibling at a time in a magical family.

Mia must have nodded and grunted in the right places because Sabrina was still talking. When she started congratulating Mia on getting the queen contract, Mia focused on what she was saying.

"We're so lucky that you and Abigail agreed to host the competition this year. We've had issues in the past, and it's better if we can keep the problems internal in the coven." She opened her menu. "I do so love the restaurant here now since James took over. The last head chef was a little boring. He thought the food at the Lodge should be all meat and potatoes. It was like eating at a hunting lodge with a really bad cook."

"James is amazing." Mia set down her menu. She knew what she wanted. She'd planned on holding this discussion off until the end of the meal, but Sabrina had given her an opening. "I wanted to ask you about Carla Manson's death."

"It's a shame about Carla. The coven board has ruled it a suicide. So it won't affect the competition. Don't you worry about a thing." She tapped the menu with her bloodred nails. "I would think that if a person had a daughter in the running, she would be more careful with the traps she set for the competition."

"So you think she was trying to eliminate the competition?" Mia hadn't expected her to say the one possible theory that would explain the death with a quick answer to end the investigation. If Sabrina was a reputable knowledge source on one thing, it was Magic Springs's coven's rumors.

"Honey, I know she was. Although her techniques were a little old-fashioned. I think her mother must have used the same spells back in the day when Carla was one of the princesses. She never had the guts for the queen position, and she must have known it. Although Kristin, she's a little more competitive than her mom was. I hear she decided to stay in the competition. Her mom's 'last wish' kind of thing. It's a terrific ace card to hold and pull out if she ever needs it."

"I hadn't heard that Kristin was continuing to compete. I would think being at the school where it happened would be hard on her." The waiter came and took their orders, then brought a bottle of wine. This lunch was definitely going on Sabrina's expense account.

"You know teenagers, it's all about them." Sabrina leaned in and smiled. "Now, tell me about you. The rumor is your ex is getting married this weekend. How are you doing?"

The good thing about the lunch was that Sabrina was more interested in what she perceived as Mia's broken heart about Isaac's new relationship status than in talking to her about joining the coven. Maybe Mia had said no enough times that they didn't think she would ever join. Or more likely, they were just biding their time until Mia needed a big favor. Then it would come at a cost.

When Mia got back to her office, she called Baldwin first. A baby was crying in the background. "You must be at home."

He chuckled. "Actually, no. Sarah and Elisa Marie stopped by to bring me lunch. Elisa Marie's not happy with the office. Sarah says she's reacting to negative vibes. Hold on a second, and I'll be right with you. Sarah's already up and leaving."

"Tell her I said hi," Mia said, then she booted up her computer and coded the lunch charges onto her marketing account with notes about the history of the festival, the appropriateness of the food trucks, and what had sold well last year. She'd decided to grab the bill during Sabrina's discussion on the spell to mend a broken heart.

The reason for coding the cost to marketing was

more than just not wanting to pay for Sabrina's lunch—when Frank checked her expenses, it would tell him that she knew about the food truck event.

She was going to be in his face about every event he hid from her. And she was going to make them all successful. Just to spite him. Of course, that meant working with one hand tied behind her back, but she'd done that before.

Mark's voice blared at her from the speaker. "Are you still there?"

She focused on the call. "Sorry, yes. I was doing some work. How are the girls?"

"Elisa Marie and Sarah are fine. Sarah says she'll stop by soon and bring the baby. We're trying to keep her a little isolated until she gets better control of a few things. If Sarah hadn't explained her special whatever, I'd be freaking out right now. She floated her stuffed tiger out of the diaper bag just now." Mark seemed more amazed than concerned.

"I've never been around babies, so I wouldn't know what to expect. I'm glad Sarah's there to help you." Mia thought it sounded like Mr. Darcy's newfound magical skills since Dorian's essence was sharing his body. She underlined the words *Call Grans* on the stickie note she'd written that morning. She didn't need a human, besides Christina, seeing Mr. Darcy's parlor tricks. "Anyway, I was calling about Carla."

Mia explained that the prevailing theory in the magical community was that Carla was the victim of her own spell. She'd been trying to fix the queen competition in her daughter's favor.

Mark was silent for a while. "Well, then. I guess the coroner's report of an aneurysm will just hold. I don't know how to explain death by misfired spell."

"At least it wasn't a murder." Mia thought she knew what Mark was feeling. An unease about something he didn't understand. "Although I hear this competition can be a little dramatic, at least for the families. Maybe you should keep an open mind this week."

"Sarah's already given me the talk. I guess it's a way for the coven to add new council members. Each of the girl children who are born in a year goes into this competition during their eighteenth year. And the winner's family gets a board seat for five years." He coughed. "I guess it's better than an election. Or a lottery, which is how they used to do it. And worse, one of the girls was sacrificed when it first started. At least that's how Sarah described the festival. That part of the ritual has been ended."

After she talked to Mark, she thought about Carla's death. Maybe that part of the tradition hadn't changed. Maybe there had already been a sacrifice. Sabrina might have just been covering for what the board knew.

Mia called her grandmother but got her voice mail. "Hey, call me. I'm getting worried about you. I haven't heard from you in a few days. And I want to chat about this harvest pageant. At least the history of it. I'm concerned."

She thought about driving over and seeing what her grandmother was up to, but then her phone rang. Work had to come first today, and the first order of business was to make sure that tomorrow's baby shower went smoothly.

Determining whether the coven still offered up blood sacrifices would have to wait until she got home. And that wasn't even the weirdest thing she'd thought about today. Oh, the life of a kitchen witch in the modern world.

CHAPTER 8

As Mia walked out of the Lodge that evening, a black Land Rover was parked in the valet area. Isaac Adams leaned against it, smoking. When he saw her come out the front doors, he threw the cigarette on the ground and crushed it with his cowboy boot.

"Mia, I need to talk to you." He stepped forward to meet her.

"When did you start smoking?" Mia walked over and picked up the filter, carrying it toward the trash.

"I don't, not really. I bought a pack on my way up here. I was nervous." He followed her to the trash can.

She spun around on her heel, trying to put some physical distance between the two of them. "Why are you here, Isaac?"

"Like I said, I came to talk." He walked back and opened the passenger door of his SUV. "Can we go for a drive?"

"I have my car." She didn't point it out to him, since he'd probably make fun of the older Camry, but the car was paid for and got her where she needed to go. Those were the two most important criteria in Mia's world now. Not how much the car cost, which was Isaac's definition of a suitable vehicle.

"Mia, please?" The crack in Isaac's voice made her look at him.

Seeing the pain on his face, she gave in. "I can't be gone long. I'm expected for dinner."

"Just a few minutes. I need to apologize." He took her hand and helped her up into the passenger seat. The car was immaculately clean.

Mia wondered if she'd left something personal in the car and whether Isaac's cleaning crew would find it before Jessica did. But she wasn't playing games with the new girlfriend. Jessica was welcome to Isaac. Mia wouldn't repay the favor of sleeping with an engaged man. Not even if Jessica hadn't given her the same respect.

They drove without talking for a few minutes, then Isaac parked at an entrance to the greenbelt that ran along the river. It also ran past the school and her apartment. If she needed to walk home, she had a plan.

They didn't leave the car. Isaac turned to her. "Tell me I'm not making a mistake."

"I can't tell you that. You and Jessica have been together since before we broke up. You sleeping with her was the reason we broke up." She watched out the window and saw the river flowing past them. "We're like the river—history. The time for us has already floated by, and you can't just go back. I have no opinions on what you do with your life now."

"Don't be like that. I told you I made a mistake with Jessica. Then you moved up here with your grandmother. What was I supposed to do?" He held out his hands like they were clean of guilt. "I thought you'd come home."

"You were supposed to only sleep with me since we were living together and were going to get married. *That's* what you were supposed to do. I hope you at least can say that you fulfilled your responsibility to Jessica in that manner." She turned her head from looking outside to look at him. "You were supposed to be mine. Only mine. You threw that away. I'm not angry anymore. I just don't care."

"You don't have any feelings for me at all?" Isaac looked surprised by the announcement.

Mia was a little surprised herself. She had thought she was over him, but this certainty hadn't hit until just this moment. "Isaac, I hope you have a good life and a lovely marriage. I sent my present to Boise along with your sister. Please be nice to Christina. She's a good person and a close friend. Even though your mom tried to mold her into an Adams."

"What's that supposed to mean?" Isaac's eyes narrowed.

Mia got out of the car. She was done. "You're not going to bait me into a fight. We broke up because of you. You chose this life. You chose her. Now, go have a happy life and leave me alone. I'm working on my own happily-ever-after."

"With a grocery store clerk!" Isaac yelled at her as he turned on the engine and gunned it. Mia slammed the door. She heard his last words through the open window. "You had a good life with me."

As Isaac drove away and hopefully out of her life for good, Mia strolled down the greenbelt. The October sun felt hot on her back, and she took off the jacket she'd worn out of the building. She'd either walk to work tomorrow or ask for a ride. It didn't matter.

Isaac was off her heart. It had taken a while, but she didn't miss him anymore. She didn't think about what could have been. Instead, she thought of Trent and her life here in Magic Springs as she strolled home. When she came close to the school, she noticed Cerby out of the yard near the fence. He was digging at a piece of what looked like white cloth.

"Cerby, stop that. Come here." Mia leaned down and snapped her fingers. The little white Maltese hellhound came bounding at her and gave her kisses as she picked him up. "What are you doing out of the yard?"

She heard a rustle behind her and turned to see Trent coming around the greenbelt where it went by the school's parking lot. "He's hiding from me. I think your cat taught him how to magic a hole in the fence."

Mia leaned down to where she'd found Cerby. "I don't see a hole, but isn't this another potion bag?"

Trent leaned down and swore. He dug the bag out of the dirt with his pen knife and then shoved the knife into the top of the bag to allow him to pick it up without touching it. "I know Mom said these were focused on the contest participants, but I don't want this one to backfire like it did on Carla."

Mia held out her jacket. "Do you want to carry it in this?"

He glanced at her coat. "Is that real leather?"

She nodded. "Isaac bought it for me years ago. Real leather and pricey."

"And you want to use it as a potion carrying case?" He took the coat from her and dropped the bag in the middle, then folded the coat around it like it was a burrito. "Make sure Mom shows you how to clean the spell off this jacket before you wear it again. I don't want you getting hurt from a rebound."

"After today, I might just burn it." She fell in step with Trent as they went back to the parking lot and the gate that would let them into the backyard. "It's been a day."

"So, should I ask you why you were walking home from the opposite side of town where the Lodge is located?" Trent opened the gate with one hand and held it for her and Cerby to get inside.

She set the little dog down on the ground after Trent closed the gate. He ran directly to the kitchen door and sat to wait for them. "I guess he's excited about his find. He's found two potion bags so far. Maybe you should rent him out as a magic sniffer?"

"'Magic sniffer'? I'm not sure that's a real skill. But the little guy is good at finding these things." Trent paused at the table and chairs that were set near the garden. "Do we need to talk?"

"No, I'm fine. I just had a visit from Isaac that didn't end well. I'm not sure what he was expecting, but he's getting married this weekend. It's time for him to figure out I'm not sitting around waiting for him to come to his senses." She took a breath, then dropped into a chair. "Okay, so yes, I needed to talk."

"Wow. Not what I thought you'd say. He drove over two hours to profess his love for you so he could stand his fiancée up at the altar? The same woman that he broke your engagement over?" Trent set the coat-wrapped potion bag on the table and sat in the other chair. "What a loser."

"I feel bad for Jessica. At least a little. She was the one who started up with him knowing we were engaged. Maybe I don't feel that sorry for her." Mia glanced at the house. "Please tell me that Christina's already left."

"Christina has left the building. Levi met her for lunch in Twin, then she left for Boise. He's at the lumberyard picking up screws for the walkway. We should have it finished by midday Sunday. Mom says the contestants want to come by and see the setup again Sunday evening." He shook his head, leaning back on the loveseat with one arm wrapped around the back edge. "Mom thinks they're going to try to get you to open the staircase and second floor for the evening gown event."

"We've already set it up so they can use the staircase. What else do they want?" Mia glanced at her coat, which held a potential murder weapon. "I'm not changing the setup. And neither is your mom. Do you think we might have found all of these spell bags now?"

"If Carla was the one setting them, yes. She wasn't alone that much in the house." Trent didn't continue with his thought, but Mia had already guessed what he was about to say.

"Seriously? We don't think Carla did this now?" Mia rolled her shoulders as she stood. "Don't answer that. I don't want to know. Did your mom make dinner? I'm starving."

"Good, because Mom's been cooking all day. And your grandmother is here." He followed her to the door. "It's nice to have you home."

Mia leaned over and kissed him. "It's nice to be here. Oh, can you drive me to the Lodge tomorrow morning? My car's still there."

The downstairs kitchen was empty, but Mia could see that Abigail had been working. She went over and opened the walk-in. Several cakes sat on the racks, waiting to be frosted and decorated for the upcoming week. Mia's Morsels wasn't responsible for any full meals during the week—except for lunches for the contestants and the judges. The night events on Thursday and Friday had a social hour before the contest started, and they were doing a variety of desserts for those events.

The coven had hired a local bar to set up and serve the drinks, so that wasn't their responsibility. At least not adult drinks. Mia's Morsels would have coffee, hot apple cider, and several flavored waters available. So as long as Carla's death was an accident and Cerby stopped finding potion bags, Abigail had the event under control.

Mia couldn't worry about the contest until after she dealt with the baby shower for tomorrow. And made sure Saturday's food trucks were staffed. Then she could turn back into Mia for a few days and help Abigail.

She realized Trent was watching her. "Sorry, I'm going through the list of things we need to do for this event. Except I keep reminding myself that I'm not in charge. So the conversation keeps going back and forth in my head."

"That must be exhausting." He put his arm around her and moved her out of the kitchen. "Let's go upstairs and see what your grandmother wants to do with this so you can get your coat cleaned and back. The temperature is going to be chilly in the morning."

"And then it's warm in the afternoon, and I won't need the heavy coat." Mia followed him upstairs, checking to see that both Mr. Darcy and Cerby were on the stairs behind them. Mia was too busy and the school was too filled with people to have those two running around on their own. Especially outside the fence. She needed a way to corral them next week while the contest was going on as well. Maybe she should ask Grans to stay for the week as their pet sitter.

As soon as Mia sat down in the living room next to her grandmother, she knew the news wasn't good from the look on Grans's face. "You can't reverse the spell."

"Yet. I can't reverse it *yet*." Her grandmother patted her hand. "Now, don't you worry on it. I'll figure out how to send Dorian packing soon. I promise. But this week, Abigail needs my help with the queen contest. Especially since Christina won't be back until Sunday. I'm glad that boy will be off the market soon, but the Adams family has a knack for picking the exactly wrong time to be in our lives."

Mia didn't want to mention Isaac's visit. Her grandmother hated him. Probably even more than Mia did at this moment. She decided to change the subject. "Cerby found another potion bag."

Trent brought over Mia's jacket and unwrapped it. The gauze of the potion bag glowed just a bit.

"Did you see that?" Mia asked as she pointed to the bag.

Her grandmother nodded and scooted closer. "That's interesting."

"It's weird," Mia clarified.

Her grandmother glanced over at Abigail, who nodded in agreement to some unspoken question. "Not weird, just active. The other two bags were inert. This one is actually set to go off. And if I'm not wrong, this is newer. Like it was made yesterday."

Trent frowned. "I thought you said Carla made the bags? Did someone else make this one?"

With a clearly muttered spell and a wave of Grans's hand, the bag glowed harder, then went out as they all watched. Grans took a deep breath and sank back into her place on the couch. "I've inactivated it. But no, this bag's maker is the same as the others. So no, Carla didn't make these."

Mia rolled her head back, not wanting to put the pieces together, but they flowed around her somewhat lackluster block. Finally, she opened her eyes. "Carla didn't die as a result of trying to manipulate the contest. Whoever is trying to do that killed Carla. So, who is going to tell Mark I was wrong?"

* * *

Friday morning, Trent came by to take her to work. He was drinking coffee with his mother in the kitchen when Mia came out of her bedroom. She hadn't slept well. Carla's death had kept rolling over in her head. She hadn't known the woman well, but when she'd been a victim of her own malfeasance, that seemed like justice. Now there was someone else to blame for her death. Someone who was walking around free right now since Mark Baldwin didn't believe in witchcraft. And the coroner had ruled it a natural death. And because Mia had told him that she'd killed herself. Now she had to go back on that story.

Abigail and Trent stopped talking as soon as she walked into the room.

"Good morning, Mia. Can I pour you some coffee?" Abigail didn't wait for an answer, just got up and went to the coffeepot, and before she knew it, Mia had a cup in her hand.

Mia sat down next to Trent. "I hope I didn't interrupt your conversation."

Trent leaned over and kissed her on the cheek. "Mom wasn't listening to reason anyway."

Abigail huffed at her son, then turned to Mia. "Just because I don't agree with what he's saying, he thinks I'm being unreasonable. His father is exactly the same way. If you know what you're doing, you'll run from this man—and as far as possible."

"Mom! Stop trying to turn Mia away from me. She already got enough of that yesterday from Isaac. Not to mention her date with Brad earlier this week." Trent framed his face with his hands. "Who could even think of breaking up with this sweet face?"

"You aren't all that, mister," Mia said, trying to hide the smile that had snuck onto her face. Abigail's words might have a string of truth in them since Trent was his father's son, but the woman loved both men with all her heart, even when she was furious with Thomas. "Did Grans go home or stay over?"

Mia had crashed early, probably tired from the energy she'd used fighting Isaac, and her grandmother had still been at the apartment then. She and Abigail were going through the coven files to get a feel for the shenanigans contestants had played with the competition in the past. Learning of all the deadly pranks made Mia realize that Thomas was in danger. And maybe, so were the rest of them.

Abigail sipped her coffee, then set her cup on the table. "She went home to gather some things. Like spell books, clothes, and Muffy." Muffy was Grans's elderly Shih Tzu. Muffy hated Mr. Darcy and Cerby, so naturally, the cat and puppy terrorized him. "Mia, I'm really sorry I got this contract. I should have realized that if we put in a bid, we'd get it. No matter what we'd charged. We have a unique perspective on any event with magical attendees, and this was just too big for them to take a chance on the Lodge messing it up."

"Like the ancestors' table at the first wake I did for the coven," Mia said dryly. "All we can do is learn to increase our prices on these special events and hope for the best. Besides, if we don't take the jobs, who will?"

"Maybe you could change the business name to Mia's Magical Morsels," Trent said.

Mia elbowed him, and his mother threw a napkin in his direction.

"And with that, I think I need to get busy working on the walkway. Levi should be here any moment." He stood and kissed Mia. "Just come get me when you're ready to go to work. I'll need a break, anyway."

Mia watched as he said goodbye to Cerby and then kissed his mother on the top of her head. After he'd left the apartment, she turned to Abigail. "I guess he's Team Thomas?"

Abigail shrugged one shoulder. "Kind of. He thinks it's better to have a united front in these types of situations. He's afraid we might miss something if his dad isn't part of the discussions."

"But you'd rather he stays away completely." Mia sipped her coffee. Relationships were hard. Normal ones or magical ones.

"Did you read some of the things that those over-eager moms offered the judges? I don't think he'd cheat on me, but I'm sure every man has a price. And what if someone threatened me or one of the boys? He'd do anything to save us." Abigail stood and dumped her coffee down the drain. "No, it would be much better if he just stayed away."

"I don't think that's going to happen. Maybe we could use a spy in all of this?" Mia threw out the one thing that made sense. They needed Thomas's inside information to make sure no one else died. Judge or contestant.

Mia had to admit that Trent's plan made sense. Since they were all involved in this mess of an event, they all needed to be talking. She watched the security monitor as Levi's Jeep was followed into the parking lot by Grans's old sedan and finally, Thomas's black Ram. It was time to put Trent's plan into motion and put up a united front.

"Time for me to get ready for work. I'm doing a baby shower for Mrs. Davis. Do you know her?" Mia stood and washed out her own cup to put in the dishwasher.

"Of course, I know Faith. She asked me to make the cake for the shower. I'll have Trent bring it over no later than three." Abigail frowned as she checked the day's schedule. "I thought I'd told you that weeks ago."

CHAPTER 9

The decorators had gone pink and blue crazy. The expectant couple had decided not to find out the baby's sex until the birth, so they used both colors to make the ballroom look like a fairy-tale nursery. Lots of white tulle floated around the room along with white silk and satin. As Mia stood in the doorway, she was transported into a fantasy version of a long-ago castle room where a royal baby was being welcomed into the world. Mrs. Davis was going to be ecstatic.

Jeani Langston, the head designer, came up to her. "What do you think? I usually work closely with the family to make sure that this is what they want for a theme, but when I called, the client told me to go with my gut. So I did. Now I'm having second thoughts. What if she hates it?"

"The party is in less than six hours. If she hates it, she's going to have to suck it up and just enjoy the celebration. Besides, who wouldn't love this? You did amazing with such short notice." Mia hoped the cake Abigail was making would be part of the fairy-tale theme.

"I've been wanting to do this room for years. No one would let me." Jeani waved at one of her assistants. "That's a moat, not a playground. You can't put a swing there."

The look the man gave her was priceless as he stood, staring at his feet.

"I guess I need to go help Ned. I swear, sometimes he just doesn't get a direction I give him so I have to work with him directly." Jeani started to leave. "No imagination at all."

"Maybe he likes you," Mia suggested.

"I've considered that possibility as well." The grin didn't leave Jeani's face. "Hey, I hear you're hosting the queen contest this year. The coven hired my sister and me to do the decorations for Friday night's pageant. Can I make arrangements with you to come over for a walk-through soon? I was going to reach out earlier, but then Frank called on Monday and wanted a proposal on this, so the contest got pushed."

Jeani must have seen the look on Mia's face because she started backpedaling. "Oh, don't worry, the decorating will be easy. Both my sister and I were in contests our senior year. Of course, neither one of us won, much to the shame of my family, but not everyone can win, right? Besides, I love my life now. The year my sister ran, the queen died the week before she was supposed to turn over her crown the next year. I didn't want to take that chance. No way."

"She died. What happened?" Mia hadn't heard this story from Abigail.

Jeani leaned closer. "I know you know about the coven, so I can tell you. It was really sad. She had plans for her future. She was dating a normal from Boise. He was heartbroken. And the baby, well, she never even knew her mom."

"That's horrible." Mia glanced around the ballroom. "I hadn't heard anything about this contest before. I'm glad my mom raised me as a normal."

"Being raised outside the coven life has its advantages. Anyway, that kid is now running for queen. Can you believe it? I wouldn't want anything to do with it, but I guess old traditions die hard." She opened her phone. "So, can I come over tonight? Or would tomorrow be better?"

"Look, call Abigail Majors to set up the walk-through. I'm sure you can do it any time, but she's the one running this. Especially if Frank asks." Mia made sure Jeani had Abigail's cell number before taking one last look at the fantasy land that would soon be party central.

Mia left the ballroom and started toward her office, but then changed her mind and headed to the kitchen to find James. He was sitting in his office working on the books. He waved her inside and stood to walk toward his coffeepot. Mia didn't want to fall into thinking about Sherry and Melody even though she was sure that was the mother-daughter duo whom Jeani had been talking about. She had too much work to finish before tonight's event.

"Tell me you saw Jeani's creation. Isn't that amazing?" He poured her a cup and refilled his own. "I swear, if she lived anywhere else, we couldn't afford her. As it is, she just squeaks by living up here, but both she and her sister are hikers. They wanted a home base here in the forest. Their folks bought them a cabin up off Spell Cast Hills."

"Jeani's great. I guess she's also decorating the school for the queen contest." Mia pretended to shrug it off. "I don't think I've worked with her before."

"Frank brought them back at the first of the year. I'm sure you've done events with them. Remember when he said the internal design staff would take over the event decorating in January? That's when they came on."

Mia sipped her coffee. She'd been too involved in her personal life and business to even wonder why her responsibilities had been cut back then. She'd welcomed the help. Now she wondered if this was a step in Frank's plan to get rid of her. If James did the food and kitchen coordinating and Jeani did the decorating, she was more of a project manager than anything else. It didn't matter. She would ride this job as long as it lasted or until she didn't need it, whichever came first.

"I wanted to check in and see if you needed more help with the food truck staffing. I have a program I use to set up shifts, and we can print out a copy to see if you have any holes." She pulled out her notebook and grabbed a pen. Then she looked at James. "If you want help, that is."

"Of course, I want help." He went over to his desk

and came back with a pile of papers and stickie notes. "I've been trying to sort this all out for hours now. I think we're covered, but I'm not sure."

Mia took the pile and put it in the tote bag she carried everywhere. "Give me the details, and I'll have you a plan before the baby shower starts tonight. So, one food truck or two? And what are your open hours going to be?"

By the time she got the information she needed from James, it was time for lunch. She begged off eating in the kitchen, but James promised to send a tray to her office in thirty minutes. "What time do you want dinner? I know you're not going home between your shift and the event."

James knew her habits too well. Of course, he *was* her "work husband," as Trent called him. "How about five? That way I have time to change into my suit before guests start to arrive."

James took her order for both meals, then disappeared into the kitchen. She needed to call Abigail and let her know about Jeani calling. And maybe ask her if the queen who had died was Melody's mother. It made her wonder if participating in the event was in the teen's best interest. Of course, that wasn't her call. It was Melody's grandmother's decision.

Instead of calling Abigail when she got back to her office, Mia dialed another number. "You caught me packing for the week. Trent's here if you need to talk to him."

Mia smiled. "I called you, not Trent. What's the story about a girl dying after her year as harvest queen? Please tell me she wasn't sacrificed."

"Oh, dear Goddess. You think the coven would do something like that?" Grans paused, then quickly added, "Don't answer that. Anyway, Sherry was crowned queen after a particularly bloody contest. Two other contestants died that year and one judge. Sherry's mom was suspected of being involved, but the local police never found a good reason for the deaths. I believe they all went down as accidents. I suspect that Sherry's accident might have been payback from the other parents."

"Seriously? Now I really don't want to join the coven. If I'd had any intentions before." Mia leaned back into her chair.

"Things were different back then. They didn't have to be worried about the local law enforcement as much. Or she could have just died in a car accident." Grans paused. "You're worried about that girl."

"Melody. She's Sherry's daughter, isn't she?"

"Yes." Grans didn't have to add anything else. Mia could tell she'd considered the danger for Melody as well.

"Do you think she knows what happened to her mom?" If Mia had lost her mother that way, she'd be more than just angry. She'd want revenge. The image of Carla Manson's face floated into Mia's mind, but she pushed it away.

"I'm not sure if Elly, Melody's grandmother, told her everything. Besides, we're not sure what actually happened. The family didn't stray far from the car accident story. The coven would have insisted and paid for the secrecy."

"Well, isn't that nice." Mia bit her lip to keep from saying the rest of what she was thinking. That the coven had tied a murder up in a nice, polite bow and paid everyone to look the other way. A knock sounded on Mia's door. "Hey, I've got to go. I'll see you tonight. Can you tell Abigail that Jeani is coming over to talk decorations? I asked her to call Abigail, but just in case. I guess the coven hired her too."

Mia said her goodbyes, and then went to open the door. Her lunch had been delivered.

After lunch, Mia pulled out the pile of papers that James had given her and was just starting to key them into her program when another knock sounded. Thinking James had sent someone to pick up the tray, she called out, "Come in."

The door opened, and there Mrs. Davis stood with a couple of bags of gifts. "I know I'm early, but . . ."

Mia stood and met her at the door. "No worries. Are you excited?"

Mrs. Davis bounced in response. And in high heels, that was a feat. "I'm so excited. This is my first grand-child. I had almost given up. We had a cruise scheduled for the end of the year. Now I've canceled it so I can stay home and play babysitter for the new addition."

Mia took one of the bags. It was heavy. "Let's take these down to the ballroom. They're just finishing up decorating, and I think you'll be happy."

She spent the next hour with Mrs. Davis, helping her bring in more gifts and talking about the setup. Then, when Mrs. Davis left to go home and get ready for the party, Mia went back to her office. She needed to make sure James got his food truck planning tem-plate by the end of the day. She'd taken the next week off to work with Abigail, and she didn't want to leave her friend in a lurch. Or have to work the next weekend. Certainly not for the Lodge. As soon as she walked out the door tonight, she was back to being a part of Mia's Morsels. At least until a week from Monday, when Frank would be back from his corporate retreat to torment her more.

Mia decided to leave after the last appetizer tray had been passed. The open bar was flowing, and the night supervisor could handle any issues. The gifts were beginning to be opened, and in another hour, the event would be over. She discreetly pulled Mrs. Davis to the side. "Is everything to your liking?"

"Oh, yes. Mia, you did amazing. Thank you so much for this." She pointed over to where a beaming daughter-in-law and son sat. "Fleur is over the moon. And Jason told me they never expected this. So, we pulled it off, even with the complications."

Mia pressed a card into Mrs. Davis's hand. "I'm so glad. I'm heading home, but if you need anything and don't feel like you're being heard, please call me. I'm just down the road, and I can be here in five minutes."

Mrs. Davis pulled her into a hug. "I can't believe there's going to be any reason I need to call you. Except to thank you once again. I promise, Mia, this isn't the last you'll hear from me."

"Well, please, don't hesitate." Mia took one last glance around the fairy-tale setting and sent a thank-you to the Goddess for blessing Jeani and her sister with such imaginations. A warmth spread over her as she walked to her office. The Goddess was pleased with her offering.

Mia grabbed her laptop, her tote, and her leather jacket. Abigail had cleaned it of all bad magic that morning. And with the chill in the air, since darkness already had fallen, Mia was glad she had the coat available.

The drive home was quiet, but when she got to the school, lights were on and shining out of the windows on all three floors. Operation Queen Contest was going well. She climbed out of her car and grabbed her tote.

Then she went to unlock the door. But it was already standing open. She pushed the door farther open and called out, "Hello?"

Loud music blared out of the gym area, and Mr. Darcy sat on the stairs, glaring at her. Mia came inside and shut the door. She went over and leaned over her cat. "Not my fault. Is Cerby in the house?"

A look toward the apartment and a nod was all she got. Of course, Mr. Darcy was a cat. She couldn't expect a monologue or a verbal report. However, she did get the guilt hit he was sending her about leaving him alone with these people.

She followed the music and found Levi, Trent, Jeani, and a second woman in the gym. Levi and the other woman were swing dancing to the song, and there were several bottles of beer scattered around the gym along with lumber, saws, and drills. No one noticed her as she came in.

Mia walked over and turned the music down, and everyone turned her way. "Hey, you forgot to invite me to the party. And someone left the front door wide open. Is Cerby down here or upstairs?"

Trent walked over and pulled her into a hug. "Welcome home. You're always invited, and yes, Cerby is in the apartment with your grandmother and Mom. Unless Mr. Darcy let him out. Have you seen your cat?"

"He was at the stairs, waiting for me to come home." She put her arm around him and smiled at Jeani. "Welcome to the madhouse."

"It's wonderful, better than I remembered. We had a senior sneak day here in the gym. You've done a lot to bring it back." Jeani had a clipboard and tape measure. "Trent walked me through the plan for the walkways and the stairway. I wanted to run an idea I had by you in case the weather turns on us."

Mia saw that Levi and the other woman had stopped dancing, and he was now stacking wood for the walkways. "I'd love to talk, but I'm beat. Oh, by the way, the Davis's party was a big success. Everyone loved your decorations."

Jeani looked at her watch. "Crap, I didn't realize how late it was. Cheryl and I will get out of your hair for the night. I'd like to come back tomorrow and finish up the measurements. I'm afraid we got to catching up and lost track of time."

"Jeani and Cheryl went to high school with me. Levi was a few years younger." Trent didn't move his arm from around Mia's waist.

"Oh, I should have realized." Mia watched as Jeani collected her tote bag and notebook, sticking things inside.

Finally, the women had coats on and were walking out the gym door. Jeani paused by Mia to say goodbye. "I should help clean up the mess."

"Don't worry about it. The guys can. I'm sure they don't want Abigail to come down and see this in the morning." Mia threw a wicked grin at Trent.

"You're horrible, and that's why I love you." Trent kissed her and then yelled at Levi. "Grab a trash bag and let's get these empties cleared up. And you're sleeping on the couch upstairs tonight."

After Jeani and her sister left, Mia started to go upstairs, but Trent caught her on the stairwell. "Don't judge Levi too harshly. He's freaked out about Christina being in Boise this weekend."

"She's attending Isaac's wedding. He could have gone too. I'm pretty sure she asked him to," Mia reminded Trent.

He glanced at the gym door. "He's kicking himself for not going now. The swing dance, it was just fooling around."

"He's not my boyfriend." Mia kissed him. "Are you and Cerby staying over? Your mom's in the extra room."

"I'll crash in Christina's room." He pulled her closer and slowly kissed her again. "I'm not sure being in your room tonight with the entire family—well, besides Dad—here is a good idea."

"I think we'd be hearing some comments about free milk and cows." She laid her head on his chest. "I'm glad you're here, though. You can keep me from killing Frank."

"You're not working next week, right?" He squeezed

her, and then she stepped away. "It should give you time to cool down."

She paused at the bottom of the stairs and winked at him. "You really think I need to be close to him?"

He chuckled as she made her way upstairs. "I don't think your grandmother would think that is appropriate kitchen witch behavior."

"She hasn't worked for Frank. Give her a week in my job. She'd see my point of view." She turned back and smiled. "As would a jury of my peers."

As both Trent and Mr. Darcy had promised, Cerby was in the apartment, asleep on a pillow by the cold fireplace. As she walked inside, a fire started up in the fireplace. Cerby opened one eye at her, then fell back asleep.

"Hellhounds like to be warm," Grans said from behind her.

Mia turned and hugged her grandmother. "So, did you set the fire, or did he?"

"Dear, you should know the answer to that. Cerby felt the chill from when you opened the door, so he set a fire. That's why I had Trent set wood in the fireplace this afternoon. I suspected with the temps dropping that this might happen. Your coat still smells of Abigail's cleaning spell. Take it off, and I'll refresh it." Her grandmother glanced at the doorway. "Are Trent and Levi still downstairs?"

"Yes, but Jeani and her sister have left. I guess they went to school with Trent." Mia took off her coat and handed it to her grandmother. Then she sat on the chair watching the fire. "I'm so tired."

"You're working too hard. That's why I haven't

pushed our training, but dear, we need to complete it sooner than later." She looked at the door again. "I know I've said this before, but you and Trent need to make some decisions if this is going to be permanent. I'd hate for him not to know where you stand."

"Grans, Trent and I are fine. He knows exactly where I stand with him." Mia thought about Brad and Isaac showing up that week. "He's not worried about anyone else. Now, Levi, he's a little freaked out right now."

"All I know is that I've always seen a strong tie between you and Trent. Tonight, I saw a faint line between him and Jeani. Maybe they have a history and that was what I saw, or maybe—"

Her next words were interrupted when Trent and Levi came in through the apartment's front door. Trent looked at Mia, then at her grandmother. "Are we interrupting?"

CHAPTER 10

Saturday morning, everyone was at the table when Mia came out of her bedroom. Levi was nursing a hangover. Most of the beer bottles Mia found last night had been emptied by him. "Good morning, family."

"Mia"—Trent handed her a cup of coffee—"how did you sleep?"

"Not as well as I should have, knowing I have a week off from the Lodge." Mia sat next to her grandmother, who was going through a yearbook. "What's that?"

"I decided to do some research on Sherry Sellers. I never knew who Melody's father was. I don't think he was ever in the picture. Maybe he was one of her classmates." She pointed to a picture of Sherry and a guy at what looked like a school dance. "Like him."

"I had the boys' old yearbooks and brought them over yesterday." Abigail set a plate with eggs and bacon in front of Mia. "According to rumors, Sherry was dating someone from Boise."

Trent looked at the picture. "That's Jeani's older brother, Ned. You could ask her when she gets here."

"Sure! 'Hey, Jeani, have some coffee. Oh, and did your brother have a love child with Sherry Sellers?'" Levi laughed, then grabbed his head. "Ouch. I'm not sure I can work today."

Trent laughed. "You can, and you will. Run home, grab a shower, and change your clothes. I'll see you back here no later than ten. Those walkways aren't going to build themselves."

Levi stood and drained his coffee. Abigail took the empty cup from him and gave him a travel mug. "Do what your brother said. This should help."

"You're a harder taskmaster than Dad," Levi said to Trent. "And that's not a compliment."

As he left, Cerby jumped on Trent's legs. "I'd better take this guy outside. I'll be back in a few minutes."

After the front door shut, Abigail turned to Mia. "You can't tell Christina about Levi dancing with that girl last night."

"How do you know about that?" Mia held her hands up. "Never mind, don't tell me. Besides, it's not my story to tell—but Levi should tell her."

Abigail sighed and then sank back into a chair. "Everything was so perfect."

"It was just a dance. They didn't go make out behind the bleachers." Mia looked up from her coffee. "Did they?"

"No, it was just a couple of dances. As you can see, Levi had a few too many beers and was feeling no pain.

Except for the hole in his heart because he and Christina are fighting." Abigail took a muffin from the basket. "That's the problem with being close to your kids. You want to fix everything."

"Not possible, and you know it. So, let's get back to Sherry. We think the baby daddy isn't from around here. Do you think he might still show up in some of these pictures?" Grans changed the subject as she flipped through the yearbook searching for random casual shots of Sherry at different events.

"Maybe, but what teenage boy has the money for a two-plus-hour trip just to see his girlfriend?" Mia waved her bacon in the air. "At my school, no one even knew where Magic Springs was located. Sun Valley, sure, but no one but the hard-core skiers ever made the trip. Too far and too expensive, especially back then. People thought I was weird for spending all summer in the mountains when I could have been hanging out at Lucky Peak and getting a tan."

"You were a little snippy about coming to stay with me during your high school years. But do you even see or hear from those friends now?" Grans looked up from the yearbook at her.

Mia thought about it. She hadn't been to a reunion in years, even when she'd lived in Boise and the location had been nearby. She brightened. "No, but a guy who was part of my friends' group has a restaurant in Twin now. Brad was someone's big brother. I can't remember his sister's name, but we'd hang out after the bonfires and talk food. Even then I wanted to be a chef someday."

"Nice to know your mom was letting you hang out

with college kids." Grans sniffed as she closed the yearbook and got up to refresh her coffee. "I should have insisted you move in with me as soon as Theresa renounced her magic. You'd be so much further along."

"I don't blame Mom. I wouldn't have had a normal childhood if she had sent me to live with you." Mia put her plate in the sink. "Sorry, Abigail. I know you raised your kids in the craft, but I liked being just Mia for a while."

"I raised my boys as normal kids. As each of the children I was teaching the craft stepped away from their birthright, I'd go to the next. Trent got most of the instruction, but now Levi has the power. I'm not sure he's emotionally set to go through with his indoctrination at twenty-five. We might have to wait for a new generation, like Mary Alice did."

"Oh, Abigail," Mia started but Grans put her hand on Mia's arm.

Abigail brushed her cheeks but not before Mia noticed the tears. "Anyway, that's that. Of all my boys, Trent had the most potential to take a power seat in the coven. Now he's running a grocery store. Not exactly the future I'd imagined for him."

Cerby ran from the open door to Mia and asked to be picked up.

Trent had heard at least the last part of the conversation. He walked over to his mom. "My future isn't fixed by what I do or by the power the family has. You know that. I love what I do at this point. When I decide to do something different, it will be my choice, not because of some council who doesn't even know me."

"I know, but Trent, you could have been in leadership by now." Abigail took her son's face in her hands. "You would have been amazing. I can still see it in your eyes."

"And he would have been working with idiots. Leave the boy alone, Abigail. I'm sensing there's going to be a change in coven practices soon. Maybe his time for contributions hasn't come to be yet." Grans opened another yearbook. "Don't you people have a queen contest to prepare for?"

"I've got walkways to build. Mia, do you want to come help until Levi gets back?" Trent leaned down and kissed Grans on the cheek. "Thank you for supporting me."

"I'm a sucker for the rebel child." She patted him on the cheek. "Just like my Mia."

When Mia and Trent got back to the gym, she shook her head. "Sorry about Grans. She's always been like that."

He turned to her as he turned the radio on. "Like what?"

"Always up in everyone's business." Mia opened the double doors to the backyard. The yard had white painted arrows on the grass. They were all leading up to a large platform that had a trellis over the top. The dais was perfect for the event, as well as a great bandstand for dances or weddings. Besides, it was beautiful. "I can't believe you finished the platform. It's stunning."

Trent's arms came around her, and he nuzzled her neck. "I believe it's some of my best work. Of course, Levi helped too. And don't apologize for your grandmother. Have you met my mom?"

She laughed and turned to kiss him. When they stepped apart, Mia kept her gaze locked with his. "I love you, Trent Majors. You know that, right?"

"I sense a 'but' in there." He pushed back a stray curl from her ponytail.

She shook her head. "Not from me, but my grandmother thinks we need to make this more official. That my seeing Isaac last week might mess us up."

"You mean, I'd be jealous of the guy dumping you out of the car in the middle of the mountains after you didn't go along with his runaway groom fantasy? I can see how she'd be confused." He rubbed her back. "Our relationship is between you and me. Not my mom, and not your grandmother. I think we have something good here. And if I haven't popped the question yet, well, maybe I was waiting for Isaac to play his last card. Now that it's on the table, things might change."

"I didn't bring this up to trick you into asking me to marry you. I'm not desperate for a husband." Mia put her hands on her hips. This conversation was going all wrong. "Not that I don't see a future together."

"That's not what your grandmother says." He gently tapped her on the butt. "Come on, desperate. Let's get these walkways finished. I'd like to have them ready to move into position so we can anchor them when Levi gets back."

At eleven, Jeani and Cheryl arrived with totes filled with fabrics and fake flowers. Jeani waved at Mia and Trent. "Good morning, construction crew. How is the work coming along?"

"Hi, Jeani. Hey, before we get started, I wanted to tell you again how happy the future mom and dad were about the baby shower. When the lights went down and the event started, it was magical." Mia remembered her own joy at the stars all over the ceiling. "It looked like we were looking up into the night sky. So, was there a bit of magic mixed in there?"

Jeani winked. "I'll never tell. But there's a reason we do most of our work up here, where magic is expected. After you put on a display like that, it's hard to go back to a normal baby shower with crepe paper, fabric, and fairy lights. It just doesn't have the pop."

Cheryl looked around the room, then as she set her tote down, asked, "Is Levi here?"

Mia glanced at her, wondering if she had misheard the desire in Cheryl's voice, but no, the woman looked smitten. She met Trent's gaze, and he shook his head.

"Sorry, Cheryl. I sent him home to clean up. Of course, he's late getting back, which probably means he's talking to his girlfriend. She's in Boise for the weekend for a family event. I'm sure you'll meet her on Monday. She's a big part of Mia's Morsels." Trent picked up the dropped tote and put it on the table. "Mia, why don't you work with the girls on your vision for the event, and I'll start putting up the walkways."

"Let Abigail know Jeani and Cheryl are here first, will you?" Mia glanced at Cheryl, whose face was beet red. She'd gotten the message. Levi was off-limits.

Jeani brought her tote over to the table. "Looks like you and your friend have the available Majors boys all tied up. Good for you. Levi's always been a flirt, but Trent was a man of mystery. He dated casually but never found the one. I asked him once who he was waiting for, and he told me he was waiting for his soul-mate. What kind of teenage boy feels that kind of certainty?"

Cheryl pointed to the restrooms on the side of the gym. "Are those useable? I need to freshen up."

"I've remodeled and updated both the restrooms. Of course, they still are gym restrooms, but the lockers are prettier, and the tile is amazing. And there's a shower room with all individual showers. I was hoping to add a pool someday. Either in this space or outside by the parking lot." Mia rattled on.

But Cheryl wasn't listening; she'd already taken off for the restroom door. Mia turned to her sister. "Sorry about Trent's bluntness. She must have fallen fast."

"Oh, she's been in love with Levi since high school. Last night just fed all the adolescent fantasies she's had since. I should have warned her. I knew he was dating your friend. But when Cheryl decides to fall in love, you can't stop her." Jeani pulled out a swatch of fabric and a sketch pad. "So, this is what I was thinking . . ."

Abigail showed up a few minutes later, so Jeani walked her and Mia through the planned decorations. Then they walked the areas where guests would be allowed and various events held. Mia opened a different classroom from the one where Carla had died. "We'll be using this for a green room. We'll have tables, rolling hangers, and full-length and table mirrors. It's big enough for contestants to have their own area to get ready. We'll provide a few chairs for each spot, but not a lot. Thoughts?"

"You should allow them access to this area for the

full week. That way you've got all the hair and makeup stuff already here. If a girl wanted to bring her full week's worth of outfits, you'll have a good setup. Do you need help with supplying this? I've got contacts with rental places. That way, it can come out of our budget and not yours." Jeani was already making notes.

Abigail nodded. "That would be great. I wasn't thinking about having it set up all week, so I'm a little behind the eight ball on getting the furniture we need."

"I do love a good challenge." Jeani winked. "So, this was the only area we hadn't seen. I'll start making some drawings, and we'll make up a list. The Monday session, it's at six, right?"

"Yes. It's a casual get-together in the foyer. We'll have passed trays. The girls and their families will meet the judges and the coven board." Abigail spun around the room. "If we can have this set up by four, the contestants can bring their stuff and get ready here."

"Sounds like a plan." Mia met Abigail's gaze and got a nod. "We're about to have lunch. Do you want to eat with us?"

Cheryl shook her head. She hadn't spoken since she'd asked about the restrooms. Having her fantasy about a life with Levi crushed by Trent had flattened the woman.

Jeani smiled at her sister. "Sorry, we have plans. Cheryl, why don't you go gather the bags we left in the gym, and I'll meet you at the car."

Cheryl nodded and hurried out of the room. When Jeani heard the door slam at the bottom of the stairs, she turned back to us. "Sorry about that. I tried to tell her, but well, she's got it bad. Can you ask Levi to be respectful of Cheryl this week? I think I can get her talking by Monday, but not if he's nice to her again."

"I can remember feeling that way about a boy." Mia didn't add the fact that she'd been in high school. She took Jeani's arm as they looked at her sketches again. "I'm so excited about working with you on this project. Abigail did the heavy lifting by getting us the contract, and I'm butting in for the week. But I took the time off from the Lodge, so Frank can't gripe."

"When has that ever stopped him in the past?" Jeani tucked her book into her tote. "He really doesn't like you. He asked what I'd charge to be the catering director, and I told him he couldn't afford me. I've worked for Frank before, and I about died when I heard the hotel chain had brought him here. I'm hoping he'll disappear to another Lodge sooner than later. But I've heard this is his last shot with this management."

"Unfortunately, the school is expensive to keep open, so I need a job. And I'm lucky enough to have Abigail to help me run Mia's Morsels." Mia smiled at her friend. "But yes, Frank and I are not on the best of terms."

Her phone buzzed. She looked at the display. "And speak of the devil."

She read the text as they made their way downstairs.

"A problem?" Abigail paused before walking Jeani outside.

Mia sighed. "Maybe. Frank asked me to attend the Monday staff meeting. He said I can be virtual if I need to be."

"Maybe it's just to set up the next week's events." Abigail called out to Jeani, who was carrying four bags from the gym. Cheryl hadn't grabbed them as her sister had asked. "Hold on, let me at least open the door for you."

Mia tucked her phone away as she went to help Jeani to her car. No, if it was an event two weeks away, Frank would just send her the schedule. If her gut was right, Frank had scheduled an event for the week she was gone. So she'd have to work. She rolled her stiff neck. No use worrying about it until Monday. But she would work as hard and as long as possible up until then. Just in case.

CHAPTER 11

Trent slammed his phone down on the table. "Where is Levi?"

Mia looked up from her French dip sandwich that Grans had made with homemade French fries for lunch. They were all back in the apartment. Well, all of them except for Levi. He was AWOL. And Trent was hot about it.

"Maybe he fell back asleep?" Abigail suggested.

Trent shook his head. "I called his buddy who lives in the same apartment building. He saw him go in this morning, then he came out, showered, with a bag, and got in his Jeep. He waved but didn't stop."

"Where would he be going?" Abigail asked, but no one answered. "He knew you needed him here."

Except Mia had a feeling. "I might know. Where's my phone?"

"In the living room, dear." Grans pointed to the coffee table.

She glanced at her text messages, but nothing had come in since the one from Frank. So she preempted Levi's surprise and texted Christina.

A response came quickly. Christina called her.

"Mom's going to croak. She had a new prospective husband for me to sit by at dinner after the wedding. I'd better tell her that I'm going to have a plus one."

Mia stepped into the living room to continue the call. "I'm not certain, but I have a feeling. And he's not in town."

"Oh, I wouldn't put it past him. I'll call if he doesn't show up in an hour. Trent can't reach him with his 'special phone'?" Christina asked. Christina knew about the psychic link between the two brothers.

"Apparently not because he's worried. Just call me or text if you see him." Mia wondered if Trent had tried, but left that information out due to his mom being in the room.

"Sounds good." Christina paused. "Hey, what happened between you and Isaac? He's a mess, and he's blaming you."

"He came to Magic Springs to declare his undying love for me. I told him it was too late. So he dumped me on the side of the road and left. Why, what is he saying?" Mia wasn't sure she wanted to know.

"He says you called him saying you were going to hurt yourself if he went through with the wedding," Christina said. "So he had to drive up to Magic Springs yesterday to talk you down from killing yourself over his getting married."

Mia burst out laughing. "He's a snot."

"Yes, he is, but he's my brother. Sorry he played with your heart."

Mia smiled even though Christina couldn't see her. "He didn't. My heart is here, and he's eating lunch and worrying about his brother. I'd better get back. Have a great wedding and say hi to your mom."

"Not today. She's already freaking out. Levi showing up might throw her over the edge." Christina paused. "I'll be back late tomorrow. We're having a family brunch before the lovebirds jet off to Europe."

Mia winced. She and Issac had planned an extended European honeymoon. They were probably using her itinerary. "See you tomorrow."

Mia took the phone with her back to the kitchen. She didn't like having phones at a meal table, but she wanted to know when Levi showed up.

"You found him?" Trent asked.

Mia shrugged and took a bite of her sandwich. After swallowing, she added, "Maybe."

"You're saying he went to see Christina?" Abigail smiled. "Levi always did have a flare for the dramatic."

"Mother Adams can beat him at that game. I'm sure she'll faint when he walks in. She had a new possible, probably uber-rich boyfriend lined up to eat dinner with Christina after the wedding." Mia took another bite of her sandwich.

"Thank the Goddess you missed that bullet. That woman is a mess. She tries to control everything. Including her adult children." Grans put her plate in the sink. "I'm going to go watch my shows in my room. Can someone let Muffy out when Cerby goes?"

"Of course, I'd be glad to take them as soon as I finish with lunch." Trent stood as Grans left the table. "Unless he needs to go now."

"Sit down, he can wait until you eat." Grans headed down the hallway. "Such a nice boy."

Mia broke out laughing as the door to Grans's room shut. "Man, she's playing with emotions today."

"She thinks that you and Trent should be moving on with your lives," Abigail whispered, looking back into the hallway. "She's told me that several times this weekend. I'm not sure what the rush is, but you know your grandmother. You can't tell her anything."

"I just wish she'd figure out the Mr. Darcy and Dorian thing. She can leave my relationship alone and focus on that instead." Mia dipped her last French fry into the special sauce Grans had made for them.

Abigail and Trent nodded, but neither of them said anything. Finally, Mia spoke. "Okay, what did I say?"

Abigail and Trent shared a look. Then he spoke. "Mia, I'm afraid it's already too late for Mr. Darcy. There isn't a spell strong enough to separate the two after this long. We didn't do it."

"You mean, Dorian's always going to be in Mr. Darcy? He's already eight. What happens when he ages?" Mia couldn't imagine what she was hearing.

Abigail pressed her lips together, then spoke. "We don't think Mr. Darcy will age. Or if he does, it won't be at the same rate cats normally age."

"I can't believe I'm just now hearing this. When was the 'cutoff'?" Mia brushed the tears off her cheeks. "He's just a cat. He didn't ask for this."

"Mia, Mr. Darcy is fine. He might not be just a cat now, but he's fine. Really." Abigail squeezed her hand.

"Look, I'll bring over some books on transfiguration. I think reading about the process will help you cope. Or at least understand what we're saying."

Mr. Darcy came out of the hallway, took one look at Mia and the others, then turned away and let himself out the apartment's front door.

"I don't think I'm ever going to get used to that." Mia sighed as she stood. "I'm ready to work. Where do you want me?"

Abigail blinked several times. "Well, we need to clean out the second-floor room for Jeani's crew to set it up. I need to start on the menu planning for each night and start baking. And we need to be ready for Tuesday's deliveries on top of anything we're doing for the contest. Oh, and Trent might need help since his brother has deserted him."

"Let's start with the planning for the week, and then I'll see what can be done early for that and Tuesday's deliveries. I'd like to be cooking unless Trent needs me." Mia and Abigail turned toward Trent.

"I need a second pair of hands, but I've got an idea." He picked up his phone and headed out of the apartment. "I'll check in at noon. Expect one more for dinner."

Abigail followed Mia out of the apartment. "Well, that sounded ominous."

Mia nodded but didn't answer. She was pretty sure who would be the addition at their dinner table, and Abigail wasn't going to like it. But they had work that needed to be done. Today. Especially since Christina and Levi wouldn't be back until early tomorrow afternoon. If not later.

Time to start thinking about food. Mia felt absolutely giddy.

The good feeling didn't last long. After they'd finished the planning, Abigail took a call. When she came back, Mia was working on a sugar cookie base they were going to make into crowns and wands for the Friday night event.

"Do you want the good news or the bad news first?" Abigail asked as she stirred the marinara sauce she was making for the eggplant Parmesan dish for Tuesday's delivery.

"Good news." Mia rolled the last of the dough into plastic wrap and marked the item off her to-do list. She carried the cookie rolls into the walk-in. "And speak up. I'm going to grab the ingredients for the next project."

"You might want to hold off." Abigail waited until Mia stepped out of the fridge and looked at her. "The good news is Jeani came through, and her rental people have everything we need to set up the prep room."

"And let me guess, they're on their way over." Mia rolled her shoulders. "That's the bad news."

"You're good at this game. Do you want me to go clean the room, or should I keep working on the sauces?" Abigail asked.

"I'll go clean the room." Mia took off her apron and threw it into the laundry hamper. Then she went to the cleaning closet and collected what she needed. "I could use the exercise."

"If you're sure. I could do it." Abigail glanced at the

pots she had on the stove. "I'd just need you to watch the sauce."

"No, I'll do it." Mia picked up the bucket filled with cleaning supplies and headed upstairs. "The good news is, I set up a cleaning closet on the second floor too, so it has a broom, cloths, mops, and all the equipment. I need to fill it with product too, but that will come. Call me when dinner is ready."

"Okay, but don't forget to clean the windows. They really need a scrubbing," Abigail called after her.

"Yes, Mom," Mia muttered, hopefully low enough that Abigail wouldn't hear. But on the other hand, she was a witch. Cerby followed her out of the kitchen, where he'd been sleeping on his bed. He stretched and yawned as he pranced after her.

Before she climbed the stairs, she stopped at the front door and looked back at her shadow. "Do you need to go outside?"

Cerby barked and sat near the door.

"I'll take that as a yes." Mia set the cleaning supplies down and opened the door to find Jeani standing there, ready to knock. "Well, hello again."

"Great timing. I'm here to measure the stage and make sure I have enough fabric." She tapped her notebook. "I won't be here long."

"Your people are due in about an hour to set up the prep room. Do you want to stay and work with them?" Mia held the door open, and Cerby ran outside to his favorite patch of grass to do his business.

"No, I'll leave them a sketch on how to set it up, then I'll come back Monday and make it pretty." She grinned as she watched Cerby come back inside. "He's so cute. Anyway, Cheryl is expecting me back home to work on a few projects, so I won't be here long. I don't like leaving her alone, especially after what happened with Levi."

"Did she really think it was more than just being friendly?" Mia knew Levi liked chatting with women, but he typically kept his interactions friendly and not too friendly. And she'd just said or thought the word *friendly* three times. No, four. She was tired.

"It's not Levi's fault. I blame her addiction to fairy-tale romance. She thinks she's just going to meet her soulmate and fall, just like that. I've told her about kissing toads, but Cheryl's always the optimist." She glanced at the cleaning supplies. "Are you heading upstairs? Can I follow you and do the furniture placement sketch?"

"Sure. Come on up. Are you okay with stairs?" Mia shut the door behind them, and they headed upstairs. About five steps up, Mia turned to look for Cerby. He met her gaze, then turned toward the kitchen and his bed. She called out to him, "Don't get lost on your way."

Jeani laughed. "I still can't believe that Trent picked a Maltese for a pet. I thought he'd go bigger, like a mastiff, or at least a German shepherd."

"Cerby kind of picked him." Mia smiled at the memory. "Trent rescued him on a rainy night."

"Oh, now, that's too sweet. If Trent wasn't head over heels in love with you, that story would get him dates for years." Jeani held open the door to the second-floor classroom. "While you're getting ready, I'll do up the sketch. If you need help moving the rest of these desks out, just tell the guys. They're super helpful."

Mia groaned. She'd forgotten there were ten or more random desks still in the room. She'd ask Trent to help, but he was busy with the walkways. "I'll get them into the hallway. Maybe the furniture guys could move them into the next classroom?"

"Sure, just ask when they get here." Jeani sounded distracted, and when Mia looked her way, she was drawing on her pad.

Mia decided moving the desks needed to be done first. Then the empty room would be easier to clean. She picked up the first desk and dragged it out to the hallway, pushing it down the hall past the doorway to the next classroom. This way, they'd be out of the way.

By the time she'd moved almost all the desks, Jeani was done. She walked over to Mia and showed the drawing to her. "Does that look okay?"

Mia took the paper and studied it. Jeani had one complete station set up and decorated, with locations for the other five. It was pretty. She looked up at the white walls. At least the paint in the room was new. Mia had started painting the second floor when she'd run out of money for the remodel but not time to work on it. Of course, now she had neither.

"This is perfect. You're talented." Mia handed the paper back to Jeani.

She blushed, and the red went up to the edge of her straight blond hair. The way she wore it, she looked a lot younger than her actual age. She could be using a glamour spell, or some women were just born with good genes. "It's what I do. Thanks again for letting me work on this project. I thought maybe since Trent and I dated, you would have an issue, but you're cool."

Mia leaned against a desk. "I didn't know you dated. High school?"

"No, it was a few years ago. But like I said, he's a lot like my sister. He knew even then he was looking for a soulmate, and I wasn't it. We had fun, but it was never anything serious." She glanced at her watch. "I need to run and get those measurements. Cheryl's going to be calling sooner than later. See you tomorrow? I'd love to do the foyer then."

Jeani took out some tape and put the sketch on the door as she left the room.

"Sounds like a plan," Mia called after her. She thought the universe might be giving her payback for her running into Brad the other day. Or maybe the Isaac incident. Old friends, old loves, old wounds. She looked up when she heard someone digging at the floor.

Cerby had come upstairs and was now trying to pull something out of a crack between the wall and the doorjamb.

"What do you have now?" She pulled at the white fabric, which felt familiar. A potion bag came out of the small crack. "Cerby, you're a real Sherlock Holmes in finding clues. So, tell me, who made this?"

Cerby barked and sat looking at her.

"What, cat got your tongue?" Mia laughed and put the potion bag on the next desk to be moved. "Don't worry about it. I'll run this up to Grans and see what she thinks."

Cerby barked, then left the room. As Mia carried the

last desk out of the room, she watched him hurry down the stairs aiming for the kitchen. The dog was better at this murder-solving thing than she was. At least he was finding clues. Even if they didn't mean much.

After running upstairs to leave the potion bag with her grandmother, Mia decided to start with the windows and work down in the room. She sprayed the first window with cleaner, then took paper towels to clean off the grime. Jeani was still here, talking to Trent outside.

Mia noticed another man working on the walkways. As Mia had suspected, Thomas Majors was the helper Trent had called in. As she scrubbed at one last fly spot, she watched as Jeani gave Trent a kiss. On the cheek—but still, a kiss.

Her arm stopped moving, and she couldn't think. Were they more than just friends? As she tried to get in control of her emotions, she saw Jeani leave the yard, and Trent's face turned up to the second-floor windows. He found her and smiled. Somehow she smiled back and then went to the next window.

If Jeani had never said anything about them dating, would she be feeling this way? And what was she feeling anyway? Envy, jealousy, anger, or fear? She pushed all her emotions away and scrubbed on the remaining windows. All she could do right now was make sure this room was spotless. And that's what she would focus on. Then she'd find something else to focus on until she understood what she was feeling.

And what it meant.

She sprayed more cleaner, making the view of Trent and the backyard blurry, just like her emotions.

CHAPTER 12

At about three, the group took a break. Together. The atmosphere was tense. Abigail didn't say much to Thomas, focusing instead on Mia or Trent. Mia, on the other hand, avoided talking to Trent. Trent and his father, sensing the tension, tried not to say much about anything. But at least they were all in the same room. Grans seemed oblivious to any tension and chatted nonstop.

When they finished the cookies and iced tea, Thomas and Trent took off to finish the walkways. The backyard would be done, with the walkways ready to stain by the end of the day. Levi would be back to help with the staining tomorrow. And Mia's backyard would be ready for the event as soon as it dried.

Mia told Abigail the prep room was ready for furniture and that Jeani had left a sketch. She asked Abigail if she'd deal with the rental company. Then she turned to her grandmother. "What about the new potion bag?"

Abigail gasped. "There's another one?"

"Yes. And we didn't even talk about using this room before Carla was killed, so someone else is definitely making and hiding these." Mia was beginning to get a headache. The best thing she could do at that moment was cook. She thought better when she was mixing up dough or baking cookies.

Grans sighed. "I can't determine who made these. They put a glamour on when they were spelling them so the bags all think Carla made them. It's brilliant, but it makes it hard for us to know who the problem child is really."

"Remind me next year that we don't want this event, even if they offer to pay us three times the going rate." Mia groaned while Abigail laughed.

"Honey, I bid it at ten times the going rate, and they still chose us. We're going to have to either figure out a way to keep the shenanigans down or just accept we're going to make a boatload of money on this and maybe that will get you freed from working the Lodge job." Abigail hugged Mia. "I'll handle the rental company. My to-do list is on the table next to yours. I don't think we need both of us cooking today, but tomorrow, it's all hands on deck as soon as Christina gets back."

"Maybe it's Isaac's wedding that's messing with my head." Mia took a long breath. "But tomorrow he'll be on his honeymoon and out of the country. That should clear the air around here."

"We'll get through this." Grans squeezed Mia's arm. "But if you start feeling worse, come upstairs. I want to make sure one of the potion bags didn't get under your skin."

"Great. Now I have to worry about stress and being poisoned while I'm trying to run my business."

"The lists will keep for a few minutes while you take some painkillers." Abigail snapped her fingers. "Muffy, Cerby, let's go outside."

After they'd left the apartment, Grans handed Mia a cup of tea. "Drink this. It will help with a headache and ward off any random spells."

Mia smelled the orange in the tea. "What would I do without you?"

"Well, I wanted to talk to you about that, but now's not the time." Grans squeezed her hand. "I would like to see you and Trent make it official soon."

"You're really on that bandwagon recently. Is there something wrong? Something I should know?" Mia sipped her tea and looked at her grandmother's face. Sometimes she could see a lie forming; other times, not. But it was worth trying.

"I've been having dreams about a break in the coven. Something that's going to affect your relationship with Trent. If you're committed, you'll weather the storm. If not, I can't see the answer there. All I know is when I see you two after the storm passes, you have a ring on your finger. When the bad dreams come, you don't."

Mia smiled as she finished her tea. "So, Trent's going to save me? I think I learned that lesson with Isaac. I make my own destiny. I love Trent, and if he loves me, we'll take that step. I'm just not sure an impending emergency is a great reason to push the timeline."

Grans lifted her hand off Mia's. Then she stood and walked to the hallway. She turned back and said, "I'm not trying to sell you off to the highest bidder. All I can tell you is what I'm seeing in my dreams. If you choose not to act on it, I can't force you."

Mia spent a few minutes alone in the kitchen. Gloria, her connection with the Goddess, was silent. Grans's forecast had quieted even the doll's giggle. Mia stood and took her cup to the sink. First, she'd get this contest done. Then she'd worry about the future with Trent. She'd tell him about Grans's prediction and see what he thought.

It wasn't a conversation they needed to have today.

As she made her way downstairs, she heard a noise in the prep room. Had the rental company guys already arrived? But when Mia opened the door, two girls stood there.

One of them turned toward Mia, and she recognized her. Melody Sellers. "Hey, Melody, what are you doing here?"

"I think I'm the butt of a practical joke. Crissy said everyone was meeting here at three, but I'm the only one here." Melody glanced at the other girl. "You'd think they would show up just to laugh at me, if nothing else. Oh, this is my friend Tera."

"Oh honey, I'm sorry." Mia stepped toward Melody, then stopped. What was she going to do? Give the girl a hug? "Sometimes kids are cruel."

"All the time," Melody corrected her. "I'm used to it. Mom died right after she had me, so I was the kid who didn't have parents. I never knew my dad. Thank goodness Grandma wanted me. She said I was her blessing. I'm fine. I'm not sure why I'm telling you my life story."

Tera shrugged. "Crissy is horrible. I don't under-stand why most people, including Dakota Marks, don't see her true colors."

"Dakota just sees her body and pretty hair." Melody laughed with her friend.

"It's been that kind of day around here, believe me. Hey, I've got some chocolate-chip cookies I made this morning. Do you want some with a soda or milk?" Mia glanced out the window and saw Trent and Thomas laughing. The school needed more laughter right now.

"That sounds great if it's not a bother. When did you know you wanted to be a chef? Tera's thinking about going to culinary school next year. I'm focusing on a four-year program, especially if I can get in some-where far away from Idaho." Melody and Tera followed Mia out of the prep room, chatting as they made their way downstairs.

Abigail joined them for cookies and milk until the rental company arrived, and soon after, Melody and Tera stood to leave. "Thanks for being such a good sport. I'm sure that's not the last trick Crissy has up her sleeve for me this week."

Tera nodded, still chewing on a cookie.

"You're the one who seems strangely okay with being teased like this. I'm sure you had something else to do today," Mia said as she walked the girls to the door.

"Not really. I was reading. I'm pretty caught up at school, so I read a lot. That's one of the reasons my grandmother wanted me to participate in the contest. To get me out of my room. But she doesn't get it. I don't fit in with the rest of the kids, and they make sure

I know it. Well, besides Tera. I'm just waiting for college to have a life outside school." She rubbed Cerby's head as she stood in the doorway. "I know, pathetic."

Tera shrugged. "College is going to be amazing."

"Sometimes you have slower periods in your life. But you're in charge of what you do and who you want to do it with. Don't wait for someone to knock on your door to start experiencing life." Mia leaned on the door frame. "Maybe you should start taking AP classes. Or get an early admission to Boise State."

"Actually, my counselor was saying something about a new program." She put earbuds in her ears and took out her phone. "I'll check into that. See you Monday evening."

Mia watched the girls stroll down the hill and take the sidewalk into town. Melody was obviously smart, if not driven. Maybe that wasn't a bad thing. Mia had only known one speed—fast. Get high school done, graduate college, get a great job, and keep climbing the ladder. It had taken her breaking up with Isaac to realize that she wasn't living; she'd been on a treadmill.

Voices from the stairs made her turn back inside. Three men were coming down with Abigail. She made eye contact with Abigail. "Hey, how's it going?"

"We're all done. The hallway is cleared of the desks as well. I think the girls and their folks are going to love this setup. Especially when I saw what Jeani was planning to do to dress it up." Abigail signed a form that one of the men had on a clipboard. "Thanks for coming, guys. The room looks great."

The one with the clipboard bowed low. "You are most

welcome. Good luck in choosing this year's harvest queen."

As Mia and Abigail went inside, Mia glanced at her watch. "Why don't we finish up the sauces and then call it a day? I'll order pizza for dinner."

Abigail glanced out toward the backyard. Toward Thomas. "Sounds good. Although I may not be feeling sociable when dinner comes around."

"You still haven't resolved it?" Mia asked as they moved toward the kitchen.

Abigail shook her head. "He's being stubborn. He doesn't realize how dangerous being a judge can be. One year, all the judges wound up in the hospital with food poisoning. Luckily, the decision had already been made on the queen announcement before they got sick."

"Maybe he's trying to be more involved in your life." Mia studied her to-do list. It was a lot for tomorrow, but she was sure they could make it. A lot of the prep work had been done for some of it today.

"If he's dead like Carla, he's not going to be involved at all, now, is he?" Abigail finished washing her hands and put on a new apron. "Not to change the subject, but why were Melody and that other girl here?"

Mia told her about the prank Crissy had played. "She seemed okay with it, though. Like she had been expecting it."

"As long as Crissy doesn't rig up some pig blood dousing if Melody wins."

Mia stared at Abigail. "Do you think she'd really do that?"

"It's a scene from that movie where the girl has powers?" Abigail shrugged. "Thomas and I always joked that we were glad to raise boys rather than girls. Girls can be mean. Boys are just reckless."

Mia thought of Levi and his impromptu trip to Boise to be at Christina's side during the wedding. It was either going to be seen as a romantic gesture or a jealous one. Although Christina had asked him to attend and had been disappointed when he'd said no. Maybe Levi was growing up—a little. Mia just hoped the two would be on speaking terms when they got back home. One feuding couple in the Majors family was enough to deal with.

The next two hours went by fast, and as Mia was putting the now-cooled sauce away in the fridge, the back door opened, and Trent came inside. "Hey, how's the walkway going?"

"It's all ready to stain tomorrow. I think Dad and I will have it done long before Levi arrives. He called, by the way. He said Christina was excited to see him, but the rest of the family, not so much. Isaac looks really mad about something."

"I don't really care what Isaac is mad about. I'm glad Christina is happy. I was getting tired of her moping around the house the last two weeks." Mia glanced around the kitchen. Abigail was finishing the dishes, and all they needed to do was wash off the prep tables and put a load of laundry into the washer. "How's pizza for dinner?"

"It would be amazing, but Dad just asked me to go to the Lodge with him." He glanced over to his mother. "I'll tell him about the offer, but . . ."

"Yeah, we can have one or the other." Mia grabbed a washcloth and rinsed it in the soapy water, standing next to Abigail. She poked her friend. "I bet he'd stay for pizza if you asked."

"I told you . . ."

Mia held up her hand. "Just kidding. Trent, have a nice dinner, and thank your dad. We'll get him paid for his help."

Trent paused at the door. "So, I'll see you tomorrow morning?"

"Bright and shiny." Mia set the wet cloth on a dirty table and went over to him, drying her hands on her apron as she went. She kissed him, holding her hands on his cheeks. "Thank you for everything. I do appreciate you."

"'Appreciate,' that's the magic word every man wants to hear." He straightened her apron strap. "What are you doing Saturday after the event? Do you want to go to the festival with me? There's a parade at ten, then we can spend the rest of the day wandering the festival grounds."

She kissed him again. "It's a date. Let me try again. You're really sexy when you work on my lawn . . . Or maybe this: I love you as well as appreciate you."

"That's much better." He stepped back and waved at Abigail. "See you tomorrow, Mom."

"I love you, too," Abigail called out as she dried a large pot. "But I'm *just* the woman who brought you into this world. Changed your diapers. Kept you alive."

Mia laughed, then watched Trent through the window as he walked back to his dad. When he brought up the pizza, she saw the reaction in Thomas's face. The men would be eating at the Lodge. She locked the door and turned back to finish the cleanup. Not her problem, not her monkeys.

She had other monkeys to deal with. Like her grandmother. A quiet dinner for three would give Mia time to chat about what was going on with her. Besides the bad dreams about Mia's future.

Mia waited until she went upstairs to call in the pizza order. Sometimes Grans wanted a combo, sometimes Hawaiian. You never knew.

"I'll have whatever you're eating," Grans said as the three of them gathered in the kitchen, three glasses of iced tea on the table.

Both Mia and Abigail stared at her.

"What? Why are you both staring?" Grans waved their attention away. "I'm not much of a diva."

This time Mia changed the subject. "Okay, Abigail, what do you feel like? Garlic chicken or a full-out combo?"

"Let's go with the combo. I feel like I never get a slice when the guys are here. They wolf it down." Abigail laid her head on the table. "I'm so worn out, and it's not even Sunday."

"Combo's better than garlic chicken," Grans said, but then she saw the smile on Mia's face. "You just said that so I'd tell you what I wanted."

"Me? Trick you? I don't think so." Mia took her phone into the living room and called in an order. When she came back, the women were talking about past harvest festivals. "So, tell me about the coven connection. Have they always been involved in the queen contest? I know most towns have a harvest festival or a fair. They started as a way to express gratitude for the generous harvest each year, correct?"

"It's an old village tradition. Coming together. Celebrating the bounty. The Goddess used to be a large part of the celebration. Then the celebrations turned a little dark when the harvest wasn't good. For the record, here in Magic Springs, we've never sacrificed virgins, but the queen contest is a way of celebrating the bounty of our so-called human crop," Grans explained. "Or magical human crop."

"It sounds a little bit like putting the prize cow on sale." Mia laughed when the other women stared wide-eyed at her.

"Mia, I can't believe you said that." Abigail started laughing, and for a minute, the troubles they'd all felt that day were gone. "Thomas used to say the same thing. Like the coven was putting the girls up for display for the virgin sacrifice part of the festival, even though they didn't follow through."

"I don't know. I guess it's tradition, but I'm glad I wasn't part of the coven growing up. I have enough self-confidence issues without the comparison-itis that comes with pitting young girls against each other." Mia sipped her water.

"And you don't do that with all your best chef shows and awards?" Grans poked her in the arm. "How many times have I caught you watching those?"

An alarm sounded as Mia watched the security monitor as a car with a Pizza Place sign on the top pulled into the parking lot. "Saved by the bell. Maybe I was just raised in the participation-trophy era. I don't like being judged only on my looks."

"The contest also interviews to see what the girls know about current events," Abigail countered. "I'm sorry if this event is pushing buttons for you."

Mia stood and stopped at the apartment door before she went downstairs to get the pizza. "It's not. I'm excited to be participating in the harvest festival. I'm not sure about what my feelings are about beauty contests, but Carla shouldn't have died trying to give her daughter a step up in the contest. That's definite."

Mia brought the pizza upstairs after locking the front door and setting the alarm. Everyone who was staying tonight was already in the building. Trent had told her he was going home after dinner with his dad. Cerby was having a sleepover with Muffy here at the school. Mia liked spending time with Trent's little hell-hound. He kept her on her toes.

When she got back upstairs, the table was set. Music played in the background. Abigail smiled as Mia came in with the pizza box. "We decided it was going to be a stress-free meal. No contest, no talking about the business or the Lodge, no talking about men."

Grans held her hand up. "I even had a report, but Abigail insisted."

Chapter 13

"Wait"—Mia set the pizza on the counter—"I want to hear Grans's report before the meal starts."

"Okay, so you both know I've been dating Robert Penny for a while now." Grans looked over to check to see if Mr. Darcy was on the kitchen window seat. When she saw it was empty, she leaned forward. "He's asked me to marry him. Can you believe it? I'm getting married."

Mia hugged her grandmother. "Oh, I'm so happy for you! Mary Alice Penny. It has a ring to it."

"Now, I'm not taking his name, and we haven't decided when or where." Her grandmother patted her back, then hugged Abigail as well. "I'm assuming we'll do it here at the school. I've got a project I need to finish and get out of my spare bedroom. We've talked about selling my house and me moving in with him. So, there are a lot of loose ends to tie up before anything can move forward."

"His house is lovely. When his wife was alive, she used to host a book club there. I'm sure you'll love living there and making it your own," Abigail said as she moved the pizza to the table. "Okay, I'm amending our rules. Mary Alice can talk about her relationship."

Grans laughed, and Mia saw how truly happy she was. Maybe that was why she hadn't been around much lately. Robert had been sweeping her off her feet. Her grandmother deserved a joyful life. "So, we need to finish my training. That's the loose end you're talking about?"

Grans nodded, then watched as Mr. Darcy came into the kitchen and curled up on the window seat. "That and a few other things. My news is over. What else should we talk about?"

Surprised, Abigail looked up from putting slices of pizza on everyone's plate and saw Mr. Darcy. Grans was being polite. Grans had been dating Dorian Alexander before his untimely death and then his consciousness being put into Mr. Darcy's body. There was no reason to rub salt into Dorian's wounds. Nodding her understanding, she passed out the plates and then set the spatula on the top of the box. "I'm pulling up my garden next week when this contest is finished, and I'll be drying herbs if anyone wants some for their supplies."

"That's a kind offer. Mia needs a vial of everything." Grans took a bite of her pizza. "We also need to set up one of the second-floor classrooms as a potion laboratory. The chemistry room would work best. We'll need to get Trent and Levi to take out most of the student tables."

"I was going to make the old chemistry lab a cooking skills classroom." Mia thought about the rooms on the second floor. "I guess we could clear out the other science lab and set up cooking skills there."

"I'm glad you see my logic." Grans used her slice of pizza to point out the many reasons the chemistry room was the best choice for Mia's potion lab. Including the fact that it was at the back of the second floor. If Mia was turning classrooms into usable space for the cooking school, she needed the magic part of her life out of the way of prying eyes.

As she talked, Mia wondered how she'd ever find the time to do all the spells and potions that Grans did daily. What was her time commitment as a kitchen witch? Five hours a week? A month? Or more? What did the job entail? Was there a to-do sheet? She really needed to talk to her grandmother about the logistics of this lifestyle she was taking on.

But that discussion wasn't on the table for today. Mia made a mental note to come back to the topic when they were alone and focused on the conversation currently being examined. Right now, Abigail and Grans were deciding how to set up Mia's witchy lab.

"This is kind of exciting. It's like when I got my first wand." Mia finished her first piece of pizza and went back for a second.

"Oh, having a potions lab is so much better. You don't have to worry about a specific spell or pronunciation. It's all in the mix. I think that's why I love baking so much—you do it right, and it's magic. Magic made out of flour, sugar, and other basic ingredients." Abigail clapped her hands together. "I've got my old cauldron at the house. The boys aren't interested, but maybe you might want it?"

Mia looked at her grandmother, who nodded. Even Mia knew that being gifted someone's first cauldron was an honor, one that usually happened in families. She was sure that her grandmother had one to pass down as well, but it wouldn't hurt to have two. Especially if Trent was going to become a part of her family. It would be a nice hand-me-down to any potential children they might have. With the thought of kids, Mia's face heated, and she refocused on the here and now. "I would appreciate that. And if you change your mind, I'll give it back, I promise."

"There are no takebacks allowed in this sort of thing. Believe me, the boys are getting a lot of stuff. Probably more than they'd ever want or need. I want you to have this. You've been a lifesaver this year with the job and your trust in me. I appreciate you." Abigail reached over and squeezed Mia's hand. "I wasn't kidding when I said I consider you and Christina, daughters. No matter what my sons do in the future."

Mia thought a lot about Abigail's cauldron and the meaning behind the gift later that night as she tried to fall asleep. Finally, she picked up her phone and texted Christina to see how the wedding had gone.

No answer.

Mia set the phone down, curled up next to Cerby, and quickly fell into dreams of open fields surrounding a castle and fire-eating dragons circling overhead.

When she awoke, she rubbed Cerby's tummy. "Were those your dragons in my dream?"

Cerby barked and jumped off the bed, running to the door to bark some more.

"Okay, you want to go outside. I promise you there are no dragons here, only birds and maybe squirrels." Mia pulled on her robe and slippers. Cerby didn't look convinced.

"Don't say I didn't warn you." She opened the door and followed the dog into the hallway. Trent met her in the kitchen.

"I'll take him. I was waiting for you to wake up before I grabbed him to run downstairs." Trent leaned in and kissed her.

"You're welcome to have him. He dreamed of dragons last night and was kind enough to share the dream." Mia rubbed her neck. "Does he usually share with you?"

"Yeah, I should have warned you. Dragons have been his go-to dream for the last week. Not sure what it's symbolizing, but there you go. That's my life." Trent handed her a cup of coffee. "Here, go get ready, and we'll be out here waiting for you."

"Sounds good." Mia turned back around and headed to her bedroom to shower and get ready for the day. She hadn't had a puppy around for a long time. Muffy had been potty trained for years. And Mr. Darcy, well, he had a box, but lately, he'd been going outside with Dorian. Mia needed to tell Dorian that he was stuck inside her cat. Or maybe everyone except her and Mr. Darcy had known how the story was going to end.

She watched as Mr. Darcy came out of Christina's

room and hurried after Cerby and Trent. Then Grans's door opened, and Muffy ran out to come along. The information grapevine shared by the animals was working fine this morning.

Mia thought about her day. More cooking. Jeani and her sister would be here to finish the prep room and decorate the foyer for Monday's event. And by mid-afternoon, Christina and Levi should be back. Mia checked her phone before getting in the shower. No text response from Christina. Maybe she and Levi had been busy making up. And now they would be at the going-away brunch for Isaac and his new wife. A new Mrs. Adams. She wondered how Mother Adams was taking the competition.

When she came back into the kitchen, Grans, Abigail, and Trent were all eating. There was a breakfast casserole on the stove, and Mia put a serving on her plate and sat next to Trent. Muffy, Cerby, and Mr. Darcy were all lined up by the stove, watching the humans eat.

Mia refilled her coffee cup and then started to eat. "This is really good. Is there polenta in the layering?"

"Good eye—or maybe good palate." Abigail sipped her coffee as she watched Mia eat. "Should we rewrite our to-do lists for today?"

"We will as soon as we get downstairs. I think we're actually going to make it. Of course, tomorrow night's going to be busy with the hot apps. Do we have enough servers?"

"I used the list you sent me and hired a server group from the Catered Cow in Twin. They were happy to get the hours." Abigail glanced at her. "I thought I mentioned this in our last weekly meeting."

"We didn't have one this week. Last week, you were still debating on asking James. It's probably good you didn't. I think Frank is one step away from having a coronary and firing me right now." Mia took another bite. "We really should put this on the delivery menu. Does it freeze well?"

"Like a champ." Abigail beamed as Mia praised her recipe.

"Let's put it on the menu coming up, then." Mia stood and took a second helping. "So, we're all about the cooking. Trent, what are you doing?"

"Finishing up the last walkway so by the time Levi shows up, we should be okay to stain. I don't like the way one of them is settling. The girls need to stay off the walkways tonight if they're coming by." Trent got a second helping of his mom's casserole as well.

"I think Bambi nixed the idea of tonight's visit." Abigail wrote something down. "I'll call her and check in. I wanted to go over tomorrow's judge reception too, but I was hoping they'd have at least one new judge to announce. Your father is still being stubborn."

Trent snorted. "And that's something new?"

Mia was making rolls when Christina came in the door. She hugged her and Abigail. "I was never so glad to leave Boise. The wedding was a train wreck, and the brunch this morning was vicious."

"So, Levi got to see the Adams family in action?"

Mia remembered her first visit, where the gloves were off. She had been scared to death and questioned her relationship with Isaac. She should have walked away from the relationship then.

"That and more. Of course, the guy Mom was trying to set me up with was a client, so Dad was furious that Levi came to the wedding. I'm so tired of being used as a client perk. Anyway, that's done, and now Mom can lean on Jessica for her shopping trips and society teas. She loves them." Christina poured herself a cup of coffee.

"Of course, she does." Mia just hadn't fit in as a potential wife for Isaac. Now, Abigail was a whole different type of in-law. She'd get Trent and Mia married tomorrow if she could. Now that Mia knew about Grans's pending nuptials, she chalked up her meddling and the bad dreams to the *I'm happy, you should be too* category. Mia was too focused on this week's event to even think about the future. Unless it was the future of her business. "If you're ready to work, we could use the extra hands."

"I'm all yours." Christina went over to the sink, where she got an apron and washed her hands. "Do you have a list for me?"

"Who do you think you're talking to? I have a different list for you if you arrived here at ten, at noon, or by three." Mia pushed the three pieces toward her friend. "Which one do you want?"

"I'll take the ten. It's not that late, and I'm faster than you think." Christina glanced down at the prep list and her tasks. "We need to write down all the things that would have made this event better, so we don't make the same errors next year."

"Who said we were taking the event next year?" Mia portioned out another roll from the bread dough.

Christina laughed. "That's what you say now, but when it's time to put in a bid, you'll forget what a pain this year was, and we'll be behind the eight ball again."

"You're probably right." Mia pointed to Christina's list. "You'd better get busy, or you'll be here late. Trent is grilling pork ribs tonight, and Grans is making a potato salad for the side."

"Yum." Christina moved toward her working station and started setting things out for the first recipe. "Oh, hey, Mom said she knew a girl who had won this contest years ago. She mentored her through the contest."

"Really? Who did she work with?" Mia hadn't expected that. Of course, Mother Adams had her finger in a lot of pies.

"A girl named Sherry Sellers. Mom said she even came down to visit her once after the contest. She was college shopping and came to visit Boise State and C of I." Christina was measuring out ingredients.

"Oh." Mia wasn't listening, but then the name "Sherry" made her pay attention.

"Mom said she brought her boyfriend to the meeting. *So unprofessional.* I guess Mom read her the riot act about not only letting him drive her to the appointment, but she also brought him inside and introduced him." Christina was pulling spices and dry ingredients from the spice cabinet. "Mom used it as a sidebar to explain why Levi showing up, unannounced, was being unpolite."

"Did she tell you who Sherry's boyfriend was?" Now Mia was interested.

Christina put the spice bottles on a tray and took them over to her workstation. She looked over at Mia. "No, but I can ask her. Can it wait a few days? She's in a mood."

"Sure." Mia figured that Melody hadn't known her father's name for years. A few more days wouldn't hurt. And just because this guy drove Sherry to an appointment, it didn't mean he had fathered Melody. But it was a start.

And this was one mystery Mia wanted to solve.

The next day, Mia got a text from James. *Check your email. The staff meeting has been canceled.*

She opened her laptop, and there was an email to her and the other department heads. Frank had been called in to corporate and wouldn't be back until the next Monday. A list of tasks was attached to the email, including the food trucks for Saturday and Sunday's festival with Mia's name and cell number listed.

She responded to all, reminding Frank and the others that she was on vacation this week, but if there was an emergency, they were welcome to call her. She added James's name and work number for the food truck contact. She didn't want to not be a team player, but she couldn't cover Frank's impromptu absence as well as this contest. There were only twenty-four hours in a day, and she needed some sleep.

Before she signed off, she got several responses back

from other department heads wishing her a restful vacation and confirming that they had remembered she wasn't going to be at work this week. They all cc'd Frank on the response. Mia was thankful for the solidarity but hoped the emails wouldn't put them on Frank's target list. Working for him was exhausting. Frank didn't reply to any of the emails.

She logged off and put the laptop back on her kitchen desk. Then she grabbed another cup of coffee and took it downstairs. Pausing on the second floor, she saw the door to the prep room was open. She stepped inside and took a breath. It looked like a movie set. Each station had a name written in glitter on the mirror along with that girl's picture. A table was set up with coffee, water, and room for snacks. And hanging on each of the clothes racks were three T-shirts with Harvest Queen Contestant lettered on the front. A note was pinned to the red shirt. Mia read it aloud: "Monday—business casual dress. Tuesday—red T-shirt and jeans. Wednesday—blue T-shirt and jeans unless you need an outfit for your talent presentation. Thursday—yellow T-shirt and jeans and change into full glamour with your dress during the evening gown section. Finally, on Friday, please wear a short dress (must be no more than two inches above the knee) for the event and then your evening gown. You may wear a (washed) red T-shirt and jeans to get ready for the event. Outfit questions are answered by Bambi Perry only."

"You're probably going to get an appropriate outfit list from Bambi too." Melody Sellers stood in the doorway, watching her.

"Hey, Melody, what are you doing here?" Mia glanced at her watch. "Aren't you supposed to be at school?"

"Grandma asked me to come get my T-shirts and outfit list so I don't have to deal with it tonight. She doesn't like driving when it's dark, so as soon as the meet and greet is over, we're out of here. And I had a free period." She glanced at her watch. "I've got ten minutes to get back before English."

Mia pointed to Melody's station. "You're over there. How are you feeling? Nervous?"

Melody went over and put the T-shirts and notes into a large bag. "A little. If I win, my college will be paid for as part of the prize. At least I'll get a partial scholarship for participating. That's what keeps me here, knowing going through with this charade helps pay my way out of this town."

"College is expensive." Mia followed her out and to the front door. "Especially the ones you're looking at."

"Those are dream colleges. With this scholarship, I should at least get out of state, but it's probably going to be Oregon or Utah. Not back East." She paused at the door. "I guess I'll see you tonight?"

"I'll be the one looking anxious and getting everyone drinks." Mia smiled as Melody turned back to look at her. "What?"

"You're just not what I expected. I mean, we heard things from the coven about the new kitchen witch, but you're really nice and approachable." Melody climbed on her bike.

"I try to be." Mia waved as Melody took off down

the driveway and turned onto the street that led to town and the high school. She wondered what exactly the coven had been saying about her.

As she came inside, Abigail was standing in the foyer, watching her. "Good morning."

"And to you. Melody Sellers paid us another visit? The girl must be lonely." Abigail glanced up the stairs, toward the prep room.

"She was just picking up the T-shirts and detailed clothes list from Bambi." Mia shut and locked the door. Trent was back at work, but she'd agreed to babysit Cerby so he wouldn't set Trent's house on fire. The dog loved his dragon play.

CHAPTER 14

The living room was buzzing with people as the judges' meet-and-greet started promptly at six that night. Mia had put up a sign, asking that everyone stay off the walkways in the backyard, but that didn't stop people from stepping out to check out the stage and the event site. She was standing outside, monitoring the wanderers, when she heard a voice behind her.

"Trent's just being overly cautious about the stain. I'm sure people could walk on them if they wanted to, but we'd probably have to touch them up again before Friday's event." Thomas Majors stood beside her, two glasses of wine in his hands—one red, one white. He handed them both out toward her. "I didn't know which you'd prefer?"

"I'm not a big drinker, but I'll take the white." She took the glass and nodded to him. "Thank you."

"You are most welcome. I have to admit, I saw you as the enemy for so long, but now I'm beginning to think you're an ally." He glanced around the backyard. "This is beautiful. You've done an amazing job with the school. I was here just before you bought the property. It was in such bad shape, I thought you were insane."

Mia laughed, then took a sip of her wine. "There were days when I *knew* I was crazy for buying the school. But it's coming together."

"You've taken a piece of Magic Springs' history and brought it back to life." He nodded back toward the party going on inside. "Kind of like what you and Abigail are doing for the queen contest. The coven needed to downplay all the pageantry a bit. Having it here allows them to do less in terms of the actual event. They're trying to modernize the contest. Make it less of a formal beauty contest."

"They have a long way to go." Mia hadn't meant to be so honest. "Sorry, I know you're a judge. I'm just not keen on what the contest represents."

"It's a way to give out scholarships to deserving young women. Yes, in years past, the event was more about the power families in the coven. But after the shenanigans that have occurred the last few years, the board decided to change up the way they assign the member a large seat." He chuckled at the look on her face. "I know, you've been told differently. The winning girl's family takes a seat on the coven board. And they do, but it's not a voting seat. And the money the family used to get is now funneled into scholarships. You learn a lot by serving as a judge."

Mia tapped her nails on her glass. "Then why was Carla so invested in her daughter winning? If the money isn't going to the family and everyone gets a scholarship, why kill for the pleasure of winning?"

"Competition, greed, or maybe just a misunderstanding of what's at stake. I told the board I'd stay on and judge, even though I knew there might be some danger. Carla's death was unfortunate, but the coven can't be held responsible for one woman's greed."

Something about what he was saying didn't ring true. She didn't want to disbelieve Abigail's husband and Trent's dad, but something else was happening, and she could feel it. "Well, I'd better go in and check the food trays. Thanks for the chat."

He waved, but instead of going back inside, he leaned against the railing that separated the deck from the rest of the backyard. The place was beautiful. But still—something else was going on. One woman had already died for this contest. And the potion bags kept showing up. Mia wasn't sure the coven's objective for a friendlier, more modern event was everyone's goal. At least not this year.

Abigail had just sent out the last run of appetizers and the kitchen was empty when Mia poked her head into the room. She glanced at her watch,—almost eight thirty. The event was scheduled to end at nine, and so far, there hadn't been any issues. When she went back into the reception area, she found Abigail and Grans watching the group. A swarm of girls was coming down the stairs, giggling and laughing. Mia recognized Crissy and the others, but Melody wasn't with them.

Abigail leaned into her. "Those girls are trouble. You can just see it on them."

Mia laughed. "Says the mother of all boys."

"You get a feeling. Levi was always bringing home the troublemakers. I knew each of those relationships wouldn't last. They were needy. They were the 'look at me—I'm amazing' types. Like these girls."

"Sounds like Levi finally figured it out. Christina's not that way." Grans moved over to a stool and leaned on it.

"She was more like that when she first got here." Mia thought about the goth girl who had come up for the summer to work and get away from her family. "She's been through a lot, and it's made her mature. Maybe that's all those girls need, some life experience."

"Life isn't always kind." Abigail nodded over to where Melody and her grandmother stood. They had arrived a little later. And they stood on the edge of the party. Not excluded by the others, but not part of any group either.

Mia saw the older woman glance at her watch, then shoo Melody toward the other groups. She could tell that Melody was being sent off to be sociable. This kind of forced social event would have embarrassed Mia to death when she was a teenager. Just talking to adults during her parents' parties had been painful. But she'd had other kids to escape with. Melody was on her own. Especially since Crissy had already played one prank on the girl.

Christina came out of the group of judges grinning as she walked over. "What are you guys doing over here? The party's that way."

"Christina, you're my social queen. Just represent Mia's Morsels, and I'll be happy to stay in my corner here." Abigail brushed a crumb off Christina's shiny party dress. "Besides, you seem to be having fun."

"I am having fun. One of the judges knows my parents, so we were catching up. Isaac's breakdown at the altar is the talk of Boise." Christina waved one of the servers over and got another glass of wine. "I explained that he was overwhelmed with emotion at the thought of marrying his soulmate and that's why he stepped off and went out of the chapel for a moment."

"You didn't tell me this." Mia shook her head. Typical Isaac, it was always all about him. He was a drama queen with all caps.

"My dad followed him out and must have said the right things because he came back and finished the ceremony. Mom gave us the party line about Isaac being so sensitive and not wanting anyone to see him cry happy tears." Christina sipped her wine as she turned her gaze on Mia. "Isaac told me later he was upset over losing you. That it should have been you joining him at the altar."

"Well, he waited a long time to realize that fact. Too long," Mia responded as she sipped her wine. "Besides, Isaac's always been in love with only one person— himself."

"I'll give you that." Christina nodded to the group. "So, come out and chat with everyone. You need to be seen as the passion behind this business."

"I'm on temporary leave from the business right now," Mia reminded her. "At any event, I represent the interests of the Lodge. I don't think going out there is the best thing for Mia's Morsels. Abigail has already shot you down. Tonight, you're the company butterfly, go do your magic."

"After the wedding, I swore I hated this stuff, but I'm having a great time here." Christina paused before heading back into the swell of people. "Maybe I just hate my mom's events."

"Good insight." Mia smiled as she waved her fingers at her friend. Abigail was right; this was where Christine shined. They just needed to stay out of her way. She turned toward Abigail. "I talked to Thomas. He said the board is changing the contest into more of a scholarship opportunity for local girls."

"He can say what he wants, it's still dangerous." Abigail pointed toward the judges' table. "Check out Tatiana in that boob dress. She's been hanging out with the judges all night. Every time a waiter brings by a new tray of drinks, she switches out their empties for them. If I'd known she was so good at cocktail waitressing, I would have hired her."

Grans chuckled. "I don't think she'd be interested in helping out anyone but those five men. I used to be desirable like that."

Mia hugged her. "You're still desirable. Besides, aren't you getting married soon?"

"One man, so many nights." Grans smiled sweetly. "How much longer is this event supposed to go on?"

Before they could answer, a scream came from the middle of the room. Mia hurried over and found Marnie Carter on the floor, convulsing. Mia knelt beside her. "Christina, call nine-one-one. Get everyone back—she needs some room."

Mia looked around and found Marnie's purse. It had a chain made of wooden dowels. She broke one off and put it between her teeth.

Rachel fell to her knees next to her mother. "Mom, what's going on? Mom, can you hear me?"

"I think she's having a seizure." Mia grabbed the girl's wrist to get her attention. "Does she have any medical conditions?"

Rachel shook her head. "No, I mean, I don't really know."

"Rachel, where's your dad?" Mia glanced at Christina, hoping she'd know what she was asking without having to ask. Rachel didn't answer her; she was staring at her mom.

"Five minutes. Levi's on call tonight, so I called him directly. Mark Baldwin's on his way too, just in case." Christina glanced around at the group, watching them. "I'm going to move everyone into the gym."

"Good idea." Mia turned back to the shaken teen. "Rachel, honey, can you call your dad? When the paramedics get here, they'll want to talk to him."

Mia watched as Marnie's body eased from the seizure and her eyes closed.

"Mom!" Rachel reached for her, but just then, the front door opened, and the emergency crew hurried in with a gurney. That was the good thing about living in a small town—everything was close.

As Mia stepped back, she heard Levi talking to Rachel about her mom's condition. Mia walked over to the door and watched as Mark Baldwin's truck pulled into her parking lot. He climbed out and put his hat on, nodding to her.

When he came up the walk, he shook his head. "Mia, we've really got to stop meeting like this. What happened now?"

"On the surface? It looks like Marnie Carter had a seizure." Mia glanced around the foyer, listening to the music that was playing softly through the speakers. It was an old Rat Pack song. Abigail must have chosen the music. Frank Sinatra was her favorite. "Or someone is messing with the contest again."

"But why would they target the mothers?" Mark watched as the EMTs prepared Marnie to move her to the hospital. "Where's everyone else?"

"Christina moved them to the gym so it wouldn't be so chaotic over here." Mia walked over to the door. "Do you need to talk to everyone?"

"She had a medical issue. Why would I talk to everyone?" He rubbed his forehead. "Look, just get me the names of everyone who was here. I'll take her glass and the contents. Was she eating?"

Rachel was standing by the wall, watching Marnie. Mia nodded toward the girl, who had her phone to her ear. "Her daughter might know."

Mark followed Mia over to where the teenager leaned against the wall. "Miss Carter? Can I ask you some questions about your mom?"

She handed him her cell phone. "This is my dad. He wants to talk to you."

Mark took the phone and stepped away. Mia turned toward Rachel. "How are you doing?"

"I'm freaking out a little. First Kristin's mom dies, now Mom has a seizure? What's going on?" Rachel crossed her arms in front of her.

"I don't know, honey, but we're going to find out." Mia saw Levi strapping Marnie onto the gurney. "They're getting ready to take her to the hospital, and I'm sure you can ride along. But before you go, can you show me where your mom was before the seizure? Was she eating or drinking anything?"

"It's after seven, so she wasn't eating anything." Rachel shrugged when she caught Mia's gaze. "It's some diet called Intermittent Fasting. She tried to get me to do it, and I told her I was, but I didn't. You basically only eat during part of the day. Anyway, she was at that table with Crissy's mom and Bambi. They were all talking about the judges. I guess one of them has been a judge for years."

Mark walked back over to Mia and Rachel. He handed the girl back her phone. "Your dad will meet you at the hospital. Do you want to ride in the ambulance with your mom?"

Rachel nodded, and Mark waved Levi over to collect her. As they walked away, following the gurney that held Marnie Carter, Mia showed Mark the table. "Rachel said she was right here and not eating."

Mark called an officer over who'd been standing nearby and pointed at the table. "Clear all that and send it to the crime lab. I want to make sure there wasn't anything in her drink."

The officer nodded and went to the table. Mark glanced at his watch and then back at Mia. "I've got to get going. It's story time at the house."

"Okay, thanks for coming out. I'll send you the guest list. I'll also have Christina take pictures of everyone who is currently in the gym. It would be nice to know if anyone's missing."

Mark tapped the table where he was standing. "You're getting the hang of this investigating thing. Sometimes it's just as basic as that. Especially with amateurs. I'm sure we're not dealing with a serial killer. This is Magic Springs."

"I'm not convinced that it wasn't anything more than a stressed-out stage mom, but you never know. If she's limiting her food, well, it might have been low blood sugar. But after what happened to Carla, well, I thought you should see this." Mia followed him to the doorway.

"Never apologize for calling. If you're being too much of a Nervous Nelly, I'll tell you and cut you off. As it is, I'd rather be safe than sorry. Especially when we've got a group of teenage girls in the mix." He tipped his hat and left.

Mia stood by the door for a few minutes, watching as the ambulance, the police car, and Mark's truck drove out of the parking lot. One thing about a Magic Springs event, it was never boring. She shut the door, then went to find Christina to have her take pictures of the guests.

Night one was in the books. Now they just had to survive four more. She sent a blessing for the event up to the Goddess and heard Gloria's giggle. Mia didn't like that at all.

The next morning, Trent dropped the newspaper on the table when he visited for breakfast. "I found this when I stopped by the store for orange juice. The reporter is calling it the 'Cursed Queen Competition.' There's a bit about Melody's mom dying years ago in the article as well."

"Maybe the coven should just cancel the contest this year. This is a lot of press, and two people have been attacked." Mia picked up the paper, glancing at the picture of her school on the front page.

"Right now, both Carla and Marnie's situations are health-related. No one's been 'attacked.' At least, that's what the normals are saying," Trent reminded her. "We may suspect magic, but there's no evidence."

"Except for the potion bags," Grans reminded him. "I'm surprised Cerby hasn't brought up another one. That dog has a strong hunting nose for a hellhound. Usually, they're known more for their strength, not their tracking skills."

"Physically, he's a Maltese. Maybe he's adapting to his limited strength by increasing other talents," Trent offered as way of explanation.

"Either way, we have three bags. And no clue on who made or set them out here in the school. And if they were set up to kill someone, they're not doing a very good job of it." Grans glanced out the window. "What's on the plan for today?"

"It's delivery day. Christina and Abigail will be heading out, and I need to get the tea and treats ready for the interviews tonight. We'll only have the judges, the competitors, and one family rep in the building," Mia explained the process. "Interviews will start at six and end no later than eight. Then the judging group will meet in the downstairs classroom until nine and do their ranking."

"I talked to Bambi this morning. Both Kristin and Rachel are still committed to competing. They will be here tonight. Rachel's aunt will step in for her mom, and Kristin's grandmother will be her chaperone." Abigail refilled her coffee cup. "Business as usual."

Mia sipped her coffee and wondered what was wrong with people. *The Show Must Go On* was kind of a dated motto, but everyone was embroidering the saying on flags and waving them high for all to see.

CHAPTER 15

Mia was alone in the school's first-floor kitchen working on the tea cakes and scones for tonight's interviews when she heard someone at the front door. Grans had just left to work on her project, and she'd taken Muffy with her. Mia didn't expect to see her for a few days. Grans was keeping her project such a secret, but that didn't surprise Mia. When she was working on cracking an aging spell, she'd worked at her house, not answering questions or returning calls. What Mia found out later was that her grandmother had a reason she didn't want to be seen in person. Now she had another project that was so important she couldn't sell the house until it was done.

Maybe getting married to Robert wasn't exactly what her grandmother wanted, and this was her way of delaying the ceremony.

Whatever it was, Mia would find out sooner than later.

The noise sounded again, this time louder. Cerby stood on his bed and barked toward the door.

"Is someone trying to get in?" She glanced at the security-camera monitor mounted on the kitchen wall. There was no one in the parking lot or by the front door. Before heading out to look around, Mia checked the locks on both of the exits in the kitchen. No use being surprised by a sneak attack. She wondered if the gym doors had gotten left open and maybe Bambi was here to set up for the night's events. Whatever it was, she would deal with it. Or them.

When she got to the banister, a white apparition floated on the stairs. She glanced down at Cerby, who was watching the ball of light. "Hello? Can I help you?"

The ghost turned toward her and nodded. It was Carla Manson. Carla floated down to the bottom of the stairs.

"Carla, you should pass over. Why are you still here?" Mia tried not to let her fear show. She didn't need to give Carla any more power over her than her presence already had.

Carla opened her mouth, but nothing came out. She grabbed at her throat, frustration oozing out of her essence. She tried again. "Sins of the father . . ."

"What?" Now Mia was really confused. "Carla, you need to pass on. Go to your next stop so you can grow. You're stuck here. It's not good for you."

The ghost tried to speak again, but nothing came out this time. Carla was already vanishing in spots. She had run out of energy. Carla needed to go and recharge wherever ghosts went to do that. Mia tried to calm her. "You just need to release and go."

Carla shook her head and pointed at something behind Mia. A scream sent Mia spinning around, and she saw Melody standing there, pointing toward Carla. Her face was white.

"What . . . is . . . that?" Melody stammered.

Mia turned back, but Carla had totally disappeared. She went over and pulled a shaking Melody into her arms. They walked over and sat on the couch. "Are you okay?"

"*Okay?* Didn't you see it? Or am I just going crazy?" Melody stared at the spot where Carla had been standing.

Mia frowned as she considered the options. Apparently, Melody hadn't been raised on a diet of fairy tales and witch development books. Mia needed to chat with her grandmother before blurting out what could be life-changing. "I'm not sure what you're talking about, but why are you here? And how did you get inside?"

"Your door was open. I heard you talking, so I pushed it the rest of the way open. I left the book we're reading for AP English upstairs in the prep room. I need it before class starts in five minutes." Melody put a hand on her stomach. "I'm still shaking. That was a ghost."

"Let's go up and get that book for you and get you back to class. It wouldn't do for one of the harvest queen contestants to miss her interview tonight because she was in detention." Mia stood and held out her hand. She was trying to avoid talking about the supernatural. "Besides, I need to get back to the kitchen and check on my scones."

"But did you see that thing on the stairs? It looked like Mrs. Manson, didn't it?"

Mia took Melody's arm, and the girl pushed herself off the couch to a standing position as they headed to the stairs. Mia ignored the question. "So, what are you reading for English?"

"*Life of Pi*. I'm not sure I love it, but at least it's different from reading *Jane Eyre* again. I swear, every new English teacher I've had in every grade put that on the must-read list. I don't think Blaine County even checks their teaching plans." Melody paused when they passed where Carla had been standing. She shuddered, then continued. "We get to choose our own book next time, and I'm rereading *The Talisman*. They're going to make it into a movie."

"Isn't that by Stephen King?"

"And Peter Straub. We read *Ghost Story* last year for Halloween, so I thought I'd report on another genre-horror book." She shook her head. Mia hoped she was thinking she imagined seeing Carla.

"I do love genre fiction," Mia admitted. "Especially living here. Sometimes I think I see things too. But usually there's a good explanation."

Melody seemed to consider her words as she hurried into the prep room and to her station, where the book sat on the table. She held it up. "Here it is."

After Melody left so she could make it to her English class on time, Mia relocked the front door as a thought came to her. How *had* Melody gotten into the school? Mia was sure she'd locked the door when Grans had left that morning. But Melody had said it was open.

Mia hurried to the gym and saw a door cracked open with one of the plastic door stands. She kicked it out and let the door close on its own. Then she checked the lock–again. Convinced all the doors were locked this time, Mia went back to the kitchen to check on the scones. Tonight, she'd make sure all the doors were secured after everyone had left the building. It could have been a complete coincidence, but it didn't feel that way. And if Melody had come in through the gym, why didn't she say so?

Nothing was adding up.

Thomas and the other four judges arrived at five thirty. Abigail had rabbited, so Mia escorted them to the gym, where they'd do the interviews. They'd set up a table for the judges that afternoon. Treats sat on a side table with coffee and tea as well as water. A matching table had been set up in the reception area where the event had been held last night. The girls and their accompanying family members would wait in the reception area to be called into the gym. Then, after the interview, they'd leave out the gym side door, where their family members would be waiting to take them home.

Bambi explained that it kept the girls from talking about the questions. Cell phones weren't allowed in the waiting room either. "It's not like most of them would be able to craft perfect answers in the time before their interview, but we want to see how they deal with being impromptu and out of their element."

Mia nodded and smiled in all the right places like she cared. It looked like the judges were thinking the same thing. Finally, when Bambi took a break from telling about the history of the interview section of the contest, Mia pointed to the doorway. "Okay, judges. When all the interviews are done, you can stay here or retire to our first-floor classroom. It will also have refreshments set up, including fresh coffee."

The men laughed, and then most of them sat down at the table. Thomas came over to where Mia stood. "Hey, I want to introduce you to the gang."

Mia smiled and followed him. "I'm a little uncomfortable about being on display. I'm supposed to fade into the background when an event is going on."

"You're too modest. You need to meet these people because they can introduce you to others who have events." He leaned closer. "And if Mia's Morsels becomes successful, you might give me my wife back."

"Thomas, I didn't mean to . . ." But Mia didn't get the apology out before he laughed.

He squeezed her shoulder. "Mia, I'm joking. And speaking of jokers, this is Zeus Eapen, our fearless leader."

The older man chuckled and squeezed Mia's hand as she reached out for a handshake. "Dear Miss Malone, your reputation precedes you. Although the file didn't have a picture or a description, you're a total knockout. I'm sure you would have won your year if you'd competed, just like your mama did."

"My mother competed in the contest?" Now, this was a story Mia hadn't heard.

Zeus shook his head. "I didn't say competed, I said won. Your grandmother was so proud of Theresa."

"I'll have to ask her about that someday." Mia glanced at her watch. "Sorry, I need to get the last details tied up and make sure the cookies aren't burning."

"Well, don't let me stop you. Cookies are a powerful thing, especially when we're trying to get these girls to tell us the truth. We'll need the sugar to sweeten them up." Zeus laughed and slapped Thomas on the back. "Right?"

Thomas rolled his eyes but nodded. "You're the expert here. Mia, Zeus has been a judge since he moved to Magic Springs thirty years ago."

"I'd love to hear the story—but cookies." Mia sprinted to the gym door. Abigail was going to owe her big-time for this. She was the manager for Mia's Morsels—she should have been the one doing the welcoming, not Mia. She burst into the kitchen, where Abigail was putting another tray of cookies into the oven.

"Sorry about that, I couldn't stand to hear another one of Zeus's stories. He cornered me last night. I think Thomas sent him over as punishment." She closed the oven door and took off her oven mitts, setting the timer.

"He said my mom competed in the queen contest. Is that true?" Mia crossed the last thing off her list for today. Tomorrow she had a whole new list, but for today, it was time to put her feet up and relax. All she, or someone she assigned, had to do was hang out downstairs. Just in case. Maybe Christina would want the job?

"Yeah, she did." Abigail didn't look at Mia. "It was senior year, and your grandmother pushed her into the competition. Theresa needed a distraction. She'd broken up with her high school sweetheart that summer. He went away to California for college and didn't ask her to follow. She was heartbroken. Of course, her freshman year of college, she met your dad, and everything was as it was supposed to be."

"I can't believe she was in a beauty contest. She always rails against them as being unfair to women and treating them like cattle." Mia took a cookie off the plate. "She never mentioned being in one."

"Maybe she was embarrassed. Maybe it slipped her mind." Abigail shrugged. "Does it change how you see her?"

"No, but I thought I knew everything about her." Mia bit into the cookie. "I suspect you don't want to babysit our group tonight? I'll check with Christina. I need a long bath."

"I'll do it. I think Thomas and I need to talk." Abigail glanced at her watch. "Besides, Christina may already be asleep. Delivery day is always hard on her."

"That's the problem with the youth of today," Mia said as she left the kitchen. "They have no stamina."

Abigail called after her, "I'm going to tell her you said that."

As Mia climbed the stairs, she thought about Carla and her statement. What did the sins of the father have to do with a harvest queen beauty contest? It had been a day of questions with no answers.

Instead of being asleep, Christina was sitting in the

living room reading a magazine, a glass of wine in her hand. Cerby and Mr. Darcy were curled up, one on each side of her. Christina closed the magazine. "I thought your grandmother would be here."

"She went to her house to work on something." Mia went to the kitchen and grabbed the wine and another glass. When she came back, she refilled Christina's glass and filled her own. "So, what's got you in a mood?"

Christina pulled her hair back and, using a band she had around her wrist, made a ponytail. "You always know, don't you?"

"You're not one for drinking alone. And you never pine for my grandmother's attention. Did Levi say something stupid? Again?"

"No. I guess I'm just thinking. The wedding was a total disaster. Jessica was in tears most of the time. Isaac was a jerk. And Mom was just worried about how Levi's showing up was messing with her seating arrangements. She always orders extra plates, so I know there was food and a spot available for him. Sometimes my family makes me wish I was adopted or an orphan. But that sounds bad, doesn't it?" Christina finally took a breath.

"Your family is a handful. I'm not going to deny that." Mia sipped her wine. "But I'm not sure why it's upsetting you so much. You know them. This is what they do."

Christina set down her wineglass. "What if they're like this at my wedding to Levi?"

"You and Levi, huh?" Mia teased.

"Stop it. You knew it was going that way. I adore his family. Even when Abigail and Thomas are fighting.

They don't bring everyone into the issue. Or have them take sides. Well, at least not too much. And Levi, he's not impressed by my parents or their house or the dresses Mom makes me wear. He's more impressed by the ideas I have and the restaurants that have been reaching out to hire me. There's a place in Portland that wants to do a catering wing and they want me to interview for the position. I guess my professors put my résumé out there with a recommendation. Now I'm getting all this attention."

"Levi should be impressed by that. But Christina, why are you still here? Find your job, find your life, marry the dude, and move." Mia sipped her wine. Replacing Christina would be impossible, mostly because she cared about her, but not for the work.

"I'm here because Levi hasn't asked me to marry him yet. And I like working with you and Abigail. And honestly, I'm a little nervous to do it all on my own." Christina rubbed Cerby's head.

"You aren't going to continue to get this kind of attention from the universe if you keep pushing it away. Levi will step up. Just tell him what you're doing, and that if he wants to be with you, you need a commitment." Mia started laughing and had to put her glass down.

"What?" Christina asked. Her eyes were wild.

"Blame it on Isaac and his wedding. Your brother owes you something, and this is as good of an excuse to be talking about your future with Levi as any." Mia glanced at her watch. "Are you beat, or do you want to watch *Kitchen Wars* with me? I have a couple of episodes recorded."

"I'll make some popcorn, and you queue it up. Sounds like a perfect way to end the evening." Christina stood and then hugged Mia. "Thank you for being my almost-sister."

"You're most welcome." Mia reached down and picked up Cerby. "Why didn't you go home with Trent tonight?"

Cerby didn't answer, just curled up in Mia's lap.

"Trent said he had somewhere to go and asked if we could watch him," Christina called out from the kitchen.

After Mia set up the show, she checked her messages. Nothing from Trent. She texted and told him she was upstairs from the event but watching television with Christina and Cerby.

It took a couple of minutes, but as Christina came back with the popcorn, an answer popped up. *Have fun. See you in the morning and don't give Cerby popcorn.*

Mia set her phone down and turned on the show. When it was over and she was tucked into bed, waiting to fall asleep, she wondered what Trent was doing. Probably something with the store. Rolling over, she saw Cerby watching her.

She pulled the little dog closer and rubbed his head. "Hey, buddy. Do you miss your guy tonight?"

Cerby whimpered a little and curled into her arms. He licked her face twice, then laid his head on her shoulder. Mia didn't speak dog, or hellhound, language, but that was a definite yes.

"I miss him too. Maybe Christina has the right idea.

Maybe we should make this situation a little more permanent." Mia started chuckling as she thought about her response to Christina. "Maybe I should blame Isaac's wedding on me starting this conversation too. What do you think, Cerby?"

The little dog didn't answer because he was sound asleep.

CHAPTER 16

The next morning, Mia poured more coffee into Christina's cup. "How are you feeling this morning?"

"Like an idiot." Christina looked up from where she'd laid her head on the table. "After you went to bed, Abigail and I stayed up talking. The wine is all gone."

"You had some things on your mind." Mia started to stand. "I can make a hash-brown skillet if you need some food to settle your stomach. You don't usually drink much, so you're probably feeling it."

"Like I said, I feel like an idiot. Three glasses, and I'm hurting. In Vegas, my roommate would drink a bottle of wine all by herself." Christina sipped her coffee. "Another reason I never fit in with that group. Anyway, if you want breakfast, I'd eat, but don't do it just for me."

"You know I love to cook." Mia stood and pulled out potatoes from the basket on the baker's rack. "Besides,

Trent mentioned coming by this morning. I'm sure he'd appreciate some breakfast."

Abigail came into the room, took one look at Christina, and went to the freezer to get out some bacon. "Girl, you still look like you're in pain."

"Not because you and Mia talked me through some difficult decisions, but because of my own actions. I'm instituting a two-glass maximum for me." Christina lifted her head and fixed her ponytail. "Or do you think I'm scared of having this conversation with Levi?"

"Until you decide what you're going to do, there is no need for a conversation." Mia started peeling potatoes. "I think you're scared of interviewing for one of these jobs."

Christina let the idea hang for a minute, then took a deep breath. "I hate it that you know me so well."

"Almost-sisters, remember?" Mia peeled a second potato. "Go take a shower. You'll feel better. Then bring your laptop out here and tell me about the offers you're getting. I can help you sort them out."

Christina stood and took her coffee with her as she walked into the hallway. "Fine. Force me into the adult pool. I liked being the little sister."

"Sorry about that. You're the one who did so well in your classes that you've got hiring teams taking notice." Mia watched as Abigail took the potatoes she'd peeled and started chopping. "You don't have to help."

"I know. I just think better when I'm cooking. If you want to sit, I'll take over. You're doing a scramble, right?"

Mia took a cup out of the cabinet and filled it with coffee. "Christina likes a southwestern flare. I think I have avocados." Mia looked around the small kitchen. "Somewhere."

"They're over here." Abigail held one up. "Grab me an onion from the basket, please."

"How did the conversation with Thomas go?" Mia handed her the last onion, then went over and put the item on her shopping list that hung on the fridge.

"It didn't. Zeus wanted to buy all the judges dinner to talk about the rest of the week. Thomas said he'd try to carve out some time today to talk. I guess with the talent practice tonight, the judge group is meeting for a round of golf, and then dinner. And he's heading to Twin to pick up something for his business. Hunting season is on us. I probably won't see him after the contest ends on Friday for a few months." Abigail glanced over at the calendar. "I probably can move home anytime and not run into him until Thanksgiving."

"That sounds lonely. You're welcome to stay here as long as you want. I think Christina is probably moving soon." Mia sat down and studied her coffee. "I know I told her to go spread her wings, but I'm going to miss the little twerp."

Abigail started laughing. "It's empty nest syndrome. I got it as soon as Levi moved into his apartment. Especially since his dad is gone so much. I guess getting time alone to think shouldn't be a problem for me, most of the time."

"You were worried about him," Mia reminded her.

Abigail nodded. "And I still am, except now if something happens, he'll be alone in that big house all by himself. I should have trusted that he understood what he was getting into. I just hate it when he goes into the protect-at-all-cost mode."

"It's sweet that he loves you so much." Mia watched as Trent pulled his truck into the parking lot. "Your troublemaker son just pulled into the lot."

Abigail looked up and laughed. "Oh, dear, you're mistaken. That's not Levi—he's my troublemaker. Trent's a mama's boy. Go let him in so you two can have a moment alone."

"Yes, ma'am." Mia threw Abigail a soldier's salute and stood. "Tell Christina I'll be right back."

"None of you kids give me any respect," Abigail called after her, and Mia just laughed. Everyone loved Abigail. So she got teased all the time. They all knew they were safe with her.

Mia hurried down the stairs with Cerby on her heels and threw open the door for Trent. She leaned up to kiss him. "Good morning, stranger."

"Good morning." He kissed her back. Then he looked down at Cerby. "Hey, little man, have you been out?"

"No, this is his first time. I should have taken him earlier, but I was chatting with Christina. She's having some life-planning issues." Mia waved him out to the yard.

Trent followed Cerby out to the yard, where he stood and watched as the hellhound made his rounds. "What did my brother say now?"

"Nothing. It's about her career. I think she's been avoiding taking a new job because of me. I kicked her out of the nest, so now she's going to start applying. I predict she'll be moving by the end of October." Mia leaned against the school, feeling the bricks warmed by the morning sun on her back. "If your brother doesn't want a long-distance relationship, he needs to step up here."

"We've had that talk." Trent leaned down and praised Cerby as he picked him up and carried him to the doorway. "I'm out of it. Whatever he does, it's on him. You're not looking for a new job in a different state, are you?"

Mia laughed as they entered the foyer, and she shut and locked the door. "I have enough jobs right here to keep me busy. Did you hear anything about Marnie? How's she doing?"

"According to Levi, she's fine. They're keeping her in the hospital for a day or so. Something about her blood sugar is what caused the seizure." He followed her up the stairs. "All I can say is I'll be glad when you all are done with this contest. It doesn't seem to be the safest place for anyone right now. And I've got too many people I care about involved in the thing. You, my parents, Christina . . ."

"And Jeani, your ex," Mia teased, but she examined his face as he answered.

"She's not much of an ex anything. We went out a couple of times, but there just wasn't any spark. No chemistry. Or to put it in a food person's vocabulary, we were missing a leavening agent, like baking powder." Trent grinned at her.

Mia paused by the door as he put Cerby down. "I'm impressed by the comparison."

"I was stocking shelves in the flour aisle yesterday

and thought about it. I just wasn't expecting to be able to use it so quickly. Now I have to think up another food-related analogy so I look witty and smart in your eyes."

She stroked his face. "You are perfect in my eyes, Trent Majors, just the way you are."

She turned to open the door, and he spun her back around to him, encasing her in his arms. "As compliments go, that one was top tier. You're not so bad yourself."

Then he kissed her.

The contestants, their parents or family members, and Bambi Perry all showed up within ten minutes of each other. Bambi called the girls and their one parent or chaperone up to the prep room. Mia followed her upstairs to listen to the plan for the evening. It was five o'clock, and all the contestants had two practice runs on the stage for their talent presentation. A presentation that could go no less than eight minutes and no more than eleven. A delivery van had set up a piano in the middle of the stage that morning, but it was on wheels so they could roll it back under the roof if it rained. Tatiana had rented it for Crissy's talent. As far as Mia knew, Crissy was the only one to be playing the piano.

Bambi turned to her as they waited for the girls to settle. "Can you do me a favor? I need a timekeeper. I'll do it for the real contest, but for now, I need to play Zeus's part of host to keep the show going."

"Zeus is the host of the show *and* the senior judge?" Mia didn't know if it was a conflict of interest, but it felt like one.

"Yes, Zeus is wearing two hats. All very legal." Bambi shoved some cards and a stopwatch into Mia's hands. "All you do is clock them from the time they step on the dais to when they stop and say their name a second time. And put up cards when they're a minute out and then again at thirty seconds. Can you do that?"

Am I an idiot? Mia didn't say that. Instead, she nodded. "I understand my assignment." She'd been hoping to sit in the back and go over next month's class schedule. She mostly had it all set up, but she needed one more class. She'd taken the class part back from Abigail since she could teach the classes at night when she wasn't doing an event. Besides, doing the classes helped her stay involved, like working on this event. Of course, she'd rather not even have taken the contract, but now that they had, she had responsibilities to her client and the customer. Like timing talent presentations for the six contestants.

She studied the six girls. No one had dropped out yet. Not Kristin, who'd lost her mom, or Rachel, whose mom was in the hospital today. Nope, all of them were still here. She made a mental note to find out when the funeral for Carla was going to be held. She probably needed to attend. Maybe she could carpool with Abigail.

Finally, Melody walked into the room with an older woman and headed to her table. This must be her grandmother.

Bambi let out a sigh of relief. "Great, we're all here. Now, get ready, the order sheet is right here on the door. Crissy, you're up first, then we'll move the piano back out of the way unless someone else needs it."

"I'm doing a piece too." Melody held up her hand. "I need a piano."

"We're the ones who ordered the piano. I'm not sure how I feel about it being used for other contestants." Tatiana stepped into the middle of the room.

"Mrs. Evans, I told you we'd provide a piano. Since you decided to provide your own, you have to let all contestants use it. Or we can use it for practice tonight, and I'll have another one ordered and replace this one for the actual event on Friday." Bambi's eyes were dark. "What do you want to do?"

"Of course, she can use the piano. I just didn't realize anyone else played." Tatiana backed down and smiled over at Melody and her grandmother. "No worries."

Something passed between the older two women that Mia didn't understand. A threat? An apology? Whatever it was, the air was thick with the emotion of the moment. And then it was gone.

Bambi studied the order of talents. "Okay, this will still work. Crissy can go first, we'll move the piano and set up a microphone for Kristin, then at the end, before Melody's up, we'll move the piano back to the middle."

Murmurs went through the room.

"This is all very exciting, I understand. But we need to stay on track. We'll start the first round of practice in ten minutes. Crissy, please be by the stage and ready then. And once we go through it, we'll take a short break, then start again. Everyone stay within earshot, okay?" Bambi glanced around the room and then motioned to Mia to follow her. "Okay, see you all in ten."

As they headed downstairs, Mia glanced over at her. "You seem calm. Do you think we'll actually be done by eight?"

Bambi barked out a laugh. "I don't think we'll actually get started in ten minutes. Wrangling girls and stage moms is a little more complicated than nuclear fission. And more dangerous."

To Mia's surprise, they started exactly fifteen minutes later. Apparently, Crissy had thought she was supposed to be in the gym, although there was no piano there. Tatiana had to go look for her. Mia was shocked by the level of talent each of the young women had prepared. Crissy did a song from a Broadway musical, Kristin recited a poem she'd written, Amie sang a popular country-and-western ballad, Rachel did a flute solo, Anne read her essay about the role of women in the development of the country, and finally, Melody sat down behind the piano and played a classical piece. Mia didn't know the song, but it brought tears to her eyes.

Melody was a prodigy. It was obvious to anyone in that practice. The group was silent right after she stopped, then Mia heard clapping from behind her. She turned and saw Trent and Levi watching. She joined in and stood for Melody. Then everyone else joined in.

Melody looked shocked, and she ran down to her grandmother. "Was it okay?"

"Melody, my love, it was perfect. You are such an amazing pianist." The woman patted her on the back. "Just like your mother."

Mia came over and congratulated her. "That was breathtaking. How long have you been playing?"

"She's been climbing on the bench next to me since she could walk." The woman turned to Mia, blocking Melody from answering. "I'm Melody's grandmother, Elly Sellers. And you're Mia Malone, correct? I knew your mother. The girls used to hang out together after school."

Another story Mia didn't have about her mother. "She was friends with Sherry?"

Elly blinked, confused. "Oh, no, she used to babysit Sherry for me. I guess I said that wrong. I did hair in my garage for years, then after Sherry got older, she didn't want to hang around with a bunch of old ladies, so your mom would come and take her to the park."

"Oh, that's sweet." Mia stepped toward Melody. "You are truly gifted."

Again, Elly blocked her. "I'm afraid I need to be going. Sherry should be home by now from school. I hate having her at the house alone."

Mia stepped back. "Sherry?"

"Yes, Sherry. My daughter?" She grabbed her purse and started digging. "Where are the keys to the Buick?"

Melody met Mia's gaze. "Don't worry about it. I'll handle getting her home. Can you tell Bambi I'll try to be back for my second practice?"

"I don't think you need one, but yes, I'll tell her."

Mia reached out and squeezed Elly's arm. "It was so nice to meet you, Mrs. Sellers."

The woman blinked, then reached for Mia's hair, tucking a curl behind Mia's ear. "Theresa, you really don't need to do anything to that hair of yours. It's perfect just the way it is. Come by Saturday, and I'll style it into an updo for your dance."

"Thank you, Mrs. Sellers." Mia saw Melody's stricken look and played along with the fantasy. She stepped back to let Melody walk her grandmother out of the yard. She saw Trent ask Melody something, but the girl shook her head.

When they'd left, and Mia had given Bambi her message, Trent came up and sat next to her as they waited for the second round of practice to start. "She's not okay, is she? Elly Sellers," Mia asked.

Trent shook his head. "I've had to drive her home several times from the store because she got confused. I think Melody's trying to keep her at home at least a little longer. It's just the two of them now."

"Melody shouldn't have to be taking care of her like this. She's just a kid."

Trent shook his head. "She's eighteen as of last month. I think everyone in town was just holding their breath hoping that Mrs. Sellers would stay lucid until Melody left for college, but this last month has been hard."

"She thought I was my mom." Mia watched as Bambi climbed the stairs to make another announcement. "Melody needs help."

"You can't step in where you're not invited. Melody's an adult now. She's able to make her own decisions, and I heard she was going to court soon to become her grandmother's guardian." Trent pointed to Bambi. "Deal with what you can control right now, which is this pageant. Then you can think about saving Melody. But talk to Mom and your grandmother first. You need to know the whole story before you step in."

CHAPTER 17

Abigail had just finished making a quiche and was putting it in the oven the next morning when Mia came into the kitchen. She poured herself a cup of coffee, then sat down at the table. Abigail joined her. "Trent told me you ran into Elly Sellers."

"How could everyone leave Melody in a situation like that? Didn't the school question it?" Mia hadn't gotten a lot of sleep last night. Melody had come back just in time for her practice slot, but then had disappeared back home to check on her grandmother. The stress of living that way must be horrible.

"Elly didn't really show signs of dementia until last year, then it seemed to get worse by the day. She was president of the PTA up until Melody went to high school. And even then, she ran fundraisers for band trips and instruments for the music program. Melody had a great childhood. After her mother died, Elly and her husband raised Melody as their own. Then Jake died five years ago. Elly was heartbroken. But she'd be furious if she knew who she was now. The women from the coven come over while Melody's at school. She's well taken care of."

"Elly is, but what about Melody? She should be going to Juilliard or someplace like that next year, that's how talented she is at piano. But she says she doesn't know if she can go to any college if she doesn't win the competition. She should be on a scholarship."

"Melody's been less than excited to leave her grandmother. One, she knows if she does, Elly will need fulltime care. Care at home, that's expensive. Going off to start a new life somewhere like New York, that's a step she may not be ready to take." Abigail sipped her coffee. "Do you understand now?"

"It's too bad about Melody's mother. If she was still alive, Melody wouldn't have to worry about who was going to take care of Elly."

"Wishes and horses, wishes and horses." Abigail refilled her cup. "Anyway, the coven has been considering setting up a fund so Elly can stay at home. She and Melody are the last in a family line who founded the Magic Springs coven. She should get something out of that, right?"

Mia nodded, but even she knew that college applications started being approved in the fall. Melody should have already applied for the schools she wanted to attend, especially since she needed financial aid.

Maybe she'd pull her aside during the contest and offer to help her with the college application process.

Melody didn't have to pretend that her grandmother was able to help with the process since Mia had already witnessed an episode.

"I see you thinking over there." Abigail pulled out her notebook. "Just make sure you talk to your grandmother before you make any plans. She has some information you'll need. Now, shall we talk about today's event?"

"Please tell me it's Thursday. I don't know how much longer I can worry about this pageant."

Abigail smiled. "Yes, it's Thursday. And it's dress rehearsal day. So Bambi will want to go over all the sections of the event at least twice. We are responsible for drinks and treats, and I have a list of what needs to be made. It's not a lot, so we should be done cooking by noon."

"Good, because I got a text from James. He needs me to go to the Lodge sometime today. He left a schedule on my desk that I need to review for the food trucks this weekend. I love how even though I'm on vacation, I still have responsibilities."

"You're just too good at your job." Abigail shrugged. "I get it. I'm that way too. Why don't you go this morning? Christina can help me cook, and you can fill in when you get back if we get behind."

"So, because I'm there instead of Mia, we're going to fall behind?" Christina walked into the room and went straight to the coffeemaker. "Challenge accepted."

"I knew you were standing back there all along." Abigail crossed Mia's name off a page and put Christina's on the top instead. Then she ripped out the page and handed it to her. "Here's your list."

"I hate making cream puffs." Christina sat down and reviewed the list. Then she leaned over and read Abigail's. "We need to switch these over to my list."

"Not on your life." Abigail pressed the notebook to her chest. "You're the one who claims to be as good as Mia. Show it."

Christina looked at Mia, who just shrugged.

"I hate both of you." Christina focused on her coffee.

A dog barked at the apartment door. Mia stood and looked back at the women at the table. "Who's here? And how did they get past the security feed? Or in the school, for that matter?"

"No clue. Should we call Mark?"

Mia pushed her emotions outward to the door and didn't feel any hostility. And she thought she recognized the bark, even though it was a little louder than normal. She opened the door to find Trent juggling a bag of groceries and Cerby on a leash.

"Thank the Goddess you heard us. I was about to drop these." Trent moved past Mia and into the apartment. He dropped the bag off on the table. "Here's what you ordered."

Abigail stood and started unpacking the bags. "Thanks. You didn't have to bring them personally. And most of these could go to the kitchen downstairs."

"I already dropped two bags in front of the business kitchen. These are for the apartment. I nabbed Mia's shopping list last night after the talent contest. Man, was Melody amazing or what?" Trent took out milk and orange juice and put them in the fridge.

"She's accomplished, that's for sure. But I think her

true gift is taking care of her grandmother with dementia, going to school full-time, and practicing the piano. She's got to be a strong multitasker." Mia stood. "Let me put away the groceries, at least."

"We've got it. It's a new service I'm thinking about implementing at the store. We'll drop off your groceries and put them away at no extra cost to you, the customer."

Mia leaned down, picked Cerby up, and put him on her lap. "Sounds labor-intensive. Besides, sometimes I don't know where I want something. How would you or your staff? Never mind, that's a rhetorical question. I'm going to work today for a few hours. Do you have time to have breakfast with us, or are you needed back at the store?"

"I'm good until eleven, but then a truck is due in, so I'll need to go unload it." He glanced into the empty sack, then folded it. "So yes, I can stay for breakfast. Besides, I wanted to drop Cerby off for the day. I don't like him in the office when we're unloading a truck. Last time I found him levitating a box off the truck."

"I would think you'd like a little help." Mia rubbed Cerby's chin.

Trent went over and poured himself coffee. "Not when the truck driver is there and watching the little freak do it. I had to wipe the man's mind of those few seconds."

"Hey, weird question, did you drive here?" Mia asked, looking up at the monitor showing the parking lot.

"You think I walked with four bags of groceries and

Cerby?" Trent followed her gaze and stared at the monitor. "Where's my truck?"

"Good question. Second question, how did you get in the school?"

Trent walked over and looked out the kitchen window that overlooked the parking lot. "The truck is right where I parked it." He pointed to an empty slot on the screen next to Mia's car.

"And you got in how?" Mia started to get a bad feeling.

"The door was open. Something weird is going on." Trent got closer to the monitor. "Your screen froze about an hour ago."

"How do you know that? Is there a time stamp?" Mia walked over and peered at the image. A time clock ran underneath the video. She checked her watch. "It's running and matches the current time."

"There's a spell on your system. You need to get your grandmother over here to end it. Someone doesn't want their comings and goings to be recorded," Trent said.

"And someone was in the house—again." Mia looked around the room. "Where's Cerby?"

They all looked around the kitchen, but he was nowhere to be found. The front door to the apartment was open. Trent moved toward the door. "Mom, check the apartment. Mia, the third floor. Christina, the second floor, and I'll go straight down to the first floor. The kitchen is locked. I checked when I dropped off the groceries."

Mia grabbed three sets of keys out of a basket.

"Everyone, take keys for your floor, just in case Mr. Darcy and Dorian are playing tricks on the little guy. And take your cells. Call if you find him."

Looking for Cerby had become an almost daily event but today it seemed even more urgent. Maybe because of the spell on the video. Or the open front door, where Trent had gained entrance. It should have been locked. Mia had locked it last night herself after making sure the bottom floor was cleared of people and the doors all locked. She didn't need a repeat of what had happened to Carla or Marnie. Not again. She had two more days to get through this mess of hosting the queen contest. She could do it.

Now someone just needed to tell her heart to stop beating so fast. She was going to hyperventilate.

She pushed a button and got her grandmother's voice mail. "This is a nine-one-one. You need to come over here, secret project or not. Something's wrong with my security system."

Mia could hear the answer from her now. "*I'm not a techie.*"

She went to the large storage room to the left of the apartment first. Unlocking the door, she stepped inside and turned on the light. She closed the door, so in case Cerby was in there, he couldn't escape while her back was turned. It didn't take long to search, and he wasn't in the closet. Then she slowly walked the whole hallway on the third floor. There were only three doors. The storage room, which she had checked. The apartment, where Abigail was checking, and the library. The door she now stood in front of. She tried the door, but it was locked. But then again, Cerby was a magical thing. As a hellhound, Mia didn't know what all his powers were, and they could include walking through walls. She knew he could make portals. Or Mr. Darcy could have opened and closed the door for him.

Sometimes living with familiars with magical powers made life interesting and fun. This was not one of those times.

The library was one of those rooms that Mia wanted to love. But it still had a problem. A ghost, or a few, haunted the room and didn't seem to be interested in leaving the school anytime soon. For a while, the wards that kept the school standing had been set to keep them here. Mia had ended that, and several ghosts had gone on to whatever destination was next.

Even after that, more than one ghost still remained. The guardian was their leader, and he had several friends who'd chosen to stay with him. Mia needed to find the time to research the library and figure out what the ghost wanted. Today was not the day. She shut the door behind her. "Cerby, are you in here? Come here, baby. Cerby?"

She rounded the corner, and a little girl stood there, holding a ghost cat. "Hello."

"Hello. Have you seen a small white dog?" Mia asked the ghost child as she leaned down to meet her gaze.

The child shook her head. "The hellhound doesn't come in here. The guardian doesn't like it."

"What's your name?" Mia didn't move.

"Annabelle. But the guardian doesn't like me talking to the living. You need to go. Peaches wants to nap in the sunshine, and I'm going to read *The Wizard of Oz*." She pointed to the door.

"You're sure the dog isn't in here?" Mia tried one more time.

"Nope. Just me and Peaches. Thanks for coming by." And the girl disappeared from Mia's view. She wondered if she and Peaches were still sitting on the floor, reading.

"Thanks for talking to me." Mia thought she could trust the girl's word, but she glanced around the room too, just to be safe. No Cerby. As she walked toward the door, a book fell off the shelf and landed in front of her. She picked it up. It was a nonfiction book: *The Care of Magical Creatures*. But instead of the book falling open to the chapter on hellhounds, it was at the golem chapter. She tucked it under her arm and left the library, locking the door as she went.

Mia met Abigail in front of her apartment. "No Cerby up here."

"Trent found him downstairs. I'm surprised you didn't get the text."

Mia's phone finally beeped announcing a text. "I was in the library. Something probably blocked it. Anyway, I'd better get going if I'm going to be back from the Lodge by the time dress rehearsals start."

"No breakfast?" Abigail followed her into the apartment, where Mia put the book down and grabbed her tote and keys.

"Not now. Keep an eye out for Grans, will you? I left her a message, but who knows when she'll pick it up. I'll call on my way home and see if she's here yet."

Mia felt her left eye twitch. She was stressed and running on empty. But she didn't have time to eat. She'd eat at the Lodge while she worked with James.

She met Trent on the stairs with Cerby in hand. She rubbed the dog's head. "I'm glad you found him. Anyway, I've got to go. I'll see you tonight?"

"Christina has offered to watch Cerby, with Mom's help. I think she's preparing for when Levi gets his own familiar. Oh, to be an innocent in the witch world."

"Sometimes it's not as fun as you all think it is. Go eat with your mom. I'll talk with you tonight." As Mia kissed him goodbye, she thought about telling him about the book, but no one had time to read it now. Maybe this weekend, once the event was over.

She hurried outside, making sure the door closed and locked behind her. When she got to the car, she looked up at the camera that watched the parking lot. It looked normal. But then again, what did a bewitched camera look like anyway? Not a question she had time to answer. Hopefully, between her grandmother and Abigail, the system would be fixed by the time she got home.

And everyone would be safe.

Mia knew that just having a security system didn't mean bad things couldn't happen, but if you knew you were being watched, you'd be on your best behavior. At least she could hope.

Driving to work, she saw a person walking down the road. Coming closer, she realized it was Melody. She came up beside her and slowed, rolling the passenger window down. "Hey, do you need a ride?"

Melody frowned at the offer, but before she responded, she saw it was Mia. "Oh, hey. I'm fine walking. I like being outside, and soon it's going to be too cold to walk."

"Are you sure?" Mia saw a car coming up behind her. The road was too narrow, and she couldn't pull off onto the shoulder. "Where are you heading?"

"Home. Don't worry about me." Melody saw the car and waved at the driver. "I'll see you tonight at the rehearsal."

"Okay, then." Mia got back up to speed as she rolled up the window. Melody's house was near the hospital, just a few miles past the turnoff to the Lodge. As she pulled into the parking lot, she wondered where Melody had been coming from. If she liked to hike, there were several trailheads sprinkled between the Lodge parking lot and the hospital. No need to be walking on the road where there wasn't even a bike lane. Or she could have been on the greenbelt, which ran behind the road and behind the school. There weren't any nearby businesses she could have been visiting.

Of course, Melody was a teenager, and sometimes they did things that didn't make sense. And maybe there was a boy who lived out here.

Mia needed to leave it alone. The girl was eighteen according to Trent, and she could make her own decision about where to walk.

CHAPTER 18

By the time Mia got home from work, she'd forgotten about seeing Melody on the road. Grans's car was in the parking lot, as was Mark Baldwin's truck. "That can't be good," Mia muttered as she got out of her car.

Mark, Abigail, and Grans were all in the reception area drinking coffee, and it looked like Mark had devoured a plate of cookies. They looked up as she walked into the school.

"There's our girl." Grans waved her over. "And before you asked, I fixed the security system."

"There was something wrong with your security system?" Mark frowned at Mia. "You should have called the company. They will come out and make repairs."

"It wasn't anything big. A bird had moved the parking lot camera, and it just needed adjusting." Grans lifted the empty plate. "Mark, can I get more cookies?"

"I really shouldn't," he said, but even Mia could see he wanted some more.

"Abigail and I will go grab some more and put them into a bag so you can take them home to Sarah. She needs all the energy she can get." Grans patted Mark's arm as she and Abigail left the room.

Mia sat down next to Mark. "How are things going? How's the baby? And Sarah?"

"They're good. And expecting me home for dinner soon. I just wanted to stop by and update you on Mrs. Carter. She's been sent home, and the doctor says she's doing well." He paused and then just shrugged. "Okay, the weird thing is she had five gift-wrapped lipsticks in her purse that were all tainted with enough botulism to make someone violently ill. Not enough to kill anyone, thank goodness, but they'd be feeling like they were dying."

"Five?" Mia sighed. First, Carla had been trying to eliminate the competition and had died from it. Now Marnie must have been trying the same thing.

"That's an odd number, isn't it? Of course, she's not talking, and her husband has told us to go through her lawyer, but I suspect that she wanted her daughter to win this contest. No matter what." Mark sipped his coffee as he watched her.

"I think you're right." Mia didn't know how to stop this, but it needed to end.

Mark stood and adjusted his hat. "If I could without it coming from me, I'd tell those stage moms to stop trying to manipulate the results of this contest, for their own sake. I'd hate to see anyone else get hurt, or worse, die."

Mia nodded. Now she understood why Mark had come by. He didn't want to ask what she knew—he wanted to send a message. And Mia was the one who had to deliver it. There was no way Mark would even acknowledge the existence of a Magic Springs coven, much less talk about magic. He'd recently found out that his wife and baby daughter were both witches, but he still wanted the idea to be a random occurrence. Not half the town.

"I'll pass on the warning." She stood as well. Coffee klatch was over. Mia had her assignment.

"Thanks, Mia. I appreciate your help with all this mumbo jumbo." He smiled as Grans and Abigail came out of the kitchen. Right on time. "Ladies, thank you for your hospitality."

"Mark, you know you're welcome anytime." Grans handed him a bag with a dozen more cookies. "These are for you and Sarah. Although if you kept them in your truck, I'm not going to be mentioning their existence to your wife."

"Oh, I'll share, but there might not be a dozen in there when I get home." He tipped his hat to all three women, then left through the front door. The women sat back down at the table.

Grans looked at Mia. "How bad is the news?"

"Marnie was attacked because she was trying to poison the other contestants so Rachel could win." Mia rubbed her face with her hands. "And Carla was trying to make it so her daughter could win. We have a karma dealer."

"This is serious, Mia. Magic is flying wild around here. People could get hurt." Abigail twisted her wedding ring. "This is why I didn't want Thomas to be a judge. When you have the power to crown the new queen, you can get hurt."

"Nothing's going to happen to Thomas," Mia promised. She just hoped she could back up that pledge. "When everyone gets here, I'm pulling them all in a room and telling them to knock it off. Is Bambi a coven member?"

Abigail shook her head. "No, she's not. She's open-minded, but not that open-minded. I hadn't wanted to mention it, but the coven is wondering if you'll take over as the event planner next year. They pay handsomely. Maybe even enough not to have to do the Lodge job, or you could negotiate at least that high. They need someone who understands the problems that having a beauty contest with magical contestants can cause."

"I'm ignoring what you just told me and focusing on the first part. I'll invite just the moms into a room for a quick chat and tell them to knock it off." Mia stood and went toward the stairs, where Mr. Darcy was watching her. "Two more days, Mr. Darcy. Or one day, two evenings. And then we'll be done with this."

The look he gave her made her think that maybe the cat knew about the job offer from the coven. And worse, maybe he thought she should take the job.

When Bambi and the contestants arrived, Mia met them in the prep room. She asked for all the guardians to follow her into the next empty classroom. The one where Carla had been killed.

"Mia, we really don't have time tonight for chitchat.

We've got to get ready for the main event tomorrow." Bambi tried to stop the moms from gathering.

"Bambi, this will just take a second and needs to be done." She glanced at the five women. There were three moms. In addition, Marnie's sister had come with Rachel, and Kristin's grandmother was here. Only Melody didn't have anyone with her to help get her ready. After meeting Elly Sellers, that didn't surprise Mia. She stood at the door and pointed to the next room. "Please meet me in there."

Melody followed the women.

"Oh, Melody, I don't need you," Mia said as she reached the door. "Go get ready for your first event."

Melody looked at Tatiana, who was just leaving the room. "Are you sure?"

"If there's anything you need to know, I'll come tell you after tonight's event. Don't worry, you won't be left out." Mia put a hand on Melody's shoulder. "I've got to deal with this."

Mia closed the door after her, and she heard Bambi call out to the girls, "Okay, let's get ready. The judges will all be at their stations, but don't let that worry you. Tonight's just for fun. No judging allowed from them tonight, even if you fall off the stage."

That sounded oddly specific. As Mia went into the other classroom and shut the door, she saw anger on the faces of the mothers and confusion on the other two women's faces.

"Why are we here? We need to be getting our daughters ready for tonight. This contest is very important."

Tatiana was the group's spokesperson. Or more likely, she always thought she was in charge.

"Police Chief Baldwin wanted me to pass on something to all of you. And you need to listen and understand what I'm saying. Both Carla's death and Marnie's accident were because they were trying to affect the outcome of the contest."

"I knew it." Elizabeth Martin, Amie's mom, turned toward the others. "I told you Carla and Marnie were up to something."

"Well, that's not the only thing I need to say." Mia met everyone's gaze, one by one. "There's a rebound on the spell. If you push it, it's going to push back—hard. So, please, no more magic. Just let the girls compete and let the chips fall where they may."

"That's easy for you to say—you don't have a child or a chance at winning the contest." Carla's mother stood next to the spot where her daughter's body had been found. "Carla did this for Kristin. Her effort needs to be honored."

"And Carla's dead because of what she did," Mia reminded the group. "Look, I know you want to help your daughters and loved ones. Everyone wants to help their children. But you have to be alive to do that. I don't know who's doing it or even how the rebounds are being cast. But I do know this building needs to be a magic-free zone through tomorrow night."

The women looked at each other and nodded. Carla's mother spoke again. "You're right, of course. We'll honor our commitment."

As they filed out of the room and toward the prep room, Mia watched and had the sinking feeling that someone was lying when they'd agreed to stop. She just hoped she was wrong.

When the judges gathered at their table, Mia went over to talk to them. Zeus and Thomas were sitting together.

"Well, if it isn't the lovely Mia Malone. What can I help you with today? Do you want to know our process? It's been a secret for years, but I could give you a hint." Zeus leaned closer, and Mia could smell alcohol on his breath.

Mia held her hands out in front of her like a shield. "Oh, no. Don't put that kind of pressure on me. I'm just the caterer. I just wanted to know if you wanted something to drink. We have coffee, iced tea, and sodas. Nothing alcoholic, I'm afraid. We don't have a liquor license."

This was why Mia contracted with the Lodge to provide bar services at events held here, but the coven had handled the bar for tomorrow night. The coven probably hadn't wanted to make it easy on Zeus to get a drink. Every night besides Friday, he'd have to go to his car in the parking lot to sneak a drink. And people would be here on Friday to watch him.

Which could have been why the security camera had been put on a magical loop last night. Maybe he wanted the cover from prying eyes.

It was only a guess about why the security system was targeted. Mia didn't know, and Grans hadn't told her if she could track down the spell caster. She sent a mental thank-you note to her grandmother for the help and got the feeling of a warm hug in exchange. The Goddess was happy with her communication, at least.

Mia still wore her protection charm so Grans could watch out for her. Even tonight in the midst of the storm. A feeling she never forgot.

Thomas chuckled and stood. "I'd love a soda. What about the rest of you guys?"

He took their orders, then walked away with Mia.

She tried to protest. "You don't have to help. I can get five sodas."

"True, but Zeus is showing way too much interest in my son's girlfriend, so I think I'll just walk with you to keep him from helping you out and putting you in a bad spot. He can be a problem." He leaned closer. "How's Abigail?"

"You could ask her yourself," Mia reminded him. "And maybe take her home tonight. She's been at the apartment for way too long."

"I didn't ask her to leave." He held up his hand. "No, we're not doing this. I know you mean well. But I won't use you as a go-between. I'm sorry I started the discussion. Just tell her I said hi."

"Okay, I will." Mia had a few things to do before the evening ended, so she gave the tray of sodas to Thomas to take back to the judges' table. As he started to leave, she put a basket of rolls on the tray. "Maybe Zeus would like something to eat as well."

"You noticed?"

Mia snorted. "How could you not?"

She went back into the kitchen where Abigail was working on trays to put out on the side tables for the girls and judges to snack on. "Thomas says hi, and Zeus is drunk."

"*Drunk* drunk, or just drinking?" Abigail asked.

Mia shrugged. "Is there a difference?"

"For the coven, yes. He knows he can't be drunk at these events." Abigail shook her head. "Don't worry about it. I'll go check. If he's over the limit, I'll call Malcolm and have him removed. It sends a bad message to the girls."

"Thanks. I don't know what's already handled and what's out of the norm with this whole thing. I'll be glad when I'm back at the Lodge just handling normal events." Mia took a mini stuffed croissant off a tray and ate it. "I should have eaten before we started. Now I'm starved and grumpy."

"There's clam chowder and warm rolls upstairs if you want to take a break. You can send Christina down to cover you while you eat." Abigail glanced at her watch. "It's about time for her dinner break to be over anyway."

"Sounds perfect." Mia grabbed two trays of treats and headed out of the kitchen. "I'll drop these off and then run upstairs."

"Tell Christina to hurry. The girls are eating like there's no tomorrow."

Mia hurried and dropped off the trays on her way upstairs. When she reached the second floor, she ran into the girls coming down to start the practice.

Bambi caught her after everyone had cleared the stairwell. "What did you say to the parents?"

"Why? Are they being awful again?" Mia knew this job wasn't what she was meant for. She decided not to take the gig next year. Gloria giggled in the apartment. She ignored her.

Bambi looked at her strangely. "No, they're being

amazing. They're being supportive and nice. Did you threaten them with bodily harm?"

Mia laughed. "Nothing that serious. We just needed to clear up something. I'm running upstairs to eat. I'll be back down in about thirty minutes."

Bambi held up her phone. "I'll call if I need you."

The rest of the night went like clockwork. And by the time everyone had cleared out, Mia thought that just maybe her message from Mark had taken hold. Maybe everyone would be positive and let the contest go on without any more interference. At least that was her hope.

Mia was up early the next morning. She had made a strada, a breakfast casserole with eggs, cheese, and bacon that used up the day-old bread too, for anyone who was hungry, and she had written out several lists. One was about work at the Lodge and the things she needed to deal with on Monday. The next was the list of upcoming classes she was committed to teaching for Mia's Morsels for the next three months.

January was coming fast, and she needed to refocus her goals. Would she return to Mia's Morsels, based on the date when Frank pulled back his requirement that any event set at the Lodge had to use the hotel's catering department? She knew it would happen, but when was another story. Or would she just bite the bullet and set her own return date, hoping she could live on what the delivery and classes brought in?

Only one of those put control of her fate in her own

hands. And that was a requirement in any goal-setting plans. Plan what you could control. Okay, with that premise set, would she go back to running her business next year or the year after?

Mia scrolled through the profit-and-loss statements and the projections for next year. And came to one conclusion. She needed to wait another year. If she hadn't burned any bridges with Frank.

Now she was depressed, so she went to shower and dress for the day. She wanted just to get back in bed, throw the covers over her head, and sink back into sleep. Instead, she decided to go for a run on the greenbelt. Like Melody had said yesterday, time to enjoy the warm, Idaho late fall was running out. And as much as she liked winter, she loved fall.

Mr. Darcy followed her out of the house, but he stayed on the dais while she moved around the fence to the greenbelt. Instead of going east toward town, she turned to go west to the end of the greenbelt. She'd get there, stretch again, then run into town and back to the house. That would be just under five miles. And if that didn't wake up some endorphins, nothing would.

When she came back from the run, her head was clear, and she felt like she could continue to slay the dragons in her life. As she walked through the parking lot, she noticed a line in the school's concrete foundation. She rarely walked this way since she typically parked closer to the front door.

"Great, right when I was feeling better, the school shows me that it has a foundation issue," Mia muttered as she walked over through the shrubs that grew next to the building. She shook the thought away and put a smile on as she repeated her mantra. "I know gratitude in all things."

As she came around the bushes, she realized the line wasn't a crack. There was a door here. A door she didn't know about. She pulled open the door and stared into the pitch-black interior. Then she heard a sound, and all of a sudden, something furry rushed at her.

CHAPTER 19

Rats? Mia had rats in the building? Holding in a scream, she moved out of the doorway, but then a small white dog jumped on her legs, wanting to be picked up. She brushed the gray cobwebs off him as she caught her breath.

"Cerby! Did you come out of the house?" Convinced that he didn't have any bugs or more cobwebs on him, Mia picked him up so he wouldn't wander. Then she went back to the open door and reached in to find a light switch. With one flick, the storage room flooded with light.

Mia had known about the storage room, but she hadn't really used it. The area was located behind the elevator and stairs and on the other side of the building from the kitchen, so it hadn't been practical for everyday storage. Mia started to step in, but then she saw footprints on the dusty floor.

Footprints that led from the door, into the storage

room. Someone else had known about the door and had come inside recently. Was this how Carla had gotten in? Mia studied the prints. These looked like hiking boots, not the stilettos Carla had been found wearing. But that had been days ago.

The bushes around her rustled, and Mia saw Trent push his way through. He stopped short when he saw her standing by the wall with Cerby. "What are you doing out here, buddy? I just left you in the kitchen with Mom."

"He apparently has been guarding this secret doorway into the house. It's not even locked. Did you know this was here?" Mia pointed to the storage room entrance.

"I didn't. When I found him the other day, he was in the storage room, but I thought he was following Mr. Darcy and got lost." Trent stepped into the room, then closed the door partway. "The door is built into the wall. I don't think you'd even see it if you didn't know it was here. How did you find this?"

"The sun was in just the right spot, I guess. I thought the foundation was cracking." Now there were more footprints in the dust. Maybe she'd seen Trent's footprints from the other day. "Anyway, we need to put a lock on this or something."

He stepped back outside and looked at the door frame. "I'll put a dead lock on the inside. All I need to do is run to the hardware store. I can do it this morning."

"Thanks. I appreciate you more than you know." Mia nodded to the doorway. "I guess we can just go in through here?"

"Ladies first." He nodded toward the entrance and then pulled the door shut after them. "I can't believe we're still finding hidden entrances in this old place. Every time I think we've locked the place down tight, something new comes up. Maybe that library of yours has a floor plan for the school. That way we can locate any other hidden rooms and entrances."

Mia made her way through the shelves until she found the doorway to the hall. It was open a crack, probably where Cerby had come into the room in the first place. Had he heard her open the other door? "Cerby seems to be finding all kinds of things in the house. He found the potion bags and now a secret entrance. I guess his hellhound tendencies are developing."

"I need to finish reading that book Mom gave me about raising hellhounds. I started, but then we got busy with the queen contest." Trent closed the door behind him, then he moved a bookshelf from the hallway in front of the door to block it. "If somebody tries to get in before I get the dead bolt on, at least we'll hear them."

"Thanks. By the way, the library gave me a book on magical creatures that day Cerby got lost. It opened up to a chapter on golems, though, not the hellhound chapter." They walked through the hallway toward the reception room. "I've got it upstairs."

"Golems? I haven't heard about those for years. There were rumors that one of the families made one for a housekeeper, but the coven shut them down as soon as they found out. They don't have souls." He nodded to the kitchen. "Mom knows all about them if you want to know anything."

"I think the library just dropped the book wrong. I might be reading too much into where it was opened to. The book does have a chapter on hellhounds. I'll read it this weekend, then pass the book on to you if you're done with the other one."

Trent rubbed Cerby's head and then set him on the floor. "I need to be as prepared as possible with this little guy. He keeps me on my toes. Mom said she would watch him today. I have to stop in at the store for a bit, but I'll grab the dead bolt and have that installed before noon. Do you need anything at the store?"

"I'm good. I'm going to go up and change, then head down to help your mom in the kitchen. Next week, I'm doing some detailed future planning and determining how much longer I need to work with the Lodge. Maybe between Abigail and me, we can tie down some strong numbers. Especially since Christina is applying for jobs now." Mia paused at the stairwell. "I don't know if she's told Levi yet, so maybe keep that between us?"

"She's told him. He came over the other night, and we talked. That's why I didn't come get Cerby." Trent looked at his watch. "I'll see you for lunch, then."

He left using the front door, leaving both Cerby and Mia watching his abrupt departure. Cerby looked up at her, and Mia shrugged. More for herself than the little dog. "I'm not sure what that was about, Cerby. Sometimes Trent's a mystery." She smiled at him. "Just like you and your investigative hellhound skills."

Cerby barked at her, then ran toward the kitchen, where Abigail was working.

Mia headed upstairs feeling lighter than she had when she got out of bed. Sometimes a run or a workout was just the thing she needed. She just needed to trust the process. Time to get ready for her day.

When she got downstairs, Abigail and Cerby were there alone. Mia pulled on an apron. "Where's Christina?"

"She had a video interview for a job in Oregon. I can't believe they got back to her this quickly. I think they really want to hire her." Abigail made an exaggerated pouting look with her lip. "Can I give her a horrible reference so they change their minds? Like, she steals food from the kitchen all the time?"

"Don't forget to tell them she never showers or washes her hands," Mia chimed in with more possible insults. "And she chews with her mouth open."

"It's impossible. They're going to hire our girl, aren't they?" Abigail put a pan in the oven and set a timer.

"Probably. If they meet her income expectations. I told her to make sure she starts her negotiation for more than what she wants. If she's moving, they need to make it worth her while." Mia glanced at the list with her name on it. "I'm going to miss the kid."

"Me too." Abigail walked over and picked up her own list. "I'm going to bake the cookies and rolls first. I want to leave tonight's appetizers for last so they don't have to be reheated."

"Can you believe we're almost done with this? Tomorrow Trent and I are going to the parade and the festival, and after that I'm just going to chill. No thinking about the business or work or even the food trucks. If they are slammed, I'm not stepping in to help. That's on James and his crew."

Abigail laughed as she took butter out of the fridge. "You know you'd totally jump in if they needed you."

Mia shook her head. "Not tomorrow. Tomorrow is my day, and I don't care what happens. I'm on vacation. Really."

"We'll see." Abigail walked over and turned up the radio. "This is the song we played at our anniversary dinner last year. I love it."

By the time Trent got back from the store and installed the dead bolt, Abigail had lunch ready for the four of them. Christina had come downstairs after her interview and started working on her list. She hadn't said much about how it went, but Mia could feel the excitement rolling off her friend. Christina had a lot to think about.

"I've set lunch up in the reception area rather than outside so we don't get in Jeani and Cheryl's way. They're decorating this afternoon." Abigail glanced at Christina. "Levi will be here tonight, but he's working today. He wants to stay away from Cheryl. She's not taking the hints or the direct statements he's given her about not being interested in dating."

"He should have thought about that before they danced the other night," Christina said, then held up a hand. "Sorry, I take that back. I know he didn't mean to lead her on, but sometimes girls want a fairy-tale ending, including being swept off their feet."

"Christina, I was there. Levi didn't do anything

wrong. They were just dancing. Jeani and I were talking about old times, we'd had a few beers, and that was it." Trent followed them out of the kitchen and over to the table, where lunch was waiting. "I would have stopped him if I'd known Cheryl was taking it seriously. Jeani says she has a history of that."

Something was bothering Mia about the conversation. "Wait. Jeani told you that? After that night?"

Trent nodded. "Last Saturday, when they were here finishing up the planning. Cheryl was freaking out because Levi took off for Boise to follow Christina. Jeani pulled me aside and apologized."

"If she knew her sister would take Levi's attention wrong, then why didn't she stop it on Friday night?" Mia asked the question that had been bothering her.

Everyone at the table was quiet, thinking about the answer.

"Look, I don't care, Christina doesn't care. Levi doesn't even care. But Cheryl's hurt from the whole encounter. Jeani had to know Levi and Christina were a couple. Why didn't she tell her sister to stop mooning over him? That it was just for fun?" Mia wasn't liking the way this made Jeani look.

Trent set down his sandwich. "I don't know."

"Well, I've wasted too much time thinking about it." Mia picked up her spoon and took a sip of the vegetable beef soup Abigail had pulled from the freezer stores. "What's going on with the contest? Is Mark going to be here just in case something happens?"

Abigail chuckled. "I didn't think about hiring security for a high school harvest queen contest, but if you think we need to do it, I'll call him."

"Just let him know he's welcome to show up. I'm not sure he's needed. I gave his message to the adults yesterday, and nothing happened last night at the dress rehearsal. So, maybe they realized they can't play their magic tricks to get their daughter that crown." Mia picked up her grilled cheese and green chili sandwich. "Although common sense doesn't seem to be working around here this week."

"Does Mark know who's been behind the retribution magic?" Trent had already eaten his sandwich and reached for the platter in the middle for another one. "These are really good, Mom."

"Thanks." Abigail glanced around the table. "I don't know if Mark can figure that out. Have you heard from Mary Alice about the potion bags?"

Mia shook her head. "Nothing more than they were aimed at anyone in the pageant and that the same person made all the ones we found. Do you think someone was sneaking into the school using that storage room door and planting them? We haven't found any more since Marnie fell under her own sickness spell."

"That was weird too. I wonder when she was going to drop off the lipsticks for the girls. If she'd wanted to do it quietly, she could have gone up before or after the introduction reception," Abigail said.

"She and Rachel came in late, remember? I heard Marnie complaining that Rachel was going to ruin her chances by being late to such an important event. I was waiting for them at the door and moved them right into the event. They were the last to arrive, and Bambi was having a cow about not starting on time." Mia thought about that night. "I'd forgotten about that."

"So, she didn't get the chance to actually implement her plan. Now our villain is reading people's intentions?" Abigail shivered. "I can't even imagine the kind of power you'd have to possess to do that."

"Well, we can eliminate Marnie and Carla since they were both victims. And I think all the girls. Crissy seems to want the crown for verification of her queen bee status with the high school crowd, but I don't see any of them having the power or the motivation to kill each other. This is more of a stage mom thing, right?" Mia looked around the table. "Christina? What do you think?"

She set down her spoon. "When I was in pageants, some of the girls were mean. Not just cruel, but vicious. If any of them had real power, like you guys have, they would have used it in a heartbeat to get what they wanted."

"Okay, so I'm being a Pollyanna." Mia smiled at her friend. "I'll take back my statement."

"Well, at least you stopped the problem before they started on the judges. I would have hated to see Dad get messed up in this." Trent finished off his soup. "Good meal, Mom. Thanks."

"Actually, I think the judges were affected," Abigail said quietly. "I put a protection stone on your dad when he decided to step into this contest. He's been watching the other judges for us. He asked that I keep it a secret. Anyway, Zeus was rushed to the hospital last night after Tatiana went to his hotel room. She said she was just talking, but I'm now worried about her. If the spell is tracking the moms and the girls, I think maybe Tatiana is going to be the next target."

"Is Zeus going to be all right?" Mia really regretted getting involved in this entire event.

"He's fine. They're saying he had a minor stroke. But if this retribution spell is as powerful as we think, maybe he had agreed to judge Crissy higher than the other girls. And maybe he was attacked for it."

"Or he refused and Tatiana took him out." Trent leaned back in his chair. "I can't believe Dad would put himself in harm's way like this. He's not a young guy."

"Don't let your father hear you say that." Abigail pointed her spoon at her middle child. "But you're right. That's why I was so mad. And then your dad said we'd use that to our advantage too. That way no one would suspect that he was watching out for the judges."

"He's an idiot," Mia said, then she held up her hand. "Don't tell him I said that either."

"I know it's all said in love." Thomas came into the reception area through the kitchen. "I wanted to know if lunch was ready. Then I hear all of you saying such nice things about me."

"I'm so sorry, Thomas." Mia felt her face redden.

"Sit down, and I'll bring you out some soup. I didn't know you were coming." Abigail stood and cleared a spot for her husband. "Tell them what you've found out."

He sat and waited for Abigail to return with a full bowl of soup and silverware. "Well, what you were saying was true. It's a retribution spell. Your grandmother pointed that out after Carla died. The coven has been watching the event for the last two years, and there's always an issue with the power usage of the contestants and their families. So, when the contract came up, they asked Abigail to bid for Mia's Morsels and me to volunteer as a judge."

"You had the contract before we even bid?" Mia repeated the idea. "The Lodge was never going to get it. Gosh, I wish I could tell Frank this."

"The coven had discussed just canceling the event. They've had too many incidents in the last few years to believe it was safe to hold it. But they thought they'd gotten through to everyone until Zeus was approached last year for a favor from one of the contestants. He reported it immediately, and the girl and her parents were kicked out of the contest. But there had been rumors of other magic-related issues." Thomas ate some soup before continuing. "But even the coven is stumped this year. They've talked to every family, and no one is claiming responsibility. And they've used a truth spell on them."

"So, someone outside the event is stirring the pot? Why?" Mia didn't understand where that left them.

Thomas leaned back in his chair, mirroring his son's actions earlier. "We don't know. My money would have been on the Evanses. They've always been on the edge of getting a board seat. The dad is always volunteering, but he never follows through. He wants the title, not the work."

"But now Tatiana is caught in the retribution spell. Is she all right? Has anything happened to her?"

Now Thomas got quiet. "She's in the hospital too. They found her nonresponsive in her bed this morning. She's in some sort of a coma."

CHAPTER 20

With three of the six contestants having parents who had been attacked by the retribution spell, Mia didn't know if that meant her suspect pool was dwindling, or if Tatiana, the last of the group to be affected, had been the ringleader of all the problems. Hopefully, she only had three more possible parent instigators. And one of those was a woman with dementia whom she could take off the list.

The group was clustered around Mia's kitchen after lunch on Friday as Abigail went through the day's events and what kinds of sabotage or problems to watch for with the judges, the contestants, or the parents. It was a long list.

Levi glanced at the clock nervously. "When are Jeani and Cheryl arriving?"

"Why? Are you looking for a new dance partner?" Christina teased, but there was a bit of angst in her tone.

"No. I thought I should apologize to her. I don't think I led her on, but if I did anything to make her think I wanted more than just a friendly dance, I want to take that responsibility and tell her I'm sorry." Levi's face was red, but resolved.

Everyone at the table was silent for a second.

"That's lovely," Abigail finally blurted out. "And I'm sure she'll appreciate it. Just don't make the apology too long or get too close."

"Mom, I know how to break off a relationship—or even the idea of one. I've done it a few times." Levi hugged Christina. "And I'm sorry if I gave you any grief in this whole thing."

"You're being thoughtful." Trent reached over and put his hand on his brother's head. "Do you have a fever?"

Everyone laughed as Levi batted Trent's hand away.

"To answer your question, Jeani and Cheryl and the staff will be back here at three to make sure everything's perfect. Then the audience starts to arrive at five thirty. We'll have soft drinks and coffee available, as well as passed trays, as they mingle on the lawn. The coven's bartenders will be here to set up an outside bar at five. At six, the ten-minute warning bell will sound—which will actually be Bambi asking people to find their seats. The judges will come out during that time, and promptly at six ten, the emcee, the current coven board president, will start the show. That's Brandon Marshall, for those of you who don't know. He's really nice and has run this contest for the last five years. Zeus had planned on doing it this year, but after last night's incident, Brandon decided to step in."

"Mary Alice, would you check Brandon for any spell work before he goes onstage? Since they couldn't get to Zeus, they may want to get someone else on their side," Thomas added to the discussion. Last night, Abigail had packed to go home, saying the event was as ready as it was going to be. Thomas had taken her luggage out to his car as soon as he arrived today.

Mia studied the group. Abigail and Thomas were solid. This whole taking-a-break thing had been a hoax to try to get the shenanigans to happen sooner than later. Mia wouldn't be surprised if Thomas had moved Abigail to the school for her safety while the contest was being hammered out. That's what family did—protected each other.

"Okay, I think that's all I wanted to say. Anyone else have anything to add? Have you seen anything odd this week?" Abigail looked around the group. "Oh, if you haven't heard, Mia and Cerby found another door into the school. It was through the storage room closest to the parking lot. So, if you see people hanging out there and looking frustrated, Trent put a dead bolt on the door, and Mary Alice fortified the wards in that area."

"So, someone was coming into the school through that door?" Christina shivered. "I thought all the weird feelings I was getting when I worked alone in the kitchen were because of the ghosts, but now you're telling me it could have been a real person? The next place I work at had better be new construction on hallowed ground."

Trent and Levi snickered.

"What did I say?" Christina looked around the table.

"New construction can actually cause spectral visits because the ghosts are angry you tore down their old family homestead or hangout. And hallowed ground doesn't mean no ghosts. It means no demons," Abigail explained to the only mortal in the group. "And boys, don't laugh. Christina didn't grow up in a magical world. She has to learn these things."

"Cerby seems to be finding a lot of things lately." Christina picked up the little Maltese as he was sleeping on the floor. He made three circles, then went back to sleep on her lap. "Is that the 'hound' part of 'hellhound'? Can we have him smell something and find a missing person?"

Abigail smiled. "Not yet, but soon. He's really going to need to go to a special trainer, though. Trent, have you picked one out?"

"I don't want to send him away, so I'm looking at trainers who are closer. The McMann family up north has a great training program. And I can bring Cerby home every weekend." Trent glanced over at Mia. "I'm sorry, I didn't mention his residential training requirements before."

"I can't believe you're sending this baby away." Mia smiled at Cerby while he slept. "Tell me he'll be a little bigger."

Her cell phone rang. The display said the call was from the Local Goat, Brad's restaurant. She stood and answered the phone while she walked into the living room. "Hello, is this Brad?"

She heard a long sigh on the other side of the call. "Then he's not there with you. I thought that maybe since he went up to have dinner with you on Wednesday, he might still be there? Like, in a coma somewhere and no one called the restaurant?"

"Brad didn't come for dinner with me this Wednesday. He was here last week." A pit was starting in Mia's stomach. Maybe talent night practice hadn't gone off quite as easy as she'd hoped. "Look, give me your name and number. If I hear anything, I'll call. Did you call the Magic Springs Police Station yet?"

"It's next on my list. I'm Diana Brown. I'm Brad's"— she paused, then went on—"sous chef. And roommate. He hasn't been home since he left to drive up to Magic Springs on Wednesday. We got in a fight because I didn't like the fact he was going to see you again. I tried to call the police here in Twin, but they said I had to wait twenty-four hours. Then I thought maybe he was just figuring out some things. We'd just moved in together. You know how that can be on a confirmed bachelor. But it's not like him to miss one night of service, let alone two."

Mia wrote down Diana's name and the three numbers she'd given her. "Call the Magic Springs police. Ask to speak with Mark Baldwin and tell him you talked to me."

After she hung up, she went back into the kitchen. The group had broken up, and now only Abigail, Trent, and Grans remained.

Abigail took one look at her and asked, "What's wrong now?"

Mia told them about Brad and the fact that he was missing. She told him how he'd told Diana he was coming to Magic Springs on Wednesday to meet her for a late dinner. "He never called me about dinner. Last Wednesday, he said he'd see me soon."

"But he's missing now." Trent drummed his fingers

on the table. "I wonder if he even got to Magic Springs or if he's still in Twin."

"Good question, but not something we can solve today. We've got an event to get through. Maybe I'll call this Diana on Sunday and we can drive down to Twin and talk to her then." Mia wrote a note on Sunday to call and get an update. Then she closed her planner. "So much for a stressless weekend. That sounds bad, doesn't it?"

"You can't save the entire world." Trent squeezed her shoulder.

Grans sniffed. "Actually we can, but we never get the credit. I'm coming over tomorrow morning with a gift for you. I'd keep it at my house, but with the wedding, I'm going to have to sell the house. Or at least move and rent it out."

Mia hoped it was furniture. Even though her apartment was fully furnished, she had little coves and outcroppings all over the school where she could put a small love seat, table, and lamp to make a conversation spot. The first floor still had a lot that needed to be done. "Trent and I are going to the festival and the parade. What time are you coming?"

"I'll be here at eight. Robert wants to attend the festival, then we're going to Boise for dinner. They never have anything good to eat at those things." She glanced at her watch. "I'm going home to get ready, and I'll be back at five to watch for any magical interference. And Robert will be with me tonight."

Mia watched as Mr. Darcy jumped off the window seat and ran to the front door. Dorian opened it for him, then the door slammed just a little too hard.

Grans sighed. "Dorian really needs to get over it. The man is dead, and he's still upset that I'm dating again."

Grans followed Mr. Darcy out of the apartment, and then it was just the three of them. "I'm running home too," Abigail announced. "Dress up tonight. The local paper will be here for pictures."

And with that, Trent and Mia were alone. He led her over to the living room, where they sat together. "Are you worried about Brad?"

Mia nodded. "A little. I mean, I haven't talked to him much since high school. It's not like the guy I knew then to just take off, though."

"But he might be a different man now," Trent pointed out.

Mia shook her head. "Not from what I felt from this Diana. She believes in him. She thinks he took off because they'd just moved in together. Like, it was her fault. I think something bad happened."

"Well, let's not add this worry to tonight's plate. We have a contest to get through. I can't believe Mom and Dad were just pretending to be mad at each other." He rubbed his face. "It's not fair to the kids when the parents fight."

Mia thought about that for a minute. When she spoke, she grabbed Trent's hand. "I think they were truly fighting. Or at least, they both didn't agree with the plan. Your mom was really scared for your dad. She was worried that something bad was going to happen. He might have thought they were on the same page, but I think your mom was just going along for the ride. Your dad can be persuasive."

"True. And I can see him making up this plan that Mom hates, but she feels like she needs to support him. Then, if everything works out, she can just say he was right and no one's feelings would get hurt. But this—this is bigger. Even Levi felt the division, and he's usually oblivious to the nuances of emotion." Trent squeezed her hand. "We need to talk."

"Uh-oh, what did I do now?" Mia sank back into the cushions. She was so ready for this event to be over. It was taxing on every level. She shut her eyes and felt the warmth of Trent's body next to her own.

"I'm just wondering if we should take this to the next level. What do you think?"

Trent's voice was soft and warm, and she could just sink into it . . . "What?" Her eyes flew open, and she sat up. "What are you saying?"

He chuckled as he pulled her back down into his arms. "I'm just wondering if you would say yes if I were to ask a specific question. Like, soon."

"You're feeling out your proposal? What am I, a scared, unbroke colt that you have to ease up next to just to get a rope on me?" She knew she was stalling. But she needed a second to think.

"No, I like the imagery, though. I know that you're a busy career woman with a second job, as well as a calling to study for and a whole new world to learn about. You've done well working on the sidelines of the coven. They respect you. They still want to give you their fancy decoder ring and swear you in on a full moon with a virgin sacrifice. I didn't want to add one more thing to your busy schedule unless you are ready. You're not going to hurt my feelings if you say no." He pulled her closer. "Okay, so you will hurt my feelings, but I'll try not to make this about me."

She took a deep breath, but he put his fingers on her lips.

"Hold that thought. We can talk more tomorrow when we're at the festival and don't have a possible murderous queen contest to get through." He stood up and then paused. "Wait, that made it sound like the contestants are murderers."

Mia stood up as well. "Maybe they are. I'm going to go read for a while before I get ready for tonight. I'll see you about six."

He pulled her close and kissed her. "I'm looking forward to tomorrow."

"Maybe you shouldn't," Mia said, but then laughed at the look he gave her. "Sorry, but you set yourself up for this. Now all the power is in my hands for a pre-engagement proposal question on how I might feel."

"When you put it that way, it sounds stupid." He paused at the door. "Cerby, come with me. We need to chat about boarding school. Your evil, soon-to-be stepmother is insisting."

"Oh, don't you put that decision on me. You're the one sending the baby away." She picked up Cerby and gave him a kiss, then handed him to Trent. "And we don't say 'stupid' in this house. Maybe 'ill-informed.' Or 'wrong,' even. But not stupid."

"That makes me feel tons better." Trent grinned, tucking Cerby under his arm like a miniature white football. "See you later."

The apartment was quiet for the first time since Mia could remember. She was totally alone. Even Mr. Darcy had left. Mia made sure the front door was closed and locked. Christina and Grans both had keys if they needed to get in. Mr. Darcy had Dorian. But other than that, she shouldn't be disturbed. She went into her bedroom and shut the door. Then she pulled out an old scrapbook from her hope chest. They should have called these chests "memory keepers." She didn't keep quilts or other items for a someday married home. She kept her yearbooks, her scrapbooks, and mementos from trips.

She found a picture from the summer when Brad had run with her social group. They'd all been out at Lucky Peak at a bonfire. It was just before school started, and everyone was mourning the disappearance of summer. She'd passed her driving exam that year, and her parents had given her an old sedan. The paint was baby blue, and the interior brown fake leather. The air conditioner didn't work, and the heater took forever to clear off the frost on her windows, but Galadriel was all hers. Mia had named her after the elf queen in *The Lord of the Rings*. She was a beauty and a terrible power, all at once.

In the photo, she and Brad were standing by Galadriel. He had a beer in his hand; she had a Coke. And they were both grinning like fools. She'd loved that picture. They'd both looked happy and had the whole world in front of them.

She sat down at her desk, clearing off everything except a white pillar candle and the picture. She lit the candle, closed her eyes, and whispered the incantation her grandmother had taught her to find lost things. It was written in her grimoire, but she'd used it enough times, she remembered the spell by heart.

As she repeated the chant, a vision of Brad, dirty and sitting in a dark room, came to her. As she watched, she saw he'd been chained to a wall. He sat on an old cot, his head in his hands. Then his head lifted.

"I can feel you. Mia? Is that you? Are you looking for me? I'm here in Magic Springs . . ."

All of a sudden, her connection was cut off, and the vision of Brad was gone. The candle had dripped wax on top of his picture, covering his face.

Mia debated trying again, but she'd found out what she needed to know. Brad was alive and somewhere in Magic Springs. She glanced at the clock. She didn't have time to try the spell again right now. And besides, she wasn't sure if the person holding Brad had sensed her and kicked her out of the basement or if the wax had broken the connection. She'd talk to Grans tonight.

First, though, she'd call Mark Baldwin and see if Diana had reported Brad missing. Then she'd tell him what she'd seen. Mark didn't believe in magic, but he also wasn't willing to ignore a possible clue—no matter where it came from. She found his name on her recent contacts list and hit the button. When he answered, she started talking.

With her phone call done, she headed to the bathroom to get ready. Brad was alive. She'd find him sooner or later. But first, she needed to make sure that all six contestants lived through the competition and the best girl was chosen for the scholarship. She hoped it would be Melody.

CHAPTER 21

Mia scanned the audience as they wandered around with flute glasses filled with cocktails, juice, or sparkling water. The waitstaff Abigail had hired were actually pretty good. Mia wondered if mentioning that she was hiring part-time catering servers would be a breach of etiquette. Probably, and it would get back to the Twin Falls company Abigail borrowed the crew from. Which would only help Frank. She smiled and took a buffalo chicken cracker from a young girl who was passing by. "You're doing awesome," Mia told her, and the girl blushed.

"Thanks. This is my first real job." She blanched. "I probably shouldn't have said that. We were told to act professional."

"Your secret is safe with me." Mia let the girl continue and turned back to check on the stage. The work Trent, Levi, and Thomas had done was perfect. She'd envisioned having something like this in the backyard of the school but thought it was at least three years out. More, if the catering side of the business didn't increase. But since the coven had paid for the enhancements, Mia was ahead of schedule. Okay, so that was something to be grateful for in this mess.

Grans stopped on her way to her seat with Robert by her side. "It all looks lovely, dear. Kind of like a fairy garden. I love the lights."

Mia gave her grandmother a hug. "Thank you, but this isn't me. Between Trent and his dad and brother and Jeani and Cheryl's crew, they made it look this way. I was just thinking how incredible it is. I need to make sure I get some of the pictures from the photographer for our website."

"You mean Abigail needs to remember." Grans touched Mia's forehead. "You've got too much going on up there. You need to let go of some things, or you're going to burn out."

Mia snorted. "Easier said than done. When I'm at work, I'm thinking about the business. When I'm at home, I'm thinking about work. It's a vicious cycle."

"Well, I think I have an answer to at least part of that." Grans's eyes twinkled with the hanging lights. "I'll be over first thing in the morning to get everything set up."

"Wait, it's not furniture?" Mia tried to keep the disappointment out of her voice.

"No, it's not furniture. Why would you think that? Anyway, it's a surprise. I'll see you in the morning. Have a great show." Grans took Robert's arm, and they moved toward the front rows of seats.

Bambi had blocked off the first two rows for family,

so Mia watched as they sat near the aisle on the third row. Robert, again, hadn't said anything. Either he was really shy, or he didn't like her. Mia couldn't tell which was the case.

Abigail joined her and brushed cracker crumbs off Mia's dress. "It's actually happening. I wasn't sure there for a while. When Carla was killed, I thought they'd shut the contest down then. I don't think they're going to find who was doing all the spell casting, but maybe this group will be held up as examples, so it doesn't happen again."

Mia scanned the area. "I'm not sure it's all over yet."

"What do you mean?" Abigail followed her gaze. "Do you see something?"

"No, just a feeling." Mia turned back to Abigail. "You did a great job with this event. Congratulations."

"Oh, you know the saying, it takes a village. It wasn't just me. Everyone chipped in. I'm just good at telling people what to do." Abigail sipped her drink.

"Telling us what to do is one of Abbie's best qualities." Thomas came up behind Abigail and engulfed her in a hug. "She's always trying it with me. I just don't listen when I should."

"And that's one of your worst qualities." Abigail leaned up for a quick kiss. Then she spun around and ran her hands across her husband's suit jacket. "You look hot."

"I'm surprised you noticed. I am a little warm under the lights," Thomas teased.

Abigail put a hand on his chest. "You never could take a compliment without turning it into a joke."

"I only care what you think, my dear. And if you

think I look hot, I'm going to wear this suit around the house for the next week or so." He nodded to the stage, where Bambi was moving toward the mic. "That looks like my cue to get the judges settled. I'll go get Zeus. He's sitting inside, out of the heat. It's unusually warm for an October evening."

Mia watched as everyone turned toward Bambi and her announcement. In the very front, a young woman helped Elly Sellers into a chair and sat next to her. The woman appeared to be fully present—at least for right now. Mia hoped Elly would be able to see and remember Melody's performance tonight. At least the talent portion.

No matter what, the playing field was completely fair tonight. Anyone who had even tried to affect the outcome had been attacked. Carla was dead. Marnie had just been released from the hospital yesterday and was already sitting in the front row on the opposite side of Elly Sellers. Tatiana wasn't here, but the rest of the family had shown up for Crissy, and they filed into the empty seats next to Rachel's family.

Mia met Abigail's eyes. "And here we go."

They were down to the final announcement. Three of the girls—Kristin, Anne, and Rachel—had been eliminated. Mia wondered if their parents' actions had knocked them out of the running—but maybe not, since Crissy was still in the mix. And grinning like she'd just swallowed the canary. Or like she was the cat—Mia didn't know the exact saying.

Crissy, Amie, and Melody were standing together,

holding hands. Amie was crying, she was so nervous. Melody kept her eyes on her grandmother. Watching for signs. It made Mia's heart hurt. Even on this night, Melody was being a caretaker. How was she ever going to have her own life?

Zeus looked at all the papers the other judges had sent him at the front of the table. Bambi had shown Mia the judges' scoring sheet. They went by points up to the top three, then each judge used a second sheet to rank his favorites. So, first, second, and third.

Mia had asked Bambi about ties, and she'd laughed. "Most of the time, the judges all have the same first place. It's second and third that might need some tallying."

If Mia was a judge, Melody would win the contest. But she knew that Crissy was a close second. Amie was a wild card. She'd been quiet during the week so Mia hadn't really noticed her until she got onstage. Then she'd glowed. Some people were just better during the actual event.

Mia hadn't sat down all evening. She was standing near the back of the seating area, watching people. Abigail stood on the other side of her, and Trent and Levi were in front of the audience, but standing on either sides of the stage, looking like well-dressed bodyguards.

Nothing had happened. Yet. Mia still had a bad feeling.

Zeus handed Brandon a slip of paper, and then Brandon took the stage. He talked about how wonderful it had been to get to know all the contestants and that the future was looking bright for Magic Springs with these types of women getting ready to take over the world.

Several people in the audience rolled their eyes. Apparently, this was his usual speech, no matter what the event. The words stayed the same; only the names were changed. Mia chuckled at the reaction. Finally, he got down to business. "The second runner-up is . . . Amie Masters. Please give Amie a round of applause as she returns to the Royal Hall on the right side of the stage."

Last year's winner placed a small tiara on Amie's head, put a sash around her neck, and then gave her a bouquet of flowers. All the girls had practiced this part of the event, but Amie was now crying so hard, Mia worried she wouldn't see the edge of the stage as she did her walk.

Brandon waited for Amie to arrive safely with the other princesses. Then he stepped back to the microphone. "The first runner-up is the person who will be there to step in if our reigning queen is unable to fulfill her responsibilities."

He paused and looked at Crissy and Melody. "Each of you would make an excellent harvest queen, but there was just something more in one of you that pushed that person over the top. The harvest queen for this year is . . . Melody Sellers. Congratulations to Crissy Evans for being our first runner-up."

The former queen put a small tiara on Crissy's head, placed the banner around her neck, and gave her the bouquet of flowers. Then, when Crissy didn't move, she pushed her toward the side. Crissy looked shell-shocked but her feet finally started to work, and she smiled. Just not as big of a smile as she'd had a few minutes ago. The girl had expected to win.

As everyone waited for Crissy to return to the Royal Hall, last year's winner hugged Melody and put the large crown on her head. Melody looked more shocked than Crissy had, and her grandmother stood and clapped for her as she strolled down the runway then back up to the stage, where the other girls came out and hugged her. Only one princess held back—Crissy.

The dark horse had won the competition, continuing her family's tradition of serving as harvest queen. Mia just hoped Melody's reign would be less traumatic than Sherry's. The event was over, and they hadn't had a second death. Mia called that a win.

She moved over to Abigail, who was greeting people as they left. She waited for her to be free, then stepped closer. "So, a surprise ending, huh?"

"Maybe for some people. I've been rooting for Melody all this time. She deserved the win. Here she comes with her grandmother."

The aide Mia had seen before was on one side of Elly Sellers, and Melody was on the other. Melody was telling her grandmother that she'd be home as soon as she changed and gathered up her things.

Bambi broke in. "Melody, we need you up front again. We're doing pictures."

The woman who was helping Elly waved Melody off. "Don't worry about a thing. I'll get her home, and my relief is coming at nine. We won't leave her alone."

Elly snorted. "You all worry too much about an old

lady. Melody, go celebrate your win. And make sure you get the paperwork on that scholarship. We need to get you off to college next fall."

Apparently, it was a good day for both Melody and Elly Sellers. Melody hugged her and told her she'd be home as soon as possible. Melody and Bambi took off for the front, and Elly Sellers leaned against her caregiver. "What a nice night. So glad the event was fair this year. Sometimes kids just don't have a fighting chance."

Mia squeezed Elly's hand. "I couldn't agree more. Thank you so much for coming tonight."

"I wouldn't miss this for the world. Wasn't Sherry beautiful tonight?"

The aide sighed and sadly smiled at Mia as she answered, "She was gorgeous."

As they went to the parking lot to leave, Abigail shook her head. "That poor girl."

"I know, right? I'm so glad she won this. Now she can go to school wherever she wants. The coven just needs to take care of Elly." Mia glanced around the quickly emptying area. The school doors had been closed with signs directing everyone to leave through the parking lot. Mia glanced at her watch. It was just after nine. "Should we gather the gang for a debrief?"

"Can we do it Monday night? Thomas and I have late dinner reservations at the Lodge." Abigail twirled in the blue sparkling dress. "Since we're dressed up, I thought we should take advantage of it."

"That's a great idea. I wish I'd thought of it." She felt someone behind her, and Trent leaned down to kiss her neck.

"Actually, you didn't have to. We're doing a double date with Christina and Levi at the steakhouse over in Sun Valley. They went ahead to hold the reservation, and we're supposed to follow as soon as we get everyone out of here. So, go find Bambi and have her help you round up the stragglers. Mom, I'll stop by Sunday morning for breakfast. Mia wants me to go looking for one of her old boyfriends she's lost." Trent shooed Mia toward the door. She hurried through the gym, checking the bathrooms for people as she went. When she got to the reception area, Crissy and her aunt were leaving through the front door.

Mia called out, but they didn't respond. But then Crissy turned, and Mia saw the tears on her cheeks. "We'll see you tomorrow for the parade."

Crissy nodded, and the door shut. As Mia was moving toward the stairs, she saw the storage room door open. She went back and turned on the lights. "Hello? Is anyone in here?"

No one answered, so she walked through the room. Nobody was in there, but as she walked back through the room, she saw the dead bolt to the door leading to the parking lot had been turned.

Had someone just used the door to leave, shutting it after them? But if so, why? She opened the door and saw a string of cars in the lot, trying to leave. No one was standing in the bushes. Which was a good thing. Mia hadn't thought about that when she'd opened the door. She relocked the door, then left the storage room, turning off lights as she went. Tomorrow she'd check the video surveillance and see what had happened.

She headed upstairs to make sure the rest of the contestants and Bambi were on their way out.

Mia didn't mention the unlocked door to Trent until they were on their way back from dinner.

"Why didn't you say something?" He turned to look at her in the darkened truck cab. "What if someone had been out there?"

"I would have said something then. Look, maybe one of the families knew about the door and thought it was fun to use it. Or used it as a shortcut to their car. Anyway, I made sure everyone was out before we left the school. Cerby and Mr. Darcy are upstairs in the apartment as secure as we can make them with the Dorian factor. And we had a nice dinner without worrying about anything for once." Mia paused. "Except now I'm worried about Brad. I think someone has kidnapped him and is holding him hostage here in Magic Springs for some reason."

"And that scenario is more likely than that he got cold feet because he recently moved in with a long-term girlfriend?" Trent asked.

"When you put it like that, no. But that's what my vision showed me." Mia rolled her shoulders. She was tired and ready to give up for the day.

"That vision spell can be co-opted if you're already worried about something. Didn't your grandmother tell you not to use it on your own problems?" Trent turned down the music so they could talk.

"Yeah, but I didn't understand why." Mia turned toward him, watching his profile in the dim light.

Trent laughed. "This is why. That's why we have

others help us. You put your own fears into the spell, and the vision will show you what you're most afraid of. That's probably why the wax covered the picture. It needed to stop the vision before you went further."

"Do you think that's true?" Mia didn't have the experience Trent had, but she'd seen Brad. And he'd talked to her. Then what had been bothering her came to the surface. "Oh, no. That's what was wrong. I couldn't put my finger on it. The Brad in my vision knew I was a witch and was doing a spell to find him. He shouldn't know I'm a witch. I never told him."

"Exactly. That was your subconscious talking to you and filling in what it thought you wanted to hear." He turned the truck onto the road that would take them home. "So, what time should I pick you up in the morning?"

"Grans is coming at eight, but now I don't think it's to bring me furniture. She said she was bringing a gift, but she wouldn't say much more." She thought about their interaction. "Hey, does Robert talk to you?"

"When he's around? Sure. We talk about the weather and golf. He loves to play. Why?"

"He doesn't talk to me. I'm beginning to get a complex."

Trent didn't say anything, but Mia could feel that he wanted to.

They were getting close to the school. "Okay, spill."

"You asked for it. I've never seen you instigate a conversation with him. It's all toward your grandmother. I think he thinks you don't like him. That you're in the Dorian camp. Especially since Dorian actually lives in your apartment." Trent pulled the truck into the parking lot. "I'll follow you up and grab Cerby."

"You could stay for a while." Mia slipped out of the truck and unlocked the front door.

He chuckled as he shut the door behind him. "Maybe tomorrow night. I'm beat. Being helpful all day has taken it out of me. Not to mention looking for any of the hundred signs Mom listed off."

"She was thorough." Mia glanced toward the storage room, but the door appeared to be closed.

"Do you want me to check it out?"

She sighed. "If you don't, I'll have to. Now it's in my brain."

"I'll check the door and be right up. Go on up and see if Cerby and Mr. Darcy have killed each other yet."

Mia hurried up the stairs but saw a light on in the prep room. She walked in, and the room was empty. No makeup or brushes on the table. There was a lot of trash in the room, but nothing else. The contest was over, and the girls had moved on. She turned off the light and closed the door. She'd call Bambi tomorrow or Jeani and see when the rental company was coming to pick up the furniture.

As she unlocked the apartment door, she heard Trent's steps behind her. "Everything okay?"

"It's fine." He leaned down and caught Cerby as he flew out the door. "Hey, buddy, ready to head home?"

Cerby barked at him. Which either meant "yes" or "I need to pee." Or, Mia thought, maybe both.

"I'll see you in the morning." She kissed him. "Lock the front door as you leave?"

He dangled his keys. "I was already planning on it. Sleep well."

Mia tried to follow his advice, but she rolled over after a couple of hours and stared at Mr. Darcy. "What's wrong with me that I can't sleep?"

The cat must have been annoyed at her constant movement, because he jumped down and ran out of the room. Christina was staying over with Levi tonight. Abigail had gone home, as had Grans, so it was just the two of them in the apartment. And she had just run off her cat.

CHAPTER 22

The next morning, Mia was awake too early for the time she'd finally fallen asleep the night before. Grans pulled into the driveway in Robert's Grand Wagoneer exactly at eight. Mia had made a casserole for breakfast along with a batch of cinnamon rolls. And she'd started a second pot of coffee. With the harvest queen contest off her worry list, she should have slept like a log last night. But she hadn't. Hopefully after a day out in the sun for the festival, she wouldn't fall asleep in Trent's truck as soon as they got in to come back to the school.

Mia rubbed Mr. Darcy's ears. "Look, Grans is here, but she brought Robert. So, if you're going to be a jerk, maybe you should hide out in my bedroom or head outside to chase mice?"

Mr. Darcy just yawned and curled up tighter.

"Okay, then. Don't say I didn't warn you." Mia headed

downstairs to unlock the front door. Abigail was coming over at ten to meet the rental company as they gathered up the furniture from the prep room. Christina and Levi were putting away the chairs and cleaning the backyard before they came over to the festival. Mia had offered to help, but Abigail and Christina told her to take the weekend off since she'd used vacation time from the Lodge for last week's event.

She unlocked the front door, and Muffy ran to her, barking a greeting. Mia leaned down and picked up the little dog. "I know, it's been forever since I saw you too."

Muffy licked her face, then cuddled into her arms. She looked back at Robert's car and saw someone sitting in the back. Robert was helping Grans out of the car, then they both turned to the back and helped another man out. Mia squinted, but she couldn't believe her eyes.

Dorian Alexander, Grans's former boyfriend and the witch whose soul was currently residing in Mr. Darcy, walked toward her. He smiled and looked around the school, but even from a distance, Mia could see that he wasn't really there. What did her dad say all the time? "*The lights are on but no one's home.*"

"Grans, what on earth did you do?" Mia hurried them into the school and closed the door. Dorian stood in the lobby, waiting.

"I told you I was working on a project." Grans patted Dorian's chest. "This is a golem. He's made up of some of Dorian's DNA, so you could say he was a clone. Like in those sci-fi movies they advertise. Abigail was right—I can't send Dorian onward. Not anymore. He needs to make that decision. But I can get him out of Mr. Darcy."

"You're remaking Dorian?" Mia didn't know what to ask first. "But the world thinks he's dead."

"I petitioned the coven, and if this transfer is successful, they'll set up Dorian in another city where he can live out his life. The new coven will watch for any degradation in the golem body and handle it if need be. But Mr. Darcy will be clear of the second soul, and you won't be stuck watching out for Dorian. Now, let's get him set up in the spare bedroom, and I'll do the transfer spell. Then, tomorrow morning, we'll know. Either way, Mr. Darcy will be back to normal in about five minutes."

Mia followed them up to the apartment. Maybe this was why she hadn't slept last night. She'd figured it had to be the missing Brad. And maybe why the Goddess had sent Cerby to Trent to watch over them.

As if she'd called out for his help, Trent came in the front door with the mini hellhound. Muffy wriggled out of Mia's arms, and she let him down before he fell. The two dogs greeted each other like long-lost friends.

Grans turned and smiled at Trent. "I'm glad you're here. Right on time."

"I aim to please." He looked at Mia and then at the Dorian golem, his eyes widening as he realized what must be happening. "Are we doing some spell casting today?"

"I need to get this Dorian project done and his new body out of my house. I can't even list it until I clean both of the bathrooms. And how would I explain a naked man hanging around the house?" Grans explained, but Mia was still in shock about seeing Dorian—or the Dorian doll—walking around her school. Mia had found Dorian's body when he was killed. Now the coven wanted to reanimate the man? Or were they just seeing how far Grans could go with the process?

As they opened the apartment door, Mr. Darcy looked up and meowed loudly.

"Get that door closed. We only have a few hours to finish the transfer before the golem starts to break down. It needs a soul to live." Grans nodded to the bedroom and went over to pick up Mr. Darcy. Holding him up to her face, she stared into the cat's eyes. "I'm sorry it took me this long to figure out an answer."

Mia could hear her cat's purring from where she stood. Dorian must be on board. She took a big breath. "I guess we're doing this. What do you need from me?"

"Just your presence. We don't need a full thirteen, but the four of us will give more of a controlled transfer process." Grans followed Robert into the hallway. "Let's go get you a body."

Mr. Darcy meowed, and Cerby and Muffy jumped up on the couch. Grans turned back to Mia. "Lock the apartment door, dear. It's better if we're not interrupted."

An hour later, the new and improved Dorian was dozing on the bed, and Mr. Darcy was running up and down the hallway in what Mia had heard explained as zoomies. He went to the door, sat there, then ran back to her, a big cat grin on his face. Or as big of a grin as cats ever got. Mia picked him up and rubbed his head. "How does it feel to be alone in there?"

The purr was immediate and the only answer she needed. Her cat was back to being just a cat. And her familiar.

Dorian opened his eyes and smiled at her and Mr. Darcy. "Thank you," he muttered, then he closed his eyes again and fell asleep.

Grans moved them all out of the room. "We'll let him sleep. The coven will come over and pick him up around noon. Abigail will still be here, right?"

"I think so." Mia set Mr. Darcy on the floor. "I could call her."

"She's downstairs. I can feel her." Grans patted Mia's arm. "I'll just let her know what's going on and ask her to stay. Then we're heading to the festival."

"So are we." Mia glanced back at the closed bedroom door. "Unless you need me to stay."

Grans shook her head. "No, the fewer people around him in the next few hours, the better. Besides, you wanted to see the parade. You two get out of here. Muffy, come here. It's time to leave."

The group moved downstairs to the front door. Mia paused and looked back upstairs.

"What's going on in your head? Aren't you happy?" Trent asked as Grans and Robert went to find Abigail.

Mia let out a big breath. "I can't believe that Dorian is going to have a second chance at life. Well, not his life—he's in a weird coven witness protection program—but he's not dead."

"He wasn't dead, or at least gone from this world all this time. His body was, but he was alive in Mr. Darcy.

There is a lot we don't understand about what makes us human. But I know one thing—it's not just our body having a heartbeat or being able to take a breath." Trent pulled her into a hug. "It's been a crazy morning, let's go have some fun at the festival. Cerby? Are you ready to go?"

The little dog barked, and Mia wondered if he knew he might run into Muffy there. Or if he was just happy to be with his human. And his human's girlfriend. Mia decided she wasn't going to think about anything harder than whether or not to have a third corn dog or to ride the Tilt-a-Whirl or the Scrambler or both. She'd think about the moral repercussions of what they'd done that morning at another time.

"Is *Frankenstein* required reading in the witch-in-training program?" she asked as she grabbed her bag.

"See, you are learning." Trent pulled her into a hug without directly answering the question.

When they got to the parade route, Bambi found them. She had sweat running down her cheek. "Oh, good. Have you seen Melody?"

Mia handed Cerby's leash back to Trent. "Not since last night. Why?"

"She didn't come to practice for the parade this morning. Now Crissy wants to step into her queen role since she's not here."

Trent rolled his eyes. "Tell Crissy to hold her horses. Mia and I will run over to the Sellers' house and find out what's going on. Did you tried to call?"

"I'm not an idiot, Mr. Majors." Bambi waved to someone across the way. "Just let me know if you find her. The parade starts in thirty minutes."

Mia and Trent headed back toward the park entrance. The Sellers' house was just a block away. They could get there and back in ten minutes tops. Mia figured Bambi hadn't wanted to walk that far in the high heels she'd worn. "Bambi's a little high-strung for this job, don't you think?"

"You should apply for the job. You've planned a magical wedding. How different could that be from a harvest queen contest?" Trent teased as they made their way off the festival grounds. He stopped a girl who was eating cotton candy as she walked by. "Hey, aren't you Melody's friend?"

The girl paused like she was going to rabbit, then she smiled. "I'm Tera. You're Mr. Majors, from the store, and Miss Malone, I recognize you from the pageant. Wasn't that crazy that Melody beat out Crissy? I bet she was mad. Crissy told everyone she was winning this thing."

"It was quite the upset. Hey, have you seen Melody? Is she here?" Mia asked.

"She was. We were on the rides, but then she got a call. She said she had to go home and change, and she'd see me after the parade." Tera held out the pink cotton candy. "She left this with me, knowing I can't help myself. Now I've eaten hers and mine. And a corn dog."

"Well, if you see Melody, tell her that Bambi is looking for her." Mia started walking again, looking over at the line for the corn dogs. "Now I'm hungry."

"I'll buy lunch as soon as we track down Melody. I'd hate for Crissy to take all the glory this early in Melody's reign."

The street was pedestrians-only until Monday so people could park at the empty lot across from the park, but since they were leaving the park and not coming in, they were going against the traffic flow. Finally, they made it through the crowd and went up to the porch of a well-maintained Craftsman-style house. When Trent knocked, the door swung open.

"That's not good." He tied Cerby's leash to the porch railing and called out, "Melody? Mrs. Sellers? Is anyone home?"

"Maybe they just forgot to close the door when they left?" Mia could feel the fear surrounding them. "Please tell me that Melody wasn't the one doing the retribution spell. She was in the school too many times by herself. I passed it off and took her excuses as valid, but Trent, please tell me that the spell is too advanced for a teenager."

Trent stepped into the house. "It is way too advanced. Besides, the coven binds the contestants from doing magic when they are chosen for the contest. It's automatic. I wish they bound their entire families, then Carla wouldn't be dead."

Mia felt better. A lot better. She liked Melody. She didn't want her to be behind the terrible magic that was happening. "Melody? Are you in here?"

A sound came from the basement. A part of her vision came back to her. "Trent, Brad's in the basement."

"Now, why would Brad be in the Sellers.' basement?" Trent asked, but before Mia could answer, something hit her head, and she fell to the floor. She heard Cerby barking from a long way away.

When she woke, she was tied to a chair, and Trent

was out cold on the floor in front of her. His hands were tied to a table. Cerby was still barking. Elly Sellers stood in front of them with a frying pan in her hand.

"Now, don't you two move. I can't have anyone stopping Sherry from winning the queen contest." Elly blinked and cocked her head. "Does anyone hear a dog barking?"

Cerby was trying to get them help. Mia blinked, shaking her head to clear the cobwebs the blow had caused. "Mrs. Sellers, Elly. The contest was last night. Melody won."

Elly frowned, setting the pan on the stove. "Melody? No, Sherry was supposed to win this year. It's her turn."

A male voice called up from the basement. "Sherry's dead, Mrs. Sellers. She was killed in a car accident, remember?"

It *was* Brad talking. She'd found him. Which wouldn't do either one of them any good since he must be tied up downstairs. "Melody played the piano for her talent. You were there. It was beautiful."

Elly rubbed her head. "Melody plays like me."

Thank the Goddess. "Yes, she does." Mia thought that maybe Elly was actually with them. Now Mia was worried about Melody. "Where is Melody? Where's your granddaughter?"

Elly shook her head and rubbed the pan. "Sherry hated practicing all the time. But I told her it would win her the contest, and look, it did."

Mia's hope faded. Elly was too far gone and lost in a world where her daughter was still alive and young. Her granddaughter, Melody, hadn't even been born yet.

"Sherry's dead, Mrs. Sellers," Brad started again, but this time Elly stood and banged on the door.

"Shut up. Stop saying such mean things. Sherry's at the contest. She's going to be queen—then her life will start, and she'll be ready to win it all," Elly screamed down the stairs.

When her back was turned, Mia saw a face at the back door. It was Melody. She waved and then held up a finger. She was trying to tell her something. One? One minute? One second? Or was it more deadly?

As Elly slammed the basement door and leaned against it, Trent moaned. Distracted by his pain, Mia didn't see when two deputies stormed into the kitchen. After taking away her frying pan, they put handcuffs on the elderly woman, who was sobbing for her lost daughter.

Mark Baldwin allowed Melody to go back to the festival with a deputy to ride the parade float. In fact, he insisted she go. Mia thought he wanted to try to piece the mess in front of him together without Melody hearing it all.

Melody paused by Mia before she left. "You'll watch out for Grandma?"

Mia wasn't sure that Elly Sellers needed much watching out for, since she'd brought both her and Trent down with just one pan. Trent had an ice pack on his head that matched her own. Brad was up from the basement now and sat at the table with them. She focused on Melody. "Go do your queen responsibilities. I'll watch out for your grandmother."

"Thanks, Mia." She let the deputy lead her away.

Mark waited for them to leave the house, then looked at Mia. "Do you want to tell me what's going on here? How did an elderly dementia patient knock all three of you out?"

Mia pointed to the cast-iron skillet. "There's your answer right there. We were here, looking for Melody for Bambi. She was worried she was going to miss the parade."

"I hate this queen contest." Baldwin glanced at Brad. "So, you're Brad Heinrich from Twin Falls? Have you been down in the basement since Wednesday? Your girlfriend is very worried about you."

Brad sipped some water, nodding. "Wednesday's my day off. Mia called and invited me to have a late dinner to catch up. She said she had some news about Sherry."

"Brad, I didn't call you. We had dinner the week before, and I was busy with the contest on Wednesday. It was talent night, and I was the timekeeper for Bambi," Mia pointed out.

"Someone called the restaurant and said it was you. That you wanted to meet at the Lodge at nine." Brad drank most of the bottle of water that was in front of him.

"Maybe it was Elly." Trent didn't seem convinced. "But how would she know where you worked? And that you knew Mia?"

"Good question. I think I have the message in my car." Brad took a second bottle of water from Mark. His eyes widened as he looked at the water. "Is this from here?"

Mark shook his head. "I carry water in the truck, just in case. So you came up for a late dinner with Mia . . ."

"*Not* with Mia," she corrected. When she saw the look from Mark, she rolled her hand. "Fine, go ahead with your story."

"Okay, so I was early. I was having a drink in the bar, then an old friend of Sherry's saw me. She came over to chat, and after a few minutes, she told me I needed to talk to the Sellers. That it was important. So I came over to see the Sellers. Sherry and I had dated before she died. She got pregnant, and we gave away the baby. Or so I thought. Anyway, when I saw Melody in pictures all around the house here, I realized Sherry hadn't given up the baby like she'd told me. Melody looks just like her."

"You and Sherry Sellers had a baby?" Mark didn't look up from his notebook as he waited for the answer.

"Yes. Like I said, she told me she put the baby up for adoption, and that she needed some time. Then she was killed in that car accident. I was just a kid. I couldn't have raised a child on my own. With Sherry, maybe, but not by myself."

Mark nodded. "So you came over to see the Sellers. I take it you didn't know Jake was dead?"

Brad shook his head. "I tried not to think about Sherry or her family. But when I saw the pictures of Melody, I asked Elly about her. She said she'd tell me everything, but she needed a box from the basement. That she kept Sherry's things down there. She'd given me a bottle of water before we went down, and I guess it had something in it, because I felt dizzy and fell down once I got down the stairs. I've been trying to get anyone to even notice me since."

"One last question—who was the woman you talked to in the bar?" Mark asked as he read what he had written in his notebook.

"I don't know her last name, but Sherry always called her Titi. They went to school together."

Chapter 23

Mia and Trent went back to the festival and caught the tail end of the parade. Melody waved at them as the float passed by, but Crissy had her hands crossed in front of her and didn't crack a smile. She was obviously still mad about not winning.

Mia was quiet as they stood in line for a corn dog.

"Earth to Mia. Should we visit the hospital after all? How are you feeling?" Trent pulled out his wallet and paid for the food. Then they handed him two corn dogs right out of the fryer. The server had slathered a paint brush serving of mustard on both.

"Just wondering if 'Titi' is Tatiana." Mia took her corn dog, and they went to sit on a bench that overlooked the duck pond. Cerby sat between them, staring at the food. "We should have gotten another one without mustard."

"The name 'Titi' is a little generic. Maybe we could find the yearbook for when Sherry was in high school.

Anyway, Cerby's fine. Contrary to the way he's looking right now, he doesn't like hot dogs. They make him sick, so no, Cerby doesn't get a corn dog, with or without mustard." Trent rubbed the top of Cerby's head. "Who was a good guard dog?"

"He was stuck outside the entire time." Mia took a bite of the corn dog. It was heaven. Then she thought about the yearbook. "I wonder if Elly kept Sherry's yearbooks. I could ask Melody once she's done playing harvest queen. I'll run by the house tomorrow."

"I'll take you there. I'm not sure if they're going to let Elly stay at home since she has started a hobby of kidnapping people." Trent looked at her. "Okay, I guess it's too soon to make jokes."

"I was thinking the same thing. I wanted to talk to Melody about the changes that are going to happen and if she has anyone to help her navigate all this." Mia watched the people walking by them. "I'm glad Cerby didn't out his other side, and actually, you and your magic."

"I *was* surprised that he didn't turn when I was attacked. For some reason, he didn't seem that worried about us." Trent pulled off a bit of the cornmeal coating and gave it to Cerby. "So, maybe I take that 'good guard dog' description back."

"But what if he knew we weren't in real danger from Elly? He barked to try to get someone's attention, but he didn't change." Mia finished off her corn dog. This was what was bothering her. "Melody said she'd discovered Brad in the basement when she came home to change. Then she ran to get Mark. She was smart and didn't try to convince her grandmother she was wrong to hold him. Elly thought she was protecting Sherry from Brad. Nothing about the contest."

"Except when we were there, she'd said it was Sherry's turn." Trent took the paper basket, napkins, and sticks and put them in a nearby trash can. "You don't think she was trying to fix the contest?"

Mia shook her head. "I think it was Tatiana. I think she spelled herself once Zeus turned her down. Think about it. If everyone knows there's a retribution spell—and they did, because I told them—then Tatiana needed to be affected, too, or she would have been outed as the person who cast the spell."

"Your logic, although twisted, is sound." Trent dialed his phone. "Hey, I know you're busy at the Sellerses' house, but has Tatiana Evans left the hospital yet?"

Mia watched as Trent listened to Mark's answer. Finally, he hung up. Mia waited, but Trent didn't say anything. She poked him in the arm, "Well . . ."

"She went home last night, after the contest. She signed herself out at nine forty, against medical advice. According to the nurse who called Mark to let him know, Tatiana was livid. Melody was crowned at nine thirty." Trent held out his hand. "I think we need to go back to the school and make sure there's not a trap that Melody avoided. Tatiana really thought Crissy was going to win."

"I think Crissy did as well. The look on her face when they announced Melody as the winner was total shock." Mia took Trent's hand, and they headed to the road. They'd walked down the hill to the festival grounds since parking was at a premium. Now Trent led her to the greenbelt, and they took off for home. When they got there, Mia unlocked the door. The house was completely empty. She could feel Mr. Darcy upstairs, sleeping in the living room, but besides that, everyone had left.

She went upstairs to the prep room and stood in the doorway, studying it. She scanned the entire room. It was empty except for several large trash cans and a small one at each girl's area. Mia went over to where Melody's prep area was located. In the trash can was a wrapped gift box. Mia used a pen she'd found in her tote to open it. The box was filled with unopened, high-end makeup, in exactly Melody's shade. A note was wadded up and also in the trash.

Mia took it out and tried to rub out the wrinkles. It was addressed to Melody and signed "Tatiana and Crissy." Mia took a minute to read the letter. It seemed harmless. A friendly gesture. Tatiana had bought the makeup for Melody because she and her mom had been close friends. She missed Sherry so badly and wanted Melody to know that even with her mom gone, she still had friends.

Mia set the note on the ground. Then, with an open palm, she asked to talk to the magic. A storm of dark energy rushed through her like it had been kept locked up for years. The magic was looking for its target— Melody. Or, Mia thought, as the power began to chatter at her, it would settle for its maker. She tried to pull her hand away, but the spell was too strong. She felt Trent pull her upright and away from the trash can, and the spell's power on her started to dissipate.

"Mia, are you all right?" Trent stared into her eyes as she nodded.

She stepped back again, and Cerby started barking at the trash can. "Tatiana was the one doing the spelling. Since nothing else had worked, she decided to attack Melody directly. She wasn't going to lose, not this time."

"Wait, what does that mean, 'not this time'?" Trent picked Cerby up and stepped away from the trash can.

"Sherry won the year Tatiana competed. I think if we look at the history, we'll find that Sherry was on her way to the next year's contest to pass on the crown. Tatiana hit her with her car and killed her." Mia leaned against the wall, staring at the trash can and trying to grasp the emotions and memories that were flowing through her.

"You got that just from opening up your magic?"

"*Emotions and the Modern Witch*, the book I read a few months back? It had an opening spell that I've been practicing. I didn't realize it would go so far back." Mia felt herself starting to black out. "I need to sit . . ."

Mia woke up on the couch in her living room. Cerby and Mr. Darcy sat next to her, one on each side, watching her. When she opened her eyes, Cerby licked her hand, and Mr. Darcy patted the other one. "You two are pretty amazing nurses, aren't you?"

"They've been there since I carried you up here." Trent came into view with a cup of what smelled like hot cocoa. "You've been out for just about an hour. I called your grandmother, and she said you'd be fine and to feed you soup when you woke up. So, I've got some chicken soup warming up on the stove. I found some downstairs in the freezer in your work kitchen."

"You've been busy." Mia sat up, moving the animals to the side so she could drink the cocoa. "Grans says this is normal?"

"I guess for the first time you try the spell on a murderous, angry woman's thoughts, it is." He sat on the other chair. "Mom found the report from the coven on the contests the year Sherry won and the next year. Apparently, Tatiana stepped in as first runner-up and gave away Sherry's crown that year. She had also appealed to get her booted because she was pregnant when she won. Mark had been given the files when Tatiana attacked Zeus."

"So, he was already looking at her." Mia sipped the cocoa, starting to feel better.

"Yes and no. He thought 'Titi' could have been Tatiana too. He's going over to the Lodge to see if they still have video from Wednesday night. Basically, he still isn't quite sure he can charge her with anything." Trent sank back into the chair. "I was really worried about you."

"I'm fine." Mia sighed. "Can't Mark link the makeup to Tatiana? There has to be something in the mix that is a human poison."

"He's coming over to get it. He said he'll have it tested. And the letter and makeup are at least enough to pull her in for questioning again."

She heard a whisper in her ear. Turning, she saw Carla's ghost.

"It's the same poison. Have them test it against my results. She did this. She wanted Crissy to win since she didn't." Carla smiled and then slowly faded.

"Mia? Are you okay?" Trent was staring at her.

"Carla just stopped by. I can't believe you can't see her." Mia rubbed her arms, then grasped her hot cocoa. The cup was already cold. Carla had been too close. "I need to warm this up and call Mark."

"I told you, I already talked to Mark." Trent followed her into the kitchen. "Are you sure you should be moving around?"

"I'm fine. Carla just told me it was the same potion. When she said the 'sins of the father,' I think she meant the parent—not just a father. That Tatiana killed Sherry. And that she was going to do whatever she could to make sure Crissy won this year. It's all about the past. That's why Carla died, that's why Marnie was attacked, and that's why Brad was kidnapped. Of course, Tatiana didn't do that, but she did set him up. I wouldn't have been surprised if she was the one who put the idea in Elly's head. And we need to check her phone records."

"I know, for the call to the restaurant." Trent nodded. "Mark's already got a warrant in process for her records."

"And the call this morning. Melody got a call from someone to go home and change. And Bambi said she hadn't been able to reach her at all. So, who called her to send her away from the parade float? And why did Crissy think she was taking over?"

After Mia got off the phone, Trent had set the table with soup and rolls for dinner for both of them. She also had another cup of hot cocoa in front of her. "Thanks."

"What did he say? I heard most of it, and it didn't seem like he was getting it. He made you repeat a lot."

Mia sipped her cocoa. "The problem is, a lot of the clues I gave him were magic-based. I mean, they happened in real life, but how I got the information involved magic. Even though he accepts that magic exists now since his daughter is a witch, he can't take it to a human court as evidence. But he did say there's a lot of circumstantial evidence that should be able to get him a warrant. Especially since the judge is also a coven member. The coven wants this done. And to set Tatiana as an example for next year's harvest queen contest."

"And we're back to that can of worms." Trent took a spoonful of soup. "This is really good."

Mia smiled. "Of course, it is. It's made with magic."

CHAPTER 24

On Sunday morning, the Magic Springs Sleuthing Club gathered around Mia's kitchen table. This time Thomas joined the group so there were seven of them. Ten, if you counted the animals—Mr. Darcy, Cerby, and Muffy—sleeping under the table. Dorian was gone. He was in a coven safe house somewhere, learning how to integrate with the golem body Grans had built for him. Mia looked around the crowded table and wondered how her life had become so full after she'd thought she'd lost everything except Grans and Mr. Darcy.

Mia's mother, Theresa, had dropped off her old yearbooks the night before and had stayed to chat about Sherry and Elly. She'd called Melody and offered to handle the legal process of the girl becoming her grandmother's guardian. Brad wasn't pressing charges for his stay in the Sellers' basement, and he'd promised to be more of a father since he now knew he actually had a daughter.

Mia thought Melody might just have all the family she needed right now. She'd stop by next week and see how things were going for the new harvest queen.

Mark Baldwin had Tatiana in custody and had swept her house last night. They'd sent Crissy over to stay with her aunt. And, he reported to Mia, all the circumstantial evidence they'd come up with against Tatiana had been verified when they found an entire project room. She'd kept a listing of all the things she'd done, what the reactions had been, and her next steps. Thomas had been listed as a possible "weak link" in the judging process since he and Abigail had been "having problems."

That morning, as Mia relayed what Mark had found at the house, he'd squeezed Abigail's hand. "I know you thought it was a risk, but she bought the cover story."

"She just never had time to put you in play. I don't think she meant for things to get so out of control, and when the theory of a retribution curse came on the scene, it took over as the way for her to get around everything," Mia added to the story. "She admitted to killing Sherry when Mark questioned her. She said everything else wasn't her fault."

"Did she think there was a statute of limitations on murder?" Levi grabbed another muffin. Mia and Abigail had been up early baking, so there was a lot of food for the breakfast meeting.

"According to her new attorney, she misspoke."

Trent handed Levi the butter to spread on the still-warm treat.

"Anyway, it's done. The harvest queen contest is over, and a suspect for Carla's murder and other assorted crimes is now in Mark's jail. Now I can go back to work and just deal with Frank and his games." Mia glanced at her phone when it rang. It was James. "Great. I guess the game-playing has already begun."

She stepped away from the kitchen to answer the call. "James, what's got you up this early on a Sunday?"

"You haven't heard, then. I can't believe it. It's like Christmas in October." James giggled.

Mia tried to rack her brain for something that would make James this happy. "Okay, I give up. What's going on?"

"You know how Frank had to go to corporate this week for an impromptu meeting? Well, he got canned. Fired. He's out of here."

"Are you kidding? What happened?" Mia almost felt bad that Frank's firing was causing such a feeling of joy in both James and herself.

"The lady with the surprise baby shower that wasn't a surprise. Mrs. Davis? She really *did* have some friends on the hotel board. Apparently, she praised you and me for working around Frank and making the shower happen. According to her, she said Frank was trying to tank it and blame us."

"Which we knew, but who knew the board would be so upset?" Mia sank into a chair. Karma was a bad thing. And Frank had gotten a full cup for his antics.

"She's a *really* close friend with several members,"

James repeated. "Anyway, I need to go. I'm getting a pedicure today to celebrate that 'Ding, dong, the wicked witch is dead.'"

Mia was just about to warn him to be careful of what he asked for since Frank's replacement could be worse, but James had already hung up. She went back into the kitchen and sat next to Trent.

He leaned into her. "Everything okay?"

"Yes. More than okay." She suddenly realized she was starving and picked up her fork.

Christina caught her eye. "Sorry, one more thing before we dig in. Levi and I have an announcement. Actually, a couple of announcements."

The room got really quiet as everyone stared at the two of them.

Christina smiled at Levi. "One, I got the job in Portland. It starts in November, so we'll be taking a trip to find a house to buy next week—unless we have a catering job, of course."

Abigial shook her head. "We're clear except for the normal Monday and Tuesday deliveries."

"Good, then we'll take off on Wednesday." Christina turned toward Levi. "And . . ."

"I've asked Christina Adams to marry me, and she said yes, surprisingly." Levi pulled her close and kissed her head. "We're getting married."

Chaos erupted with everyone hugging everyone. The pets moved from their spots under the table and now stood by the hallway, watching the humans.

Finally, everyone sat back down.

"Well, isn't this an exciting time for the two of you!"

Trent caught Mia's gaze and smiled. "Of course, with you two moving, it puts a huge hole in our sleuthing club."

"And I'll have to hire someone else for the business," Abigail added. She leaned into Mia. "With your help, of course."

"I don't think we can ever replace Christina," Mia said, then wiped the tears off her face. "I knew this day would come, when the little girl I met so many years ago would grow up and start her own life, but I thought it might still be a few years down the road."

Christina reached over and squeezed Mia's hand. "You were too good of a surrogate parent. You made me a good person."

Mia shook her head. "I'm not doing this. No crying allowed on this special Sunday. Why don't we all do dinner at the Lodge to celebrate tonight?"

"Dress-up dinner!" Christina bounced in her seat.

Levi and Trent exchanged glances. Levi suggested, "What about pizza and a game night instead?"

Thomas laughed. "Sorry, boys, this is too special of an occasion. You don't want to hear about this for years to come."

"Now, Thomas, when have I ever—" Abigail started, but then he put a finger on her lips and kissed her.

After he returned to his plate, he looked up at his sons. "See what I mean?"

"Levi, let's go downstairs and call my mom and dad. They're going to be so surprised. And I'm sure they're going to want to talk about dates. Maybe we should plan it for next June? And do we want to do it in Magic

Springs? You know Mom's going to want to have it at the Cathedral of Saint John in Boise. It would make for some amazing wedding shots." Christina took Levi's hand and led him out of the kitchen like a lamb to the slaughter.

Abigail took a deep breath. "I hope Christina's mother lives through this wedding, because if she doesn't, I'm going to be at the top of Mark Baldwin's suspect list."

Thomas pulled her into a hug. "We can get through this. Besides"—he looked over at Trent and Mia—"after Levi, we only have one more to dump on an unsuspecting bride."

"Thomas, you're so bad." Abigail stood and picked up his plate. "You need more of Mia's strada. I think you're hangry."

After breakfast, Mia and Trent took Cerby outside for a short walk. Grans had already left with Muffy to start packing up her house. Mia and Trent watched as Christina and Levi pulled out of the parking lot in Levi's Jeep. Trent put his arm around Mia. "Remember when I asked if you thought it would be okay if I asked?"

"Vaguely. A lot has gone on since then." Mia leaned her head again. "Now what? Are you thinking about asking again?"

"Very funny. Anyway, I'm thinking that with the Levi and Christina announcement, we should either plan a double wedding and get it over with or hold off on me asking that question for a while."

Mia groaned. "There is no way I'm doing a wedding with Christina since Mother Adams will be running the show. It's just not happening."

Trent turned her toward him, then leaned down and kissed her. "Okay, then, I'm going to find a perfect time to propose that doesn't involve us doing a joint ceremony. I don't think I could watch Isaac mooning over you without saying something. We don't have to invite that family to our wedding, right?"

"Exactly. Now you're getting my point." She leaned into him. "The chill is starting to hit. I think fall has fallen, and winter is coming."

He rubbed her arms to warm her. "Just be aware, I am going to ask. And soon."

"I hear you." She turned toward the school. The day was a little overcast, and the lights inside made the three-story building look warm and cozy. A place to build a life. A place filled with family, friends, and love. And a lot of food. "And just to warn you, I'm going to say yes. When you ask, that is."

"Then we understand each other," Trent said as they moved toward the front door. "Do you want to watch a movie this afternoon? Something that maybe Cerby would like?"

"We're picking movies based on your dog's interests?" Mia laughed as they closed the front door, leaving the cold air outside.

"Our dog. I thought it might be good practice for when we have to do family-friendly movie nights." He laughed as he headed up the stairs. "You should see your face. You were so into it."

"I was not," Mia cried after him. "I was playing along."

As they made their way upstairs to the apartment on the third floor, Mia felt the joy the school could hold and experience. This was home. And when she moved out, it would be someone else's home. But no matter who lived here, the school would be filled with love.

She'd make sure of it. Mia Malone was a kitchen witch. It was what she did.

ACKNOWLEDGMENTS

Mia and her journey to be a kitchen witch was one of my first attempts at learning to be an author. For several years, I'd get into a story, then drop it at the magical fourth chapter, where I'd realize I didn't know where to go next. After I learned to finish books, I returned to Mia and her grandmother, Mary Alice.

The book started, like many of my story ideas do, with the setting. The idea for Magic Springs came from a Future Homemakers of America state conference at the Sun Valley Lodge as a teenager. I'd never seen something as magical as the lodge that spring as we attended our meetings. When my friends and I were sitting in the hot tub later that first evening, the snow started to fall. That moment is one of the many images I carried around for years before I knew I was a writer. We're all magpies, holding on to special memories, until we can use them in a story.

Many years later, I still feel that same magic when I start to write a story in Mia's world in Magic Springs. And six books later, I'm very thankful that the team at Kensington saw my vision. And I'm very grateful for my new editor, Michaela Hamilton, who has championed my books, which she inherited. I also am blessed to have Jill Marsal as my agent, helping me navigate the sometimes-stormy waters of being an author.

RECIPE

A Kitchen Witch Staple—Chicken Soup

Dear Readers:

My mother had one motto—nothing goes to waste. That meant if the freezer was down to what the fancy chefs call "sweetbreads," it was a liver-and-onions night at the farmhouse. (And I had a peanut-butter sandwich.) Or if we had roast chicken on Sunday, you can be sure that there would be chicken noodle soup sometime the next week. I'm not continuing the liver-and-onions tradition, but I do like to make homemade chicken noodle soup.

My mom cooked out of one cookbook (my sister has it) and her own memories and feelings. Recipes that were handed down were simple and had measurements like *add lard the size of a walnut*. What kind of walnut? Big, little, shelled, or whole—that secret died with my grandmother.

So, when Mia needed a pick-me-up from a nasty magic spell, it was only natural that Grans would prescribe homemade chicken noodle soup. It's one of my go-to soups, especially when I'm not feeling my best.

I hope you enjoy,

Lynn

Homemade Chicken Noodle Soup

In a large stockpot or Dutch oven, put the carcass of a roasted chicken and any leftover meat from the chicken. Add a roughly chopped onion; two peeled, roughly cut carrots; a teaspoon of minced garlic; and salt and pepper. Cover the ingredients with water and simmer for 30 to 45 minutes or until the meat is falling off the bone.

Drain the liquid into a bowl, then return to the empty stockpot.

Clean the meat off the chicken carcass and shred it. Return the meat to the stockpot with the liquid (off the heat). Chop any onion and carrot bits into bite-sized pieces and return that to the broth as well. Add enough store-bought chicken broth to have approximately eight cups of broth (probably at least four more cups).

Put back on the heat and bring broth to a boil. Salt and pepper to taste. You can also add ½ teaspoon dried thyme and ½ teaspoon dried oregano if you'd like.

Add either twelve ounces of egg noodles or home-made noodles from recipe below.

Boil until noodles are done, then serve.

Homemade Noodles

These are the best, carbs be darned. Mine turn out a little thick, but I like them that way.

Combine one large egg, two tablespoons water, and ½ teaspoon salt in a bowl. Add one cup flour and stir until a dough forms, adding more flour as needed, a little at a time, for the dough to come together. Roll out and cut into thin noodle strips. I've used a noodle maker before, but I love the hand-cut noodles.

Cook in the hot broth for ten minutes or until done.

Are you over the moon about Lynn Cahoon?
If so, you won't want to miss her other series,
including the delightful TOURIST TRAP mysteries.
Keep reading to enjoy an excerpt from her next
scheduled release . . .
VOWS OF MURDER
A TOURIST TRAP Mystery
Coming soon from Lyrical Press, an imprint of
Kensington Publishing Corp.

CHAPTER 1

The South Cove, California, January's business-to-business meeting's agenda was pretty light. I had volunteered to run the meeting since Darla Taylor was on vacation this week with her boyfriend, Matt. I looked down at the list of things we still needed to cover in the last thirty minutes before people would abandon the meeting to open their businesses. I didn't blame them. My own staff members, Judith Dame and Deek Kerr, were both busy helping customers who were wandering through the bookstore and lining up for coffee to get them through a busy day of shopping. Everyone was looking for the perfect system to reframe their New Year's resolutions.

"The city council wanted to let you know that next year, they're closing Main Street the weekend of Thanksgiving through New Year's Day. It's to protect Santa's workshop. There have been complaints that cars have been parking where Santa's sleigh and reindeer are supposed to park." I looked around the room. "They say it's a safety hazard. This isn't up for debate here. If you want to complain, call City Hall."

My best friend, Amy Newman Cross, gave me a dirty look. She would probably be the one fielding those calls. "Call your city council reps instead. I'm sure they'd love to hear from you. And besides, they'll probably forget before next Christmas."

"It makes it hard for people to carry big-ticket items from your store to their cars if the street is closed," Josh Thomas spoke up. He ran Antiques by Thomas next door to my bookstore. "I suppose you expect everyone to provide delivery service?"

"Or they could go behind your store and pick up large items in the alley," I pointed out. Josh always wanted to complain without looking for another alternative. "Anyway, there are a few more items for today, but they're related to the winter festival starting on the fifteenth, so I'll have Darla send out an email next week. Don't ignore it, please. One more thing, if you haven't received your invitation yet, Greg King and I are getting married next Sunday at the La Purisima Mission at three p.m. sharp. After that, we'll have a reception on the grounds as well. Hopefully, the weather will hold out for as long as the band wants to play."

At least I hoped we were finally getting married. It had been scheduled for June, October, and now, January. I hoped Greg's mom would feel up to making the trip this month. If not, we were still getting married. Come hell or high water, as my aunt always said. I thought that maybe saying it aloud was tempting disaster.

"It should be lovely," Brandi Leaven, the owner of the newest business, a jewelry shop, added. "My husband and I went there just last week to walk around and tour. Of course, we didn't see the ghost, but it was early. Hopefully, he'll show up for your festivities. His appearance is supposed to be a blessing."

"Hopefully not," Amy murmured.

Brandi turned her head and glared at my friend.

Before she could say anything, I jumped in. "Unless there is anything else?"

Kane Matthews stood and held up a hand. "Sorry to delay closing, but I want to invite everyone to our open house at the compound the next Friday. We still have all our holiday decorations up and would love to have our neighbors come and see our new home."

The Central California Society for the Advancement of the Mind and Body was a new addition to our town. CCSAMB—or Cscam—as most locals called it, was a group of over a hundred people who lived on a ranch outside of town. The first thing the group had done when they'd purchased the property was put a stone wall all around the hundred acres. Then they'd added a black gate and guardhouse that was staffed twenty-four/seven. Before they'd registered with the city as a religious organization, the townsfolk had assumed that a celebrity from Hollywood was moving in.

Instead, now we had our own cult. Greg hated it when I called Kane's organization by that term, but it seemed like the description fit. The women who visited town wore their hair long and in braids or in a bun. They were always in modest dresses, no pants. And the men wore jeans and button-down shirts. Kane Matthews wore a black suit with a purple dress shirt with no tie today. He wore a variation of that outfit every time I saw him in town. Or driving his gray Hummer.

The one good thing was that the residents of the compound bought a lot of books. Reading must be an approved activity for the group.

I realized Kane had stopped talking. "Oh, how fun. Will there be open-house hours?"

He smiled at me, and I felt the chill going through my body. Maybe some women found him attractive, but I never had. He looked mean. "Of course, the gates will be open from eight to eight. I do hope you all will come by. The rumor that we are some sort of cult has been circulating, and we just want to show you all that we're good neighbors."

I hoped I wasn't blushing since I'd been one of the ones who'd thought that. I scanned the table, but no one else seemed to want to make an announcement. "Okay, then. You'll be getting an email from Darla regarding the winter festival. Please read and respond. And I'll see you all next month, unless I see you before."

"I'm not sure a winter festival is appropriate based on the lack of snow," Kane said to the person next to him.

"Okay, we'll see you all later." I wasn't going to get into a discussion on Darla's favorite festival without her there to defend it. Besides, festivals brought in tourists who bought stuff. Kane's group wasn't really a business, so I didn't understand why he was even attending our meetings. The mayor had invited him originally. Of course, the mayor rarely attended the meetings himself. A fact that pleased me to no end. I banged the gavel, and people started fleeing the store.

Kane Matthews looked around the now-almost-empty table, then smiled. "I guess I'll have to fight that battle next year."

After he'd left, Amy came over and started helping me move tables back to the dining room setup. "He's creepy. I can't believe you stood up to him. Now if you disappear, at least I'll know the first place to look. That ranch of theirs. But with so many acres, I'm not sure we'll ever find the body."

"Stop it. They're nice people. At least the women who come into town to shop are nice. He's just a little off. Maybe it's the mantle of leadership that has him all in everyone's face."

"I heard Kane and Pastor Bill got into it Sunday after services at Diamond Lille's. The guy came over and challenged his beliefs, if the story I heard was true." Amy moved to another table. "Did Sadie say anything?"

"No, but I haven't seen her this week. Since Aunt Jackie retired, I'm only working the morning shifts on Thursday through Sunday. A schedule Greg doesn't understand. He wants me to work Tuesday through Thursday. That way our weekends are free." We'd had the discussion this morning again before I'd come in for the meeting.

"Like Greg ever takes a weekend off," Amy said, supporting my own observations.

"It's just that me being gone on the weekends makes it hard to plan for festivals and impossible to take out the food truck." I was pretty sure Greg was just grumpy thinking about his mom and her health. She'd had it hard the last year. Hopefully, she was in full remission now, and he could relax a little. We'd had to put the wedding off again. Now it felt like something we had to do rather than something we wanted to do. Weddings could be stressful. "Anyway, I told him we could revisit my schedule after we got back from the honeymoon."

"A week in Hawaii on the beach. I'm jealous." Amy glanced around the dining room. Judith and Deek had jumped in to help as soon as the meeting adjourned, so we were already done.

"Don't be. He's being cagey about where we're going. I'm thinking we're probably going to Alaska or Antarctica rather than Hawaii." I went over to the counter and refilled my coffee. "Is it too early for lunch?"

"Yes. It's only ten. And I can't get away today anyway. Mayor Baylor has me doing a new PR campaign to bring more retreat groups to South Cove. He thinks that maybe Kane's group will allow the town to host a yoga retreat or something out at the compound."

"Is that what he's been working on?" That made a little more sense than inviting a group with religious tax exemptions to the area. "If they host a retreat, they'll have to pay taxes, right?"

"Or at least our tourist counts will increase in the off months." Amy grabbed her purse. "I think he's in bed with the devil, but it wouldn't be the first time."

Amy was right about that. Our mayor had a habit of supporting big developments for the sake of lining his pockets. Whether or not the town wanted the new business. He'd tried to get me to sell my house and property for years. Almost since I'd moved here.

My phone buzzed with a calendar reminder. I had final fittings on my dress in Santa Barbara at noon. It would take at least an hour to get there. I'd take a book and eat lunch at my favorite Mexican restaurant there after the fitting. Or maybe I'd be on carrots and water until after the wedding. It all came down to how the fitting went.

I grabbed my tote and said goodbye to my staff. Deek held up a hand, so I stopped by where he was stocking books. "Do you need me?"

"Your aura is really funky orange today. Did you and the dude have a fight?" Deek Kerr was the son of a fortune teller. So, he thought he read auras. Or maybe he really did read auras, and I was just a nonbeliever.

"We're fine. Greg's just a little freaked out about the upcoming wedding." Greg had been worried about something else. He hadn't talked about it, but Esmeralda had let it slip. He was being courted for a job by a state law enforcement agency. He'd always said he'd never leave South Cove, but I thought this one might just be tempting him. I'd made him a résumé last night and had planned on giving it to him this morning. Now I'd just have to send it to him. He needed to review it and see if there was any missing work experience or if the dates were right. I'd heard that the agency was a stickler for absolute accuracy in the application process. "I'm hoping by the end of the month, he'll be back to normal."

He set back down the book he'd been shelving.

"Orange is a serious color for you. Maybe you should chat with my mom or Esmeralda about everything. Sometimes having a professional's take on life helps."

Professional? Rory Kerr and Esmeralda DeClair were fortune tellers, not mental health counselors or even life coaches. I shook my head. "I'm not much into taking advice from the beyond. Anyway, I need to go."

When I moved to open the front door, a woman came inside, holding a stack of flyers.

"Excuse me, have you seen this girl?" The woman thrust a flyer into my hand. "You can't really tell from this picture, but she's just turned eighteen. She went to Cal Poly this fall, just down the road in September. She didn't come home for Christmas, but she said she was skiing with friends. Then I go to her dorm last week to visit, and I learn she's been gone since October. Following this Reverend Matthews. I hear they have a church here."

The picture was of a typical blond, blue-eyed California girl. It must have been her senior high school picture. She grinned at the camera like she'd had her life in order and a plan to go conquer the future.

I didn't recognize the girl, but only a few of Matthews's followers came into town. A few of the men drove a van into town once a week to pick up mail, deliver their crafts to the artist shops that let them do commission, and drop by the bookstore. I'd heard from others that they did their food and supply shopping in Bakerstown. I felt honored that they came into South Cove for books at least.

I tried to hand the flyer back, but the woman shook her head. "Keep it. Maybe you'll see her. Her name's

Carolyn. But she likes going by Carlie. She was study-ing engineering. And she worked so hard to get admit-ted to the school. I don't understand what she's thinking."

"I haven't seen her, but Deek here will put the flyer up on our community board. Maybe someone in town has seen her." I handed the crumpled flyer to Deek, who looked up after seeing the picture and shook his head.

"Sorry, I haven't seen her either. I'll take another one for my writers' group. Maybe someone has seen her around here." Deek held out his hand for another flyer.

"Bless you. It's just the two of us after her dad died last year. I thought she just needed some time at school." The woman was gently sobbing now.

"Deek, why don't you get"—I turned to look at the woman—"sorry, I didn't get your name."

"Molly. Molly Cordon." She sank into a chair at a table. "I'm so tired."

"What do you want to drink, on the house?" Deek listed off all the coffee drinks with a little flair.

I smiled at him and left Molly Cordon in good hands. Getting a free coffee and some friendly atten-tion from Deek wouldn't bring back her daughter or solve the mystery of why she'd disappeared, but maybe it might just brighten her day for a few minutes.

Walking home, I noticed all the flyers in the win-dows of the local businesses. If Carlie was really with Kane's cult, he wouldn't be too happy when he came back into town. But keeping him happy wasn't my problem. I felt for the woman sitting in my coffee shop right now. She might have her own issues, but no one should be faced with losing a child and not knowing why.

Josh Thomas was sweeping off the sidewalk in front of his antique store. His wife, Mandy, now worked for him along with his assistant, Kyle. I'd seen a softer touch to the store's decorations since their marriage. And if my unscientific count of increased customers was correct, adding her to the business had been a good thing. He picked up one of the flyers that some-one must have dropped. "Did you see this?"

I nodded. "Her mom's in my bookstore right now. She looks like she needs a good month of sleep."

"I know the feeling." He glanced over at the book-store windows. "I can't imagine having your child go missing."

I thought that out of everyone in town, Josh was the one person who could imagine it, since Mandy had dis-appeared before their wedding. I didn't bring up the past; I knew it still was painful. "Hopefully she'll be able to make contact with her. If Carlie's in the"—I al-most slipped and said "cult"—"I mean, at Matthews's compound, someone will see this and have her call her mom."

"I hope it's that easy." Josh took the flyer and his broom back inside his shop.

"Me too," I muttered under my breath. I needed to get home and get the Jeep so I could get to my fitting. Then, maybe later this afternoon, I could take Emma for a run. As long as nothing else slowed me down.

As I hurried down the hill to my house, I saw a slight woman slowly walking up the hill. She had short salt-and-pepper hair and was wearing a pink T-shirt. When she saw me, her face filled with a large grin.

"Jill, I'm so glad to see you. I just got in a few minutes ago and left the car at the house. I thought I'd walk up and surprise Greg at work. If he's there." Amanda King, Greg's mom, had arrived for our wedding. A week earlier than we'd expected her.

I might not make my fitting today.

Visit our website at
KensingtonBooks.com
to sign up for our newsletters, read
more from your favorite authors, see
books by series, view reading group
guides, and more!

BOOK / / / CLUB
BETWEEN THE CHAPTERS

Become a Part of Our
Between the Chapters Book Club
Community and Join the Conversation

Betweenthechapters.net